OF THORNS AND BONES

THE HADES AND PERSEPHONE DUET: BOOK 1

HELOISE HULL

HENWIN PRESS LTD

Copyright © 2021 by Heloise Hull

All rights reserved.

No part of this book may be reproduced in any form or by any electronic or mechanical means, including information storage and retrieval systems, without written permission from the author, except for the use of brief quotations in a book review.

Cover by Etheric Designs

❀ Created with Vellum

A NOTE ON GRAMMAR

There are special rules for possessive nouns that are from the classical tradition, i.e. Socrates, Hades, Zeus. If a noun has two or more syllables, it only needs an apostrophe. If a noun only has one syllable, it needs an apostrophe and an S.

Socrates' writings
Ramesses' spear
Zeus's thunderbolts
Hades' Helm

Technically, Zeus needs an apostrophe and an s but I thought it would look wrong to readers if Hades didn't have the extra s and I'm fairly certain most of you don't care about Merriam-Webster and their rules, so I didn't do that. Apologies if you do care.

Plural possessive Nouns MW

OF THORNS AND BONES

I don't want your kiss. I don't want your crown. I want to burn your kingdom to the ground.

I haven't seen Hades for fifteen hundred years, but he is the key to the one thing I desire above all else: revenge.

After what I did to him, it's going to take a lot more than batting my eyes to get him to trust me. For weeks, he ignores my requests and my gifts, so I do what any jilted wife would do. I sneak into the Underworld, breaking every rule that has been in place since our separation.

But he can't ignore one thing.

The mythical passion that burned our land from the inside out left us both with scars, and it's reigniting with every second we're in the same realm. One stray spark could destroy us both.

Indulge in this new twist on the Hades and Persephone myth where the grudges are as ancient as the gods. An intense romance that begins with Of Thorns and Bones and concludes with Of

Flames and Thrones. Perfect for fans who want C.N. Crawford to have a baby with K.F. Breene.

Flectere si nequeo superos,
*   Acheronta movebo.*

If I cannot bend Heaven,
    Then I shall move Hell.

— Virgil. *Aeneid*. In the Mouth of Juno.

PROLOGUE
HADES

If my name makes your neck bristle and your body shudder, it is not because of me.

It is because of her.

I would prefer to let you go. Go, die. Let the worms eat your flesh.

If you fear me, it is only because she gave you hope of a life after death. It can hardly be my fault that it was a lie. Instead, the blinding pain of mortality ends, and I am standing over you. I may look different than you expected or speak a tongue you can't quite match, but you still understand.

I am the balance of life and death, and you are standing on the edge of it.

Right now, I may be a breeze on your neck or simply a feeling creeping up your spine. You believe someone is watching you.

I assure you, I am much more concerned with other things. You don't need to shake and tremble and beg. You may try to ask for her, but she is gone. I am your judge. I am your salvation. And I am laid bare.

Abandon hope, all ye who enter here.

For she didn't merely mislead you. She betrayed me, too.

I am not violent. I am not a terrifying beast. I am merely nothing. You may think of me as the god of absence.

It is she you should fear.

1

PERSEPHONE

Varna, Bulgaria
Summer, 2001 CE.

THE GOD of death was watching me. I could feel his gaze linger. Good, let him enjoy the show.

The manticore dressed in a stolen Adidas tracksuit accessorized with fake gold chains and a white baseball hat was also watching me. But he didn't know any better. He was too busy congratulating himself for finding such an easy target.

Music pulsed from the row of nightclubs in the resort district, reverberating through my skull and making my chest thump as I picked my way over the cobblestones. The Eastern Bloc came alive in the summer, and stilettos clacked loudly as young women tittered and laughed on the arms of the wealthy oil tycoons and military contractors vacationing on the Black Sea.

I swerved into a darkened alley and took stock. Two rats throbbed with life energy, and another teetered on the brink of life and death. A mortal registered five meters away at the edge of the chain link fence, but he was walking fast the opposite way.

As for the manticore? Well, he simply radiated death.

The demon rimmed his lips with a blood red tongue and smiled with two, bright gold teeth that I knew were fake because I'd sold them to him last week. A tiny wave of apprehension skated over my skin, leaving goosebumps to pimple my arms. Finally, what I'd been waiting for. A chance.

I'd been waiting for something to come. Not exactly him. Manticores were nasty creatures. They took joy in ripping off the limbs of mortals one by one to suck the marrow from the sticky centers of the bones. Add my forbidden magic to the mix, and I was downright irresistible. A mystery. Something to be savored and devoured all at once.

My advice? Always let them underestimate you.

My pulse thrummed at my throat as the warm summer breeze off the bay kissed the backs of my knees. The manticore moved closer.

"I knew something smelled off about you," the manticore said, stumbling a little as he entered my orbit. He didn't notice his misstep, though. Instead, he stood watching me, his eyes dilating in his excitement. The gold chains around his neck jangled together like a delightful sea shanty. "The moment I stepped foot into that pawn shop, I said to myself, I said, 'there's something off about that one.' And I'm never wrong."

Resisting the urge to roll my eyes, I put my hands together in a prayer position. "Oh please, good sir." Here I winced. That might've been laying it on thick. When was the last time 'good sir' was in vogue? I couldn't keep track. "Oh please, sir. Why don't you swing by the pawn shop tomorrow? I'll give you a real good price. Whatever you want. Jewelry, watches, more teeth. All yours."

"Cute. But you know what I want." His red tongue skimmed his lips again. "I'd rather you not scream. Others might hear, and then I'd have to share you. Trust me. You do not want to be shared, girl."

Girl. That word. It was abhorrent to me in the old tongue. It was equally detestable in any language, and the very reason I refused to ever look younger than thirty in any incarnation. Believe me, I did not look like a girl. I looked like a woman in her mid-thirties who was tired of putting up with handsy tourists. I even had the crows' feet from frowning to prove it.

My patience for playing the gullible part pulled at the threads. While it was true that I was practically neutered in this realm and my stockpile of hoarded magic dwindling by the week, I was still a goddess. I let my cloak of magic diffuse in rose petal pink and enjoyed the way my prey's eyes feasted on it.

He wanted me. Badly.

"What's a girl like you doing with magic like that in this realm?" he asked.

Hm. So perhaps not as thick as I thought. Honestly, he didn't look like he had two brain cells to rub together to keep himself warm. And there it was, again. That abhorrent word.

"Black market," I tried, stretching my toes in preparation to lunge.

"Nah. I know everyone that comes through. You? Never heard, seen, nor sensed you before."

I lifted an eyebrow. "Oh do you?"

The manticore picked his lion fangs with a sharpened bone. "Yeah. I do." He tossed it over his shoulder to clatter against the cobblestones and cracked his neck in both directions. He shook out his mane as he transformed from mafia to manticore. His hands widened into paws the size of my head, and a serpent's tail flicked back and forth. I had the distinct feeling he wanted to whip me with it first.

Good luck, buddy.

The goddess inside of me wanted to obliterate him with carefully curated death magic, but the been-too-long-on Earth goddess settled on jabbing my fingers into his windpipe and flipping his body over my shoulder as he gagged and coughed.

He squealed in surprise as his tracksuit tore along the rough stones before scrambling back to his feet. Instead of warning him off, my attack enraged him. He had no caution whatsoever, which suited me fine. I lifted my chin in a quick, jerking movement, egging him on.

"That wasn't very ladylike," he commented.

"Oh good. I thought for a second I was being too delicate."

The manticore narrowed his eyes, but I tossed a lentil seed at him, willing it to sprout before he could flick his deadly tail again. My seed somersaulted through the air, spreading its arms like some grotesque but adorable alien. They curled around the manticore's head and clung tight as he stomped through the alley, roaring and demolishing dumpsters. I smiled grimly as the network of shoots finally managed to gag him.

The shoots continued to grow, wrapping their vines around his back and trussing him like a pig ready for slaughter, forcing him to his knees. I couldn't see his face anymore, but every line of his body twisted in rage.

For a moment, my body glowed oil-black with my true form. Glittering stars cascaded down my hair and power churned through me. I felt fanged and dangerous, hungry for more—and I liked it. It was sweeter than the ripest strawberry on my tongue, and I savored the power burst.

"What are you?" he gasped. "I deserve... to know... what slayed me."

I bent down to whisper my name in his ear. As his body shuddered one last time, I added. "And I want him to know it was me."

Too soon, the power coursing through me dissipated as his essence splintered like dried spaghetti, and he left this world for the next. With it, I sent a prayer: *I don't want your kiss. I don't want your crown. I want to burn your kingdom to the ground.*

2

HADES

The Underworld
   Summer, 2001 CE.

When I thought of my wife, I imagined cracking her head open like an egg and examining her brain as a priest might do to the entrails of dying virgins.

Why does she think the way she does? Was the answer written in the lobes and folds, or was it branded on her cortex like a scar? Was this recklessness from some childhood trauma, or was she simply always a brat and I was too blinded by her youth and beauty to see it? How I wished to probe her more deeply. To understand her.

To crack her.

"Basileus?"

King.

I pulled myself to the present. A map the size of a small mountain glittered in onyx, the lands of the Underworld outlined in gold and the rivers in silver. With a fling of my finger, I moved a few pieces of cabochon rubies representing three phalanxes of Kako demons out of Tartarus and over to the far east bank of the River Styx.

Thanatos looked up sharply. "All of them, my king?"

I nodded. "Tartarus is gone. We may as well accept it now and hold what we can."

As we spoke, fire bombs rattled the windows of my obsidian castle and blasted a section of the serpentine tunnels. I grimaced at the deaths. Waves of energy pulsed against the stone walls, but they held firm. For now.

"As you wish." Thanatos turned on his booted heel and went to withdraw his troops.

Nyx and Hecate paused their conversation. They lived in their black cloaks with fox skull epaulets and Stygian bladed boots, constantly at the ready to do battle. We'd been living in this war room for a week now, although it felt as if no time had passed.

We were at war. We were at war, and the sirens were drowning. They died by two and threes and tens and twenties. I still tasted the sulfur on my tongue and felt the burn in my lungs and throat from when I'd swam across the Styx, suffocating as the siren's arms wrapped desperately around my neck. I dragged her to the shore as she convulsed with one last request that I could not honor. *Save my babies*. If I couldn't protect my demons, how was I supposed to save anyone?

"What?" I asked my companions wearily. The diamond of my breastplate sparkled in the light of the flickering reed torches along the walls. Except for the fire crackling in the hearth, the room was deadly still.

"Have you considered sending messages to Olympus?" Nyx asked carefully. "We have some stores of magic that might make the journey."

My jaw ground. I knew what she was asking. "No."

Hecate conjured a ball of light, her pole cat's eyes reflecting the same green color. "I can show you what she's doing. Perhaps she is—"

The slam of my fist didn't startle them, battle-hardened as they were, but it did shut them up as the reverberations echoed through the stone chambers. Nyx's crow cawed softly at her shoulder, but she stayed silent.

I straightened the greaves along my arms. "I said no."

Nyx retained her mild expression as she called for servants to bring wine and food, although I couldn't stomach the thought of eating. "You have always been a prudent god. Even mortals say so, despite their fear of death. So you don't want to consider her. Fine. Then at least consider surprising everyone for once."

"Stop being prudent, you mean."

"Precisely."

"And what did you have in mind?"

"Besides the idea you dismissed out of hand?" Nyx asked.

"Preferably."

Hecate knocked over a few rubies. "You could cut off access to the Underworld. When the dead begin walking around with no place to go, mortals would take notice."

"And what would that achieve?" I asked wearily.

"How would I know? It's never been done before. That's why it's the opposite of prudent." Hecate's face shone with an inner zeal that would make zealots tremble.

"Leave me to think on this."

"As you wish."

Where before the mortals worshipped us Olympians as gods, now they scorned us. Worse? Many had forgotten us, a consequence of their mayfly lifespans. After the Titan war, when the Olympians ousted the Titans from the Heavens and sent the most vengeful of them to Tartarus, the possibility of peace stretched to the horizons, but it was not stable. The Greek golden age lasted only until the end of the Roman Empire when the humans grew tired of the gods' demands and sided with the demons.

The Demon War was long and the battles threatened the existence of all. They rent the sky to reach the gods, and eventually, a human was able to unleash the caged Titans and turn the tide of war. Zeus surrendered and the Accords were struck. Humans no longer needed to smoke their sacrifices to him or to any other god. In fact, they no longer needed to recognize us at all.

Now it was the Olympians who were locked in their prisons on high, silent and forgotten, a footnote in mortal myth books. I alone of the Olympians emerged as a new god, one of death. After what happened at the Accords with Persephone, I embraced it. Death, after all, was a necessity of life. Traveling between the three realms was also made impossible. Magic was outlawed on Earth. Equilibrium was attained. I never saw my wife again.

But this newest conflict?

This guerrilla war had come from nowhere a century ago. It marked exactly the fifteen-hundred year anniversary of the Accords. It felt pointless and also malignant. As if my realm bled great gouts of demons for nothing. Recently, my enemy had grown stronger, and still I wasn't quite sure who it was I fought.

Unfortunately, imprisoning the most vile beings from any realm tended to make my enemies rival the number of stars in the universe. It could truly be anyone—or anything —fighting me from the shadows.

Anger boiled beneath my surface and rattled my bones. I stood abruptly. Nyx and Hecate both joined me, their heads bowed. Guards stationed around the room clanged their swords to their chests. They were ready to follow in my wake, whatever form I may take.

I rematerialized along the black shore of the River Styx. Out of the five rivers encircling my kingdom, it was by far the most famous. A shame. I quite liked the idea of the River Lethe. I wondered what drowning in it would feel like. Peaceful, I suppose.

A slight displacement of air shuffled somewhere to my far left. Most wouldn't have noticed it until it was too late. Before he landed, Scally was already transforming into a beak-nosed man holding something tightly in his fist. A drop of black blood dripped through his fingers.

"There was an incident, Basileus."

Infinite scenarios rolled through my mind. At my look, he clarified, "A dead demon. A manticore."

Irritation laced my words, and I strode down the banks as curls of sulfur rose from the black currents. "We're in a war, Scally. There are dead demons everywhere."

"He wasn't from this realm," he said.

I stopped my long strides, and Scally hurried to catch up. "What?" I demanded.

A hint of nerves entered in his voice. He tended to screech when he was anxious. He was, after all, part screech owl. "The manticore's body washed up on the shore with these." Scally opened his hand to reveal two gold teeth on his palm.

"What are you showing me exactly?" I said in disgust. Manticore slime still clung to the roots.

"There was a spirit note attached."

Surprise welled up at once. It took a lot of power to send this sort of message. Power that shouldn't be on Earth anymore. No demons in. No demons out. Those were the rules after the Accords. Whichever demons had decided to stay on Earth were there for eternity. The same went for the ones that decided to live in my realm and those on Olympus.

"Show me."

Scally blew on the teeth with an icy breath that dissolved the gold into dust. Out came a voice as thin as gossamer webs. The way Scally tilted his head told me that only I was privy to this message. Why encode it?

Anger, disillusionment, and even a bit of fear surged upon hearing the message. Her voice kept repeating the words like a drumbeat over and over until Scally broke the spell. It was only three words, but they shook me to my core. I might have let her voice spool over me for eternity. My name on her tongue was sweeter than any ambrosia or nectar we used to grow drunk on.

I hated her for that.

"What did the message say?" Scally asked softly.

Shaking myself, I lied. "Nothing important. Not to us, at least. Go see if Thanatos needs anything for his retreat."

Scally looked unconvinced, but did as I ordered. He took flight, soaring silently on owl wings as I was left to try to ignore the words that had already tattooed themselves on my soul. There would be no safe harbor from them tonight. Even my feet pounded to their cadence, soft and feminine, just as I remembered her.

Help me, Hades.

Help me, Hades.

Help me, Hades.

3

PERSEPHONE

Just like our marriage, at least the end of it, Hades ignored me. I wanted to scream, but being married to the lord of darkness for millennia would boil anyone's brains.

It had been three days since I killed the manticore. One day for every word I sent and nothing in return. Not a team of demonspawn horses to pick me up, a secret portal, or even a wandering ghost shade with a message telling me to piss off. If that was how Hades wanted to play it, I would continue to send dead demons until he was drowning in them. Just as soon as I figured out where to find more impossible magic. I had almost run out as it was.

Clicking open the safe I held together with a regular padlock and a small spell of death magic—minor, really—I took stock and tried not to grimace. Typically, I moved between the realms with ease, making it easy to gather lost magical items. To my knowledge, I was the only creature who could. It was my second most closely guarded secret. Or third.

I had a few top contenders.

But suddenly, about a century ago, that power faded,

and I ran into a literal dead end, banging my nose on some invisible wall every time I tried. No longer could I move between the realms. Worse, I was stuck on the Earth side, growing weaker by the day. For a century, I resisted the need to ask for help, but with the last of my magical objects almost gone, I would soon wither. I wouldn't die on Earth, probably, but I preferred to keep my breasts above my knees, thanks.

Also, the not-dying thing was only a working theory. The weaker I became, the more of a target I presented to roving magical creatures who chose Earth in the Accords. We all learned well the lesson that gods could die at the hands of demons, even if the simple passage of time didn't kill us.

Here I had swallowed all of my damn pride to ask Hades for help, and he hadn't deigned to answer? Not even a no. Despite traveling between Olympus and Earth during the past fifteen centuries like it was a revolving diner door—those are adorable, by the way—I'd always felt the pull of my old home. Surely, even in my weakened state, I could still get into the Underworld. At least, that was my gamble.

Into my bag went a small, dented square of matchless material, purloined from Hades' Helm of Invisibility. While it wasn't as powerful as the real thing, taking it meant Hades couldn't ever be completely invisible again, and the square provided some cloaking aspects. That, friends, was what they call a win-win.

Next I stuffed inside my favorite dagger. Its pale pink color matched my immortal aura, and the handle was inlaid with pale, celery-green jewels. I tucked a second dagger of bronze and bone into a holster on my leg and twisted my dark hair into a bun.

The door to my apartment swung open, but I barely stopped my frantic search for any last remnants of magic. I'd sensed Dawn a mile away, trudging home from her own dead-end job as a bank teller. In immortal years, she was basically a zygote. In mortal years, I think she was in her mid-twenties.

She paused at the open door, a plastic bag of take-out dangling from her arms as she took in my outfit of leather corsets studded with silver bolts. "Are you headlining a midlife crisis dominatrix convention? Or is this a real midlife crisis? Please don't say you have a moonlighting gig I don't know about."

"Ha, ha, ha. You really missed your calling as a funny person."

"A funny person? You mean a comedian?"

Despite all my time on earth, sometimes human things escaped me. "They're the ones who tell jokes, right?"

Dawn shut the door and laid out the food. "God, you are so weird sometimes. But I'm serious. That look is for a very specific taste."

"Noted." I continued my frenetic pace. I refused to waste any more time waiting around for a man. God of the dead or not.

"That's quite the packing style," Dawn commented through a piece of broccoli beef. She threw her feet on the bean bag chair we used as a semi-hazardous coffee table and took a swig of cheap, pink-flavored wine.

"Thanks. I'm thinking about trademarking it."

Dawn sat up so fast the bean bag protested by coughing out a cloud of Styrofoam balls from a hole at the bottom. "Wait! Are you leaving for good? I can't afford rent on my own. That was the deal. I let you have the master bedroom and all of the bathroom cabinet space in exchange for ninety percent of the rent."

"Yeah, great deal."

Dawn stood now, her chest heavy, and I could feel her panic dripping off of her. I threw her a small bag from the back of the safe. "Go buy a nice flat, nothing too flashy. Save your paychecks. And stop taking handouts from Naveed. You don't need his drama in your life."

Dawn mumbled incoherently as jewels poured out of the bag into her palm. She looked up, even more terror in her eyes. "What did you do?" she whispered. "Or what do you do? This is about the moonlighting thing, isn't it? Jesus, why didn't I ask more questions on the sublease?"

As Dawn continued to question her life choices, I eyeballed a vial at the back of the safe. A little something I'd shown Circe how to brew. Luckily for me, I'd hoarded a few magically enhanced objects from various demons and witches over the years. You'd be surprised how many magical folk chose neither Olympus nor the Underworld after the Accords. There were plenty of them here on Earth, and plenty of them that found ways around the no-magic rule in this realm. I had merely run out of time and patience.

"Shouldn't we be celebrating?" I asked, keeping my last potion from her view. "I just handed you a bag of priceless jewels to buy your own place. I also imparted the wisdom of middle age on you."

"But... I don't..." she stammered, moving the sparkling precious stones in her hand with her index finger.

I grabbed a chipped, ceramic mug from the cupboard and poured myself a glass. Then, with a furtive gesture when we clinked, I poured the vial in her glass and threw my own back.

Dawn's eyes crossed and she blinked twice. "Wait," she asked, starting to slur a little. "What's wrong with Naveed? He's not bad to look at, and he's working his way up from bar back to bartender. He could get to be a manager eventually."

I put my hands on her shoulders and gripped her tightly for a moment. "The worst ones are never ugly." Hades' dark lines and darker swagger wavered in front of my vision for a moment, but I quickly shook free of its hold. "Listen, I've got more middle-aged advice, since I'm so much more advanced in years."

"Oh great. Here we go."

"Get yourself happy first."

Dawn snorted. "Oh, blah, blah blah. Then boys will notice how happy you are and how you shine on the inside and fall in love at first sight. Give me a break. That only works in the movies."

I lifted an eyebrow. "Of course not. They'll notice how happy you are and want to fuck it up. Come on, Dawn. Psych one-oh-one."

She burst out laughing. "God, I'm going to miss you. Where are you going?"

I nudged her glass. "Drink up! Thatta girl. I'm going home. I have something important I need to do. Didn't you say you needed to use the restroom?"

Dawn mechanically set down her empty glass. "Oh right. Yeah. Thanks."

By the time she'd come back from whatever it was the magic made her do in the bathroom, I had finished sweeping the apartment of objects and remnants of me. I smiled sadly at her confused expression.

"Are you leaving?" she asked, tilting her head and blinking slowly.

"Got to. The gendarmerie are on my case, and they're about to crack it wide open. Remember what I said? What do snitches get?"

"Ditches. Snitches get ditches."

I pretended to wipe a fake tear. "They grow up so fast."

Dawn's blinks were getting longer. "You can't leave. What will I do without you?"

Instead of smiting her as some gods were wont to do, I showed her the last object in my safe. "Here, I want you to have the magical amulet of the deathless, dread Persephone. Sounds fancy, doesn't it?" My real name sounded odd on my tongue after so long. I quickly wiped it clean, adding, "Only the best for you."

Dawn rolled her eyes. "You know I don't believe in your magic stuff. It doesn't exist."

I waved my fingers and spouted voodoo lines we'd heard on an American television show once. "That's what you think."

It was adorable how humans refused to see the truth. Never change.

I shoved the amulet in her hands, knowing it would offer her protection. Perhaps even better than I could offer, sucked dry as I was here after too many years and too little access to real, teeth-rending magic. Magic I could only access on Olympus—or the Underworld.

When the Accords were signed with the human leaders, we gods really got the raw end of the bargain. Stay on Olympus or else. I tossed my hair over my shoulder, remembering how much we gave up. And now, only a few humans were gifted with the truth every few generations. And they were so frightened that gods and demons truly existed that they shut themselves beneath their basilicas and refused to emerge. Believe me, I tried getting their help. There wasn't much I hadn't tried over the last one hundred years.

Except for this.

Desperate times.

On the off-chance someone had intercepted the manticore and his message before Hades had seen it, I was going to send one more. And if that didn't work?

I shuddered.

Really desperate times.

I brushed my lips over Dawn's crown. "See ya, kid. Don't go down alleyways at night."

"Is that another magical thing or a middle age thing?" she asked, still fighting the effects of my potion. At least she'd sleep well tonight, all traces of me wiped from her memory by morning. It was for the best.

I shook my head. "Just a smart thing."

She was snoring before I reached the door. The only thing left to do was meet the night as one met the day. I shouldered my bag and marched into the chilled and salted Black Sea air.

4

PERSEPHONE

Olympus
    Millenia ago.

Olympus was a lot bigger than I expected. The cotton blue sky opened to infinity, and even the gods felt like simple players on its stage.

Demeter gripped my hand so tightly, I feared it would break my fingers. She hated that I was here. While I was fond of her, the fact remained that she had lied to me for centuries.

I was trying to forgive her.

So far, I was failing.

"Don't look anyone in the eyes. Remember to accept no food or drink. Try not to wander too far," she whispered for my ears only.

I nodded my assent. At this point, I would say anything to get to Olympus. A place I detested with every fiber of my being, but if I was to plan accordingly, I needed to see it. I needed to understand it.

I dropped my eyes as we passed a few gods in colorful robes with neon hair and slick skin, but I could feel their gazes linger. I risked a furtive glance and almost stumbled at their predatory look. I kept telling myself it was just my nerves. No immortal looked that hungry. There was too much food and drink.

A little goddess floated by wearing a bored expression. She offered us her tray of ambrosia squares and drinking cups of nectar. Flakes of gold leaf sparkled at every turn in the brilliant light of Olympus. I desperately wanted something to take the edge off, but Demeter waved her away.

"Take nothing, Kore," Demeter repeated, low. As if she hadn't drilled it into my head for weeks.

More servants, demigods, and favored mortal lovers, lounged on cushions, drinking, talking mutedly, and strumming their lutes. All of their faces were blank. If Zeus said something, their laugh always sounded a beat too slow. Their smiles were too wide and revealed too many teeth. It made me ill to watch them for long, so I let my gaze slide from one face to the next without lingering.

Zeus was a fool. He wanted everyone to see his throne room and quiver before the dais. He staged these parties for himself and himself only, as if anyone could relax and have fun. I'd only been here a few minutes and already I had gathered that.

I felt the gaze of a few male gods and even a few female ones as we strolled. Some were merely curious. Who was that girl with Demeter? Surely not a glamored mortal. Certainly not a god of Olympus. *I wondered what they'd give to know the truth.*

Instead of clenching my fists, my first instinct, I kept my eyes straight and my smile faint, as if this were all too much. Too beautiful, too dazzling, too magnificent. When indeed, I felt too exposed, every inch of my skin on display under the gauzy material of my pale pink chiton.

When I first put it on, it felt as if I were wearing moonlight. Crocus buds had been arranged in a corona around my head and at my ankles. My face was left fresh, scrubbed raw with salt and honey. The nymphs had patted white lead into my skin and snuck me a little crushed mulberry to use on my lips, but I hadn't painted it on. Demeter watched my every move, and she wanted me bare. In her mind, the plainer I appeared, the less attention I would draw. Unfortunately, it had the opposite effect, making me appear out of place with such a sweet, young, unadorned face.

"What are we going to see?" I asked.

"The gods in their natural habitat. Then, perhaps you will understand their depravity, and why we should not even bother. They are trite at this point, and I tire of them easily."

"What If I don't?"

"Kore..." *Demeter's voice was woven like strands of wheat. Soft if you rubbed them the right way, but sharp enough to prick if you did not.*

"It's simply a question."

"It's not."

I crossed my arms petulantly, feeling low on the day I was supposed to feel exalted. Demeter always meant well, but it didn't make it any easier to bear when our desires did not align.

She led me to a quiet courtyard with a fountain that spouted shimmering rainbow water. Clearly, Iris had touched it. I knelt to drift my fingers through the lotus blossoms perfuming the pool, letting their silky petals swirl in tiny whirlpools around my fingers. It was scented with jasmine, and iridescent in the eternal sunshine. Me? I preferred a nice rainy day every once in a while. How else would flowers come to their full potential without a little rain? How else would we appreciate the glory of the sun?

"Let's settle near the hedges," *Demeter murmured. She needed their greenery to feel safe, I guess, only a tall god blocked our path. He sparked with latent energy, and his gold robes shone so brightly that he could've been seen from the earthly realm. In one* hand, he clutched an entire amphora of nectar. I could smell it on his breath from two stades away.

Zeus. Lord of the gods. This time, I did not try to hide my scowl or the way my fingers clenched together. As if it mattered. Zeus wouldn't meet my eyes. The coward.

Addressing Demeter only, he said, "I didn't think you'd come, grain goddess."

"Am I not welcome?"

Zeus laughed heartily as if she had made the best of jokes. Demeter's face soured, but it wasn't as if she could stand him, either.

"Don't be ridiculous. You're an Olympian like everyone else. If Hades is welcome, then you certainly are, beautiful sister."

As if by speaking his name he had conjured him, a cold wind swept through the courtyard, cutting through the delicate material of my dress. I had to admit I was curious about this black sheep. Demeter barely spoke her eldest brother's name and, when she did, it was only in derision. Now, his bitter magic crashed through the elegant party, turning every head. I felt it in my core without having to look.

Both Zeus and Demeter started at his presence, although they tried to hide their jerks. Hades, the loathed god of the Underworld. I always wondered why he was so feared. It wasn't as if Hades was the god of death. He left that to his generals. Hades was simply balance. It must've been something about his very essence that riled them.

He stared at me. I knew it, felt it in my chest. If I turned around, our eyes would meet. So this was what unadulterated masculine interest felt like. No wonder Demeter feared it. She loathed pleasure. Although she wasn't known as a virgin goddess, she might as well have been. This type of gaze frightened her.

Zeus flicked his eyes over my shoulder. His mouth turned

down, and he shot a look to Demeter that seemed to say the world without uttering a sound.

"I'll leave you both to enjoy yourselves." He inclined his head, finally acknowledging me. "Kore."

I didn't return the gesture. Instead, I watched as Zeus intercepted Hades, clapping a heavy hand on his shoulder, bolts sparking where it hit bare skin. "Brother," he boomed loud enough for all to hear. "What brings you here? Come, where's Hebe? Let's get you a drink, eh?"

I couldn't hear Hades' response, but I didn't need to. The deathless god had not stopped watching me. And I was intrigued.

5

PERSEPHONE

The man in canvas overalls and work boots brandished a paint scraper and held himself entirely too still. Not even his eyes tracked me, although I knew it was because his kind didn't need visuals to hunt. His body was restrained violence threatening to break free from its mooring and consume me.

The nervous need to pat my pockets and check my trinkets overwhelmed me, but I held steady. *Please work. I promise blossoms if you work. As your once Dread Queen, I demand it.*

These were all I had left. I'd run through my magic more quickly than I'd expected, leaving me at the mercy of the creatures that had chosen Earth after the Accords. Still, I crooked my finger at the demon, beckoning him closer. His forked tongue flicked out to test the winds. To be perfectly honest, I didn't recognize his type, which was odd. As once queen of the Underworld, I knew them all, but the only thing that mattered now was sending him to Hades.

A waxing gibbous moon illuminated the golden sands of the beach. Hornbeam and white oak trees thickened on the far side, and astringent ribworts carpeted the ground. Even if I had no magic left, even if the very earth dampened any magical efforts, I could always feel the plants.

The cave complex was created a few centuries ago, and there were even older cave monasteries from the time of the war. Monks as far back as the Byzantine emperor, Justinian, prayed, left offerings, and buried their dead among its karst cliffs.

A local treasure demon used it for his horde until recently, but that's for another story. Now, it was a popular tourist attraction during the day. At night, I could see why the treasure demon chose it.

Haunting cliff ledges, old mosaics and frescoes, and ledges carved from limestone added to its appeal. I led the unknown demon away as we tumbled through the horsetail grasses. A magnificent red deer licked her haunches. She paused to raise her head as I passed a few meters to her left, but gently went back to her bath.

I had no idea what the demon thought was about to happen, only what would. I had no more seeds, no more vials of potion. Magic had been forbidden in this realm, and while the manticore implied there was still a black-market trade, I had no access. I didn't know where it was, who ran it, or how it worked. All I had now was a regular knife, my Totenpasse, and my pink dagger. I felt its cold comfort on my thigh and took courage.

"Did you come from a job or something?" I asked as the demon followed me deeper into the cave.

He didn't respond. I didn't even know if he'd understood the question. He must've copied some workman's style after he'd borrowed his clothes. Probably his skin too. I could still see bits of hair and flesh hanging from a button.

"Hello? Did you forget to take the man's voice, too? Tsk tsk. Always remember to take their voice."

The demon cocked his head at a nearly ninety-degree angle. I winced as I heard tendons and sinew crack at the treatment. No mortal was coming back from that. I clapped once. "Well, let's get this over with. I need you to go to the Underworld. Would you like the easy pass or the more difficult one?"

The demon lunged with the paint scraper, attempting to take my skin next. I parried and ducked, flinging myself against the cave wall. Just a little closer. I heard skin and cloth ripping as the monster's true tentacles emerged from his borrowed back.

I pretended to trip and stumble, and the demon whipped his tentacles to clutch me. I slashed down with the knife and severed one from his body, yet the demon made no noise. He lurched and reached for me again, hitting me on the temple with the edge of the paint scraper. I had to ignore the trickle of blood, though, as more tentacles emerged from his back.

Damn. I really did not want to use my pink dagger. Before I ditched my magic to hide, I'd imbued some of my essence, my true magic, inside its blade, hence the primrose pink color that matched my aura. I knew I'd need something trustworthy and powerful in the mortal realm. Something that couldn't run out of magic or fail. Yet, I only used it when absolutely necessary. I didn't want to risk damaging it or exposing myself.

A second tentacle wrapped around my leg, this time unseating me. I hit the ground hard and swore harder. A third and then a fourth oozed stinging suckers around my limbs. I could feel them through the leather.

"Screw it!" I screamed and stabbed him in the face with my dagger, my back spasming from the effort in this older, mortal body. My breath came in clumps. I had to get to the

Underworld, soon. There was a gurgle as green liquid poured from his mouth, but that was it. The eeriest part was watching him convulse and twitch as he died without blinking or making a sound.

Finally, he was still. With a heave, I rolled his body into the abyss as my offering.

Now, all I could do was wait.

Help me, Hades.

* * *

I WAITED a full day in the cave, shivering in the chill night and sleeping during the day. Still, Hades did not show himself. Still, he did not come.

The bastard.

Things were getting desperate, but I had one trick left. One thing I hadn't tried. The gold of the Totenpasse felt cold in my hands. It was a kind of passport for the dead, the kind they used to offer to me. This was a particularly impressive specimen. Gently, I took off my shoes and dipped my toe in the sea where it lapped at the cave. At least the summer currents were warm.

I sat on the ledge of the inky black water. It swirled at my feet, the abyss of the cave absorbing all light. I dropped without thinking too much. It was easier that way. My legs kicked, treading water as I fumbled with the gold object, repeating the ancient lines to grant easy passage to the Underworld.

"I am the daughter of Earth and starry Heaven, but Heaven is my birth. I am the daughter of Earth and starry Heaven, but Heaven is my birth."

I waited for the chill waters of the deep to bubble up and claim me, to recognize their once-Dread Queen. Except I must have given up too much; I was barely above a mortal at this point, begging pointlessly against the implacable.

"I am the daughter of Earth and starry Heaven, but Heaven is my birth," I said, barely hearing myself above the ringing of the waves. They were getting higher now, my neck the only thing above the water.

"Heaven is my birth..." I was fading.

It was beautiful, the moonlight on dark water. I gave this realm that. The mortals lacked understanding, but that gave them the ability to see beauty, even in death. Except that I might actually die if this stupid piece of hammered gold didn't start working. "Come on," I muttered, repeating the phrase over and over.

Why wasn't it activating?

The waves were relentless, becoming more feral in their pounding. I knocked my skull against the craggily cave wall twice before I managed to grab hold of an outcropping that scraped the palms of my hands.

As I clung to the wall, I had to duck between the waves and try to catch my breath on the upswing. That was the thing about passing to the Underworld. If you weren't already dead, you had to at least be willing to die.

The waves crashed again, and again I went under, but it wasn't just the warm water of the Black Sea. It swirled cold and forbidding in sudden streaks. The entrance to the maw was opening. It sensed death.

I would not let it be mine, even if I was willing to toe the line. Clearly the Totenpasse wasn't enough by itself. Time to get there the old-fashioned way.

As I braced myself for another wave, I closed my eyes and felt for the nearest life force. An octopus hunted casually nearby, its movements languorous, as if it wasn't truly committed to the cause. I, on the other hand, was committed as shit.

My hand snapped out to grab its bulbous head and dash it against the rocks, but it panicked, lacing its tentacles around my arm and up my bicep like some grotesque version of haute couture, sea style. I gritted my teeth against its stings and crushed its skull with a bare hand. The octopus frantically squeezed tighter, dispelling clouds of ink as it thrashed, but its movements slowed. I held its lifeless body out.

Black-haired Hades, ruler over the departed, accept my offering thus.

Hades used to feed lines to his favorite poets. He was particularly proud of this one.

Headlong from some towering mountain peak I will throw myself into the waves. Take this as my last dying gift!

Me? I never cared much for Virgil myself. He completely mischaracterized Queen Dido. Don't worry. He's not playing tour guide with Dante. That rat bastard was suffering eternal damnation beneath the rock I'd stuffed him under the last time I'd cared to check. In fact, it might be fun to revisit him once I finished my task. Maybe I'd check in on all of my former favorites.

With that pleasant thought, I sucked in deeply, thanked the octopus for its sacrifice, and threw myself headlong into the abyss. And this time when I plummeted, I actually felt fear.

6

HADES

My wife was here.

She had a very specific scent that clung to her even as it pervaded an entire realm. Although she'd tried to mask it, nothing else matched it in all of the realms. She could have rolled in demon shit and it wouldn't hide her pomegranate, spring rain fragrance.

So, after so many years of absence, we were to begin another game.

I wondered if she knew I was embroiled in a war, quite possibly a coup, or if she just got lucky. She thrived on the desperate hope of warfare.

Shocked? You thought she was all pomegranates and innocence? War brought despair and hope in equal measure. It merely depended on what side you were on. Of course, she exploited war when she could.

"Basileus?" Thanatos prodded.

By my war council's expressions, they thought I was growing complacent. How many times had they needed to nudge me to the present this week alone, my thoughts swirling of Persephone? They didn't know what occupied me exactly, but I still worried them. If they suspected it was her, the fighting wouldn't just be outside the castle walls.

With a tight look, I tapped the ever-in-motion map and said, "I'm getting some air."

Hecate rolled her eyes, the only one who I would allow to get away with such impudence. "Is it that time already?"

"Rituals are good, as you well know," I reminded the witch. "They ground us."

"At least my rituals could melt off your face, but you go have your alone time."

That got a barked laugh from me as I made my escape and strode down the cold corridors, torches flickering every few feet. The draft didn't bother me.

It was nearly dawn. Eos, rosy-fingered goddess of dawn, Nyx, and Hemera of the day were no longer needed in accordance with the set laws. The sun rose and fell as it must, and Nyx stayed with me while her daughter, Hemera, chose to go with the Olympians. The Demon War had torn the gods bitterly down the middle. What would they call this new war, I wondered? The War of Hades? How Hades Failed? Cumbersome, but true.

And now, Persephone was sucking me back into a vortex of our own twisted history. She was forcing me to think about her outside of my designated time. She was forcing me to track her. And when I found her, she would force me to hurt her. Anything to get her out of my realm and keep her out. She had made her decision centuries ago. With her decision, she robbed me of mine.

Guards snapped to attention as I approached the iron gates. The white elm tree of False Dreams shone brighter than any star over Olympus. It was the centerpiece of my courtyard, here before me and, if I was being honest, here after me. The primordial chthonic gods whispered to me as

I walked. Eons before, they roamed as I did, complete masters of their domain. As such, I was under no illusions that I would reign forever. Nothing lasts forever. Not even the gods. Instead, I had their whispers. I had the resonance of their hopes and dreams, their lives, their wrongs, and their rights.

Sometimes, after my designated half-hour to think of Persephone—never Kore, as "Kore" was nothing but an illusion—I tried to commune with them. Who were you? Were you good and just gods? Did you love your people? Or did you abuse them for your own pleasures? Am I destined to live as you? To eventually be forgotten? I was already so close to being nothing but a memory. Would anyone care? It was then, in the depths of my questions, that I felt most mortal and most at peace. Indeed, nothing lasts forever.

I walked across the courtyard and sat under the tree only to appease Hecate, should she be watching. It was exhausting work, pretending to observe a ritual I had no pleasure in doing at the moment. Persephone was here, and I had to track her down.

But not yet. It would raise too much suspicion.

I forced myself not to look at the leaded windows of my castle. I never did during my half-hour. It would be odd to do so now. Instead, I focused on the mint plants. That sharpened my anger like a knife on a whetstone.

It was persistent, the mint. My cooks used the delicate stems and leaves in their nightly preparations, pulling them from where they grew among the cracks in the black granite paver stones. New shoots immediately unfurled once the old ones were plucked. Lichen and moss in their varying green-grays subsumed the rest.

Don't think of her. Goddess of spring. Of light and warmth and flowers.

Fuck that. Persephone was adjacent to those things at best. She didn't embody them. She destroyed as easily as she created.

The minutes crawled by as they never had before. Finally, my penitence over, I rose slowly, as I always did, despite the adrenaline surging through my veins. It heightened the dull colors around me and urged me forward.

Now, it could begin.

I counted on Thanatos to watch over Tartarus, on Hecate and Nyx for the war, and on Cerberus for the dead. Together, we worked in tandem. Now, I could search for my dear wife. I could strangle her thin, swan-like neck with my own hands. I could crack her skull and bring it to my soothsayers. I could understand.

I strode from the False Dreams and leapt over the wall, spreading my wings in flight as I plummeted. Only once I reached the eastern edges of the desert did I drop to the sands and kneel, plunging my fingers in the dunes.

I rubbed the grains between my fingers and brought them to my nose. Her scent was faint but distinctive. Despite the utter shit of it all, I smiled.

"Oh, Persephone. You have finally made a mistake," I whispered.

7

PERSEPHONE

Passing through the realms was the closest immortals could come to feeling human. Some hungered for that weakness like a drug. Eventually all users veered too close to toxicity. It was that knowledge that helped the mortals win their war against the gods, which didn't exactly help my nerves now. While I used to traverse with no problems, something had happened, and whatever it was that had closed the realms to me was fighting me now every step and slog of the way.

My body flooded with cold adrenaline as I found the spot. Its dizzying fray felt like slipping a thin, white Hemlock flower under my tongue and sucking its perfumed oils. Then, a hand slick with moss gripped its fingers around my ankle and yanked. At least, that was what it felt like. I had no doubt that no hand existed, but still, things that resided in this space liked to pull you under.

This time, I went down harder than usual. The speckled marks on my arm from the demon and the octopus's death throes stung in the salt water, but that was nothing compared to the poisoned water of the Styx.

My breath caught in my chest, my throat a lead-blocked

tube as it tried to scrabble up. The waves were relentless, and I thought maybe I hadn't escaped at all. I was still stuck in the cave, doomed to drown in the Black Sea with an octopus.

No, I was Persephone and I would break *through*.

There. Ahead was something a little lighter than black. I just had to follow it. My legs kicked, my hands beat the water. I angled for the surface and finally broke its viscous seal.

The minute my knees hit the cold, loamy-smelling earth of the Underworld, a gulp of power slid down my throat. I almost moaned in ecstasy. This was something worth touching true death for. This was worth getting caught. I wanted to suck it into my lungs and absorb it to my core. Raw power. It infused my bones and made me weak and formidable all at once. I could collapse right here and luxuriate in this sliver of my old powers.

I could. But I had bigger dreams to realize. This was a mere taste. Like every good appetizer, it left me hungry for more. I inhaled roughly again, the cold, stinging air of the Underworld bruising my nostrils as I took in its tantalizing odor. And I had waited a century to sneak back in? My patience should be the stuff of literal legends.

There was something else. Something acrid. The air was thick with it. I couldn't quite place it, but something felt off. My memories were tinged with bitterness, but that was reverie. This was real, and it made my mouth curl in dismay.

Finally, I pulled myself up and took stock of where I'd entered. By the smell alone, I was somewhere near the confluence of the River Lethe and the River Styx. I forgot how wretchedly beautiful this place could be. Black curls of sulfuric steam danced and bent as the deadly undercurrents met with a crash before swirling away. The Lethe sparkled crystalline blue on its own, but became muddied and unfathomable where it met the Styx.

Lightning struck haphazardly without the rebound of thunder. The strikes lit up the rivers and the darkened mounds of rocks along the shores. I cocked my head as the lightning faded.

Like a fishhook in my belly, I felt a tug, and I set off at a brisk trot, power tingling in my fingertips. I was back, and it was glorious.

Three walls of bronze protected the Underworld, or so Zeus claimed. In reality, he placed the walls there to protect himself after the three brothers carved up the world between themselves. All of the gods feared the power of the Underworld, untouched and ungoverned by their rules. Hades accepted no sacrifices, and mortals didn't even try. This place existed outside of immortality. It frightened the mortals. And it frightened the gods.

This, of course, always made me giggle.

What can I say? I had a dark sense of humor. It went with the whole Underworld-queen vibe.

Inching my way along the lichen-covered walls, I felt for the object of my heart's desire. It wasn't a man, I can tell you that much. Demeter may have been right about that, but then again, even broken clocks are right twice a day. Men, especially the mortal ones, were highly overrated. Hades was different, but in the end, he too turned out to be a disappointment. Unfortunately, not in the sex department. He was quite adept at that bit.

I kept sucking in air and power. It wasn't enough, but it felt wonderful compared to the way I'd been forced to live. Here, everything was a study in gray. The sky was gray, the walls were gray, the mosses and lichen were gray, and the air held its breath.

Together, the shades of slate, silver, and ash painted a tapestry worthy of the gods, if one took the time to examine the tableau of the Underworld. It was hard to believe I was back.

As I hiked, I kept my right side to the outer bronze walls. There was a door near the castle, invisible except to me. At least, I hoped it still was. I had left six precious little magicks in that door. Once I reached them, half of my problems would be solved. I longed to roll the seeds between my fingers and savor their crystallized powers. My eyes closed for a second to fully appreciate the dream. Then, letting their sweet memories carry me, I practically flew across the lichen and deeper into the Underworld. Black mud soon turned to thick, sucking sand, but even that gave way to rolling dunes, illuminated by a sliver of silver moonlight. There hadn't always been moonlight. Hades had done it for me.

I once mentioned missing the moon, so he hung a string of them suspended in the endless night. Crescent, waxing, waning, gibbous. Like charms on a bracelet or a paper string fashioned to hang in a child's bedroom. I didn't let myself dwell on his kindness. We both did lovely things for each other at one point or another. It was a marriage, after all.

Tiny succulents in perfect nautilus patterns scattered in my wake. I bent to press a nail in one, piercing the waxy leaf until clear juice ran down my thumb. Then I licked its peppery nectar.

Once again, something was off. The taste was tinged with bitterness. The land seemed more barren than I remembered. If I paused and listened quietly, I could hear a low moan. The land was hurting. What had Hades done in my absence? Despite the Underworld no longer being my home, I felt a twinge of self-righteous outrage. This should be protected at all costs. What the hell was going on here?

I had always loved that expression.

I got to my feet and continued my trek. I needed my magic. I needed to shed my old skin like a snake sloughing off its scales. Only finding my seeds would do that.

My feet dug into the dark sand while my fingers struggled to find purchase along the smooth walls. The endless night was silent, which seemed a little out of character. Even in these far desert reaches of the Underworld, there was life. Shocking? Of course not. Life thrived everywhere.

So where was it?

I heard it then. Soft footfalls and near-silent breathing. By the way it hid its presence, it was predatory. Someone was with me. *Damn*. He knew. And he was coming for me.

In only the barest of movements, I pulled out my bronze dagger and balanced on the balls of my feet. How long until—

A fist like iron slammed into my back, and I was thrown against the smooth bronze of the inner wall. His energy merged with mine, icing and blackening where it touched bare skin.

Before I could so much as gasp for oxygen, a powerful body pressed on top of mine. One hand covered two-thirds of my face while his other took my wrist and slammed it against the wall. My dagger fell as I cried in pain.

He yanked back to expose my face, ensuring it was as bad as he feared. It was. It was truly me. My breath grew shallow at our closeness, this meeting centuries in the making. His cold fingers swallowed my wrist and I shivered. But so did he.

What was he doing at the far edges? Had he seriously sensed me so soon? It was possible I'd tripped some sort of alarm. His eyes were black pits, his cheekbones sharp angles. His lips were pale, even more so by the way he pursed them in anger.

I aimed a knee between his legs, which he easily blocked, but it gave me enough of an opening to twist and duck under his arm.

Beautiful curses inked on his skin as we danced. His gleaming, black eyes met mine as he blocked my thrust. "What are you doing, dear wife?"

"Getting help," I said as cheerfully as possible with his curses battering my body. *Block, stab.* "I thought that was obvious. Wait. Don't tell me you didn't get my message?"

Hades slammed his elbow down against mine, reverting to pure, animalistic rage at my intrusion into his realm. Coming here probably felt like a violation of his very body, and he even forgot his magic in his desire to hurt me. Using magic wouldn't have felt as good as physically dragging me, anyway.

I twisted to the side, breathing heavy. It wasn't an act. Fighting manticores and sea serpent demons in the mortal realm was one thing. Fighting Hades on his home turf after a century of diminishing magic? Quite another. "Please, Hades. I need you. And it looks like you might have a need for me." I let my power of innocence suffuse my voice. "The land is screaming in my ears. Surely you sense it, too."

Uh-oh.

Hades' dark eyes sparked in outrage, and I began to panic. All traces of trickery fled as I begged for my life. "I have nothing to do with whatever is going on here, I swear it. Please, Hades. At least listen to what I have to say."

"That sort of trust died eons ago," Hades grunted. His magic clashed with mine, and it was deliciously dark. He went left, but it was a feint. Agony flooded my senses as

Hades gripped my wrists in hands that felt like iron manacles. I wiggled like a worm caught on a hook.

"You're hurting me, Hades. I was stuck on Earth and my magic is fading. I'm practically mortal."

He lifted me with one hand until we were face to face. Despite the pain in my arms and shoulders, my stomach swooped at the intimacy. I'd forgotten how he radiated power, and how the power made him loom larger than the other gods. It was why they feared him. And it was why I should be more afraid right now.

"It's good to see you, too, my dear," I managed to say.

"You should not have come, wife."

And there was no mercy in his voice.

8

HADES

Per usual, it was a wretched good time on Olympus. Zeus' glamored favorites laughed as they cuddled naked on long couches. Small winged creatures, held fast by transparent pithoi, hung throughout the great hall.

I came because I couldn't afford not to. Despite the revelry, whispers abounded and plans were made here. I could not let my brothers gain the upper hand merely by drinking and laughing together. So I gritted my teeth and I attended.

Typically, I would find my brothers in short order, make a circuit around Olympus, take a sip of nectar, and leave, careful to avoid Hebe. Sweet as she was, Zeus did still create her of his loins. I had a feeling she was his most lucrative spy during these events.

Sometimes I'd wear my Helm of Invisibility for a circuit as well, but the gossip for the last thousand years had become mundane, even when they thought no one was listening. Perhaps it was all some long game, where Zeus and Poseidon thought to lull me into a false sense of security, but from the varying degrees of inebriation evident on their flushed faces, I doubted it.

From a distance, I nodded hello to my sister Hera with all the enthusiasm of one greeting a plague. She had her moments, but the fundamental truth remained. She may have hated how Zeus acted and took her own petty forms of revenge, but she was, at heart, his enabler.

"Hades, how good of you to come and support your brother," Hera said as she drifted closer. She wore a matronly veil over her dark curls and a thin band of pure gold across her forehead.

"Have I ever failed to support him in the past?"

Hera smiled slightly with only half of her mouth. It looked mournful to me. "You are above reproach, brother."

"That's not what I meant—"

Hera waved away my defenses and started walking. "Follow me, Hades. It's been too long."

"I don't mean to stay."

"You never do."

I gave her a frown. "You're in a mood tonight, sister."

She sighed and picked at a square of ambrosia from a passing silver platter. "Zeus is seeing someone again. He always throws these little parties to try to distract me."

"I see."

"Do you, brother?" Hera asked suddenly. "Would you betray one sibling to save another?"

"I—"

"Sometimes I wonder," she continued over me. "What would it have been like to choose you? Would we have been happy?"

"No."

Hera jerked at that. Her eyes widened at my callousness before she burst out laughing. "See? So straightforward. Something must be said for that."

"Why do you play games with Zeus?"

Hera absently turned and wandered the opposite way, grazing citrus fruits with her hands and plucking olives off of *trees. "It is our way. At its core, our marriage is successful. Why should I want to tarnish that?"*

"Because you're both miserable?"

"Anyway," she said, unbothered, "we have our moments."

"Where is our dear brother?" I asked, eager to end this. A morose Hera never led to any good.

She shrugged and spit out an olive pit into a bush of yellow broom flowers. A naked dancer brushed against my bare leg, their glamor practically seeping out of their pores and coating my skin.

As I grimaced, the atmosphere changed. There was a shift in the air, like a displacement, but I barely processed what I'd felt—until I saw her.

Diaphanous pale pink fabric skimmed her thighs and clung to her hips. She smelled more exquisite than Aphrodite, although I would never say such traitorous thoughts out loud. Wars had been waged for less.

Her smell bloomed fragrant and fresh, like white orange blossoms. A shock after the sulfuric scent of my domain. This girl was the antithesis to everything I ruled. The craving that started hot in the base of my belly grew as it spread like roots. Hera was still talking about some slight from last week, but I couldn't have parroted back a single word, even if a spear was at my throat.

Every one of my muscles contracted, desiring nothing but to sweep up this slip of a girl and carry her away from this place forever. It was raw and powerful and completely unknown. I had my Underworld nymphs, but this... this was something new.

The idea that this was dangerous, that she was dangerous, unfurled in my mind like a map of all my future mistakes. But all the rivers and roads still led to her. My legs moved almost mechanically as she looked up—and met my eyes.

I calculated a thousand scenarios of what that look meant, but I couldn't begin to fathom which one was correct. All I knew was that she was beckoning me, and I couldn't deny those eyes. No, quite the opposite. An all encompassing need pounded through my veins. It mingled with the warning signs flashing in my brain, making an intoxicating brew. If I could have self-flagellated as I walked to her—no, ran—my outward appearance would have matched my inner war. Already, it was the long, slow walk of a mortal man going to his doom. Trust me, I knew it well. But my state matched the pain in her eyes, and I wouldn't have had it any other way. Make me mortal, if just for one night. I would bear the consequences.

Just as I arrived, Demeter swooped in. Odd, I hadn't noticed her before. I hadn't noticed anything except for the girl.

The girl looked back down, breaking our eye contact. She didn't feel glamored, but she didn't feel quite right, either. What was she? What was Demeter hiding?

Thunder rebounded near my ear, and Zeus appeared, spinning me around to walk in the opposite direction. "Hades, you came, brother. I'm impressed."

Only with the greatest effort did I pull my gaze from her. Indeed, it would have looked comical if I had not. "When have I ever denied you?"

The laugh from Zeus' throat sounded strangled. "Come, let's get you some nectar. Where is my daughter, Hebe?" *he roared.*

All music ceased in that moment, until the little goddess Hebe appeared with her tray of gold-flaked nectar. "Father." *She bowed.*

Zeus took two cups and handed me one. "Drink up, brother."

Dutifully, I pretended to take a sip. Old habits die hard. "Who was that girl with Demeter?" *I asked.*

"Eh? Demeter?"

"You know what I said, brother."

Zeus gave me a sidelong glance. "You're interested?"

"*I merely would like to know whom Demeter has suddenly*

become so attached to," I lied, still trying to piece together this mystery. If she wasn't glamored, was she a goddess? A secret one?

Zeus was still acting cagey. He shifted his weight twice before answering. "If you must know, Kore is my daughter."

And the sky fell out from beneath me.

9

PERSEPHONE

"Hades, please—" I begged.

"Silence."

He didn't yell. He never raised his voice. It was infuriating how even-tempered he was. Scream, beat your chest, show emotion, show something!

He never did.

The Bare King, I used to taunt. No emotions, no feelings. Devoid of life itself. This time, I snapped my mouth shut. He had changed. His presence filled the cavern, and his predatory posture actually frightened me for a moment. I hadn't lied. My shoulders felt like they might come out of their sockets at any second. The cool breeze from the rivers brought his scent to me, and I almost gasped at the familiarity of it. It was something I thought I'd never smell again. Iron and earth, the bloom of a pure narcissus flower. The death of one. Masculinity encapsulated in a single god.

Hades' voice was both soft and hard, with a dangerous undercurrent that made his position clear. This was a mistake, and he would not be forgiving.

"You will sit in the dungeons until I decide what to do

with you. If you attempt to talk to me en route, I will gag you. If you attempt to escape, I will hobble you. Be happy that is all I plan to do." I could almost see his fingers twitching in their desire to wrap around my neck.

"But—"

"Starting now," he said as he bound my wrists with nightless cuffs and began a search for weapons.

"Not even a hello, how have you been, before you're already pawing at me. Well? How is it? Is everything as you recall or do you need a closer inspection?"

"I have no desire to hear what new untruths you've come up with this time, goddess of spring." He straightened up from where his face and his lips had been dangerously close to the soft skin of my belly. He'd found everything, including my Totenpasse, which he crumpled easily in a fist.

Well, almost everything.

"You didn't answer. Are my breasts as fabulous as before? Because I've been stuck on Earth for a while and gravity is a real thing there."

"If you say another word, I will seal your mouth myself. Be quiet, goddess. That is the last time I will ask nicely."

My jaw clenched. So this was his new game. I couldn't even speak to defend myself for fear my very voice would tempt him. Without bothering to look at me again, he unfurled his wings and soared into the air with me curled under his arm. Typically, I would resist, but this time? This time I believed him. If there was one thing the war with mortals taught the gods, it was that we were not invincible.

The silence of an abyss followed as we flew in the direction of the castle. At least there was that, I thought, as I considered my options. At least he wasn't taking me to Tartarus. Yet. That must mean something.

Below, the landscape changed from an oil-slicked blackness to smudges of gray. Something felt off, though, just like at the rivers and the desert. Blotches of charred land belched smoke into the air as if there had been a recent burning—or a battle. I ached to ask, but one glance at his stony face stopped my tongue.

The closer we drew to the castle, the more devastated things became. Broken fencing, bombed out craters. Even the mountains with their snow capped peaks and glittering lakes smoldered. Once-giant pines were broken in half at the tree line. Before Hades jerked me sideways, my body swaying dangerously through the thick air, I saw a horde of armed demons grouped outside of the castle walls. And then we were over the top, through a black veil of magic, and into the courtyard.

My old home. Except, it didn't look like the one I loved. It looked, instead, like it wanted to devour me, body and soul, in one slick bite.

Spiny towers shot into the black sky, needles piercing velvet. They were so delicate, they appeared as if one good exhale from the north wind would crack them in half, but I knew they were built by Hades himself. He had a gift with precious metals. Those obsidian towers withstood fierce fighting and the infrequent inmate uprising. The white elm tree bloomed as the brightest thing in any direction, the snowy leaves so bright, only Hades could look at them without going blind. Well, Hades and me.

I used to sit in the afternoons staring at the underbellies of the leaves, the kaleidoscoping images unfolding and dancing across them. There, I used to sit and dream.

My heart wrenched for a moment. I had lived here on and off for millennia. And then not all. It was another thing I thought I'd never see again, which had felt fine at the time, but now it seemed unimaginable that I had wanted to stay away. And unimaginable that I didn't anymore. That it felt... nice.

I stole a quick look at Hades, but he merely nodded from the air at the two Kako demons guarding the footbridge into the castle grounds. It was devoid of decoration, sparse and unwelcoming. At least, that was how I'd pictured it the first time I came to the castle. Now, I saw how it fit Hades in every way and, in more subtle ways, how it also fit me.

"You're in a war, aren't you, Hades?"

"That is not silence."

"I never was good at listening. Anyway, you're silent enough for the both of us."

No response. I crossed my arms, brushing his side accidentally, and my touch made his hardened stomach recoil. So, he wasn't indifferent to me. There was, at least, that. Idly, I wondered how long he'd been at war. I wondered if it coincided with the fact I had been locked out of the realms for a century.

"A recent war or a long-standing one?"

Still, silence. That was fine. It didn't matter much, now that I was here.

I looked back down at the castle. I hated the idea of returning home a prisoner. In fact, I refused it. "Put me down," I demanded, struggling against him as the wind buffeted us. But his hold was too strong. Hades was the deathless god, after all.

Feeling a little pin-prick of heat at my shoulder blades, I said a little oath. *Give me strength, and I will feed you blossoms.*

Faster than the next streak of lightning, I pulled out my second, pale pink dagger from its hiding spot. Its magic seeped into my bones, spurred by the motherland's power. I pricked him—barely, in my humble opinion—and wriggled out of his grip, focusing on forcing my wings to do things they weren't able to do in a century, stuck in a magic-less realm.

It felt like a band of leather had tightened around my chest. I couldn't breathe, and I couldn't break through to free my wings. The wind ripped the screams from my throat as I plummeted, and still they refused to spread.

Hades swooped down, looking remarkably unconcerned by my imminent crash. "Would you like me to catch you?" he asked mildly.

I pawed at him across the thin air, and he veered just out of reach. "What's the magic word?" he taunted.

How well I had taught him! To be fierce, to be unforgiving, to be vengeful.

"Hades, I will bury you under Tartarus and feast on your liver every night for dinner myself if you don't save me!"

Hades lifted an eyebrow. It felt like I was plunging faster.

"Please."

Faster than a cobra's strike, he jerked me to his chest and shot upwards again. I clung to him and tried not to think too many bitter thoughts of revenge, since my husband couldn't even save me without exacting some tribute.

We swooped far away from the front of the castle in dizzying patterns. He was disorienting me on purpose, and it was working.

"Where are you taking me?" I gasped.

He performed an aerial maneuver that would have made birds vomit and soared to a back dungeon I hadn't known existed. It must have been new. With a light landing, his wings retracted. He parted a thick curtain of vines and winterberries and shoved me inside. Instantly, the bright light from the white elm disappeared, and Hades' hand of steel gripped my bicep and led me deeper into the black.

The corbeled walls seeped moisture and felt soft, probably covered in fuzzy moss.

"If you wanted me in the dark, all you had to do was answer my original message," I quipped.

His breath quickened, and I smiled to myself. With a snap of his fingers, a ball of blue light appeared in his palm. His features flickered under its steady flame, but it meant my tricks in the dark wouldn't work as well.

I slowed my pace so I could get closer, forcing him to remember what my body felt like next to his. What I smelled like. I knew it was what lured him to me the first time we met. After so long apart, I was hoping it would re-shock him and give me a slight advantage.

"What is that horrid smell?" he sniffed.

Oh for—Eternal damnation. I caught the lingering scent of the sea serpent and putrid tentacles on my leather corset. That would be a pain to get out.

Unfortunately, I had taught Hades a little too well. For every small maneuver I attempted in the tunnel, he countered it. We did it without speaking, a dance only we knew, one whose steps we had created long ago. A dodge here and a thrust there. Neither of us even needed to comment on my attempts. It would be more shocking if I didn't try any trickery.

After a half hour of walking in peril, the tunnel widened into a long corridor of archways. I peeked inside one. Individual cells. My brow furrowed. "When were these built?" I asked.

Of course, Hades didn't answer. He produced a long bone and inserted it into a complicated shadow lock. The stone door squealed in outrage at being forced to open. Like some grotesque interpretation of a gentleman, Hades held the door to a tiny dungeon and smiled. "Goddesses first."

I peered around his arm without moving. There wasn't a bench or a threadbare mattress. I sensed no living creatures. Not even a rat to keep me company. I turned to him, my eyes wide and, hopefully, innocent-looking. Hey, it'd worked before. At his core, Hades was but a dick.

Hades scowled.

Damn. I held my wrists out in supplication. "Thank you, my king. At least it's not Tartarus."

Hades scowled. "This is your last warning. Do not speak to me. Until I come to a final decision on your fate, you will stay down here."

I bowed over my bound arms, head down. "So I am supposed to sit around for an eternity like this while you figure it out?"

His diamond-tipped bident appeared from the ether. Hades caught it in mid-air and slammed it to the ground. His dark magic exploded, shattering the stone where it struck and leaving a smoking, black crater. I flew backwards into the room at its power and landed hard on my side. The leather pants I wore from the mortal world ripped loudly, and I swore at the sudden pain. Hades blinked once, but it was the only sign he gave that he was surprised at my sudden and odd weakness. Instead of probing me, he turned and stalked back the way he came.

"You know what I think?" I shouted, struggling to my knees. "I think I took the one thing you cared for. Now your heart is hopelessly lost, and you're nothing but a shell. A monster."

"And I think you know very little about me, despite it all."

Desperation clawed at my chest. No, I couldn't rot down here. He would leave me for an eternity. And that was not histrionics. That was history. It was kind of Hades' thing. Eternal imprisonment.

My voice was low. "What would Melinoë say?"

Finally, he paused, his thick shoulders stiffening at her name on my tongue. He turned around, refusing to meet my eyes.

"Not much, if I were to guess, seeing as she's dead."

"How can you stand to be so flippant—"

"I am king in this realm. You revoked your status as queen. For the last time, hold your tongue, Persephone."

The stone door slammed shut in a very final sort of way, leaving me in endless night. I hoped I wasn't as mistaken as I felt at that moment.

"Well, that went well," I muttered.

I never was very good at listening to instructions.

10

HADES

For the second day in a row, I dragged myself to the courtyard, because I had no choice. If I didn't, Hecate would grow suspicious. I arrived in disarray, my thoughts scattered like disturbed crows all taking flight at once.

It felt infinitely strange to sit under the length of the white elm tree and look up at the trembling leaves knowing she was here. Within every vein of every leaf was inscribed a False Dream, and they waved in the breeze like little warnings.

Before the Accords, Zeus used to request they be sent to various heroes and mortals who annoyed him. Dreams of cheating wives or cheating neighbors. Dreams of a lover's star struck eyes or impending destinies of battlefield glory. False, all of them.

Now, unless I sent one, the dreams hung limply. I rarely did. What use did I have for a False Dream? I lived one.

Sometimes I would watch them twist and coil, like oil and water. I watched tales of false lovers and battlefield betrayal. Lover's remorse and lover's guilt. All lies. My entire existence was built on them. But those were just on Mondays.

Mostly, I sat and rolled a single pomegranate seed between my fingers. Thumb to forefinger and back again. I watched the castle servants go about their business and quietly thought about Persephone, resolutely limiting all thoughts of her to this one half hour. She used to sit in this spot every Monday during the months she was stuck in this realm. I felt it morbidly fitting.

Hecate liked to tell me how dreadfully predictable I was, although when it came to the afterlife, I would say that was a good thing. Hecate also enjoyed mentioning how my dour attitude had a direct correlation on my sex life.

Oh, gods. Did I really think I could keep my wife a secret from Hecate? She would sniff her out like Cerberus with a new bone.

Why had Persephone been slipping into my thoughts more frequently? I did not get foresight or premonition when the magicks were gifted to the gods. Yet, for the last few months, I thought of Persephone in the morning while stoking a fire, remembering the few times she had stirred in my bed, her long hair clinging to a sweat-sheened cheek. I remembered the way she blinked sleepily as she sat up and parted her long hair with her hand. Of the way her eyebrow quirked up in that way that made my ichor quicken.

I thought of her in the afternoon as I walked the boundary to check on Cerberus, just as we used to do together. It was one of the only things that united us as king and queen. Of the way she kept special treats in her pockets to satisfy all three of his heads, or the way his noses would sniff and whoosh to her pockets like an excited pony.

But mostly I thought of her in the evening. Before the Accords crashed our reality to pieces, Persephone could be mercurial during her six month stay in the Underworld. Like a spring day, I never knew if she would come down stormy and vengeful or with a sunny smile that melted even the coldest hearts of my realm.

Lately of course, the war had ramped up, and I hadn't had as much time to think of her. And still, she seeped in. Why couldn't I ignore her pull after hundreds of years?

Now she was here. What did it all mean? It had been a gut punch to see her. I had hoped I was mistaken, and yet I feared it was a mirage at the same time.

Ladies and gentlemen, our relationship.

She was the same, yet not. Clearly, her time on Earth had affected her, slowly leeching away the magic from her bones. Her eyes had damson-dark circles ringing them, but her lips were still full and perpetually pursed, as if she had just bitten into a tangy piece of fruit.

I could force her to Tartarus. Whatever demons were camping there would surely take care of my roseate problem. The urge to smash something, to destroy, amplified with every picture I conjured of Persephone, both the before and the present Persephone. Both angered me. Both betrayed me. What could she possibly want?

If only I could ask her, but sweetened lies poured from her mouth. They were very pretty, always very pretty, but they were still lies.

Finally, my self-appointed half-hour passed, and I left the white elm in relief. Hecate met me near the courtyard entrance. Her cinnamon hair fluttered in the ever-present breeze, and her green eyes were on fire. For a moment, my guilty conscience feared the worst. Had she already uncovered my secret?

"Going to see Prometheus is folly," she said by way of a greeting.

"I haven't gone yet, have I?"

"Why?" she asked, already suspicious. "It's unlike you to delay once you've decided something."

I clapped my hand on her shoulder. "So you're saying I can still surprise you? Mark it in the calendar. That's one for the books."

Hecate scowled. "I don't like jokes."

"Which is why I will continue to make them. It keeps you sharp."

She didn't reply. She probably didn't want to encourage me.

We began to walk through the protected area within the walls of my castle. I'd had to erect them for this new war, which didn't send the best message. It told my hungry-eyed inhabitants that I was vulnerable. That I had no choice. That fear beat beneath my breast. It was a new feeling. The only time I'd ever felt vulnerable was the first day I brought Persephone to the Underworld. The day I'd let my heart hope.

The lesson learned was worth the price of heartbreak.

"You look preoccupied," Hecate commented. "All of the time, actually."

"A hundred years of war would do that to any king."

Hecate laughed softly. "Basileus, I know you better than that."

"I have no doubt."

Hecate's weapons clinked as we walked, but I knew it wasn't the ones I could see that were the most deadly. Those she kept hidden away for the most dangerous foes, the most dire emergencies. Then it struck me, although not as literally as the first time.

Persephone's second dagger. Her mysterious pink one. Persephone had managed to hide it from me during my search of her body long enough to stab me with it mid-flight. My hand ran over my scalp through my hair as I considered the consequences.

I would need to pay a visit to my queen sooner than I hoped.

11

PERSEPHONE

Into the deepest part of the never-ending night of the Underworld, I paced. While I couldn't say my plan had worked *exactly* as I imagined, at least I was here. No matter my feelings on Hades, this had been my home for so very long. It had sheltered me from Olympus when I needed it. I had emotional resonance here, regardless of how much I hated its king.

And eventually, I would figure a way out.

A few Kako demons in bronze helmets and long sarissa spears rounded the corner. They patrolled the corridor every few minutes, usually stooping to sneer and spit into my cell through the peephole before continuing their route. I only ever saw their fangs and the bristle-boar hair of their snouts through the opening, yet I could feel their hatred. I wondered when they would get tired of the posturing or when their mouths would dry out. One hundred years? Two hundred?

And suddenly...

The demons scuttled away, and my heart thumped faster. Fog crept under the door and pooled around my feet.

It was cold and glittering. The temperature dropped again. That could only mean one thing.

Hades was near.

"Stand back from the door," he ordered in a low, gravelly voice. It was like rocks scraping together in the pit of my stomach. Once upon a time, it used to comfort me.

Dutifully, I went to the far edge of the cell. If I was going to convince Hades to make these visits a regular thing, I would have to be patient... and on my best behavior. I could wait, bide my time, figure out his motives. I mean, shit. It'd only been a day by my calculations. I'd expected at least a year before I saw him again. Perhaps I had unnerved him more than I realized.

His magic burst through the lock and he stormed in, looking more like his brother, god of storms, then I think he'd ever want to admit.

I did the "good wife" act and bowed so he could see my spine running down my neck into my corset. Pro tip: it was humble, yet showed strength. It lets your opponent know you respect them, but you're not afraid of them. It can backfire though. Depending on who wins next. It can also look reckless.

"My lord," I called from under the deep bow.

"I have not commanded anything other than silence."

I lifted my head with a wry smile, pulled my fingers across my lips, and flicked away the imaginary key. My hands were still bound in front of me by the nightless cuffs, but he got the picture. I chose to be cheeky and unafraid.

Hades stalked toward me, and damn it if I didn't back up a step. *Reckless*. Weak and reckless. What a great mix to show the deathless king!

"Give it to me," he ordered.

Because it seemed he was really quite serious about the

no talking command, I did a little shimmy and bobbed my chin, my lips squeezed tightly shut. Oh, I gave it. I gave it my all.

Hades responded by grabbing me by the cuffs and pulling me close. "You hid that dagger using magic from my Helm. I'm going to ask you one more time. Where is it?"

I wiggled my closed mouth back and forth and shrugged. That got an eye roll from him.

"You may answer when I ask a question."

I pretended to let myself out of the lock. "I've really missed this banter."

"Keep to the question," Hades said, warnings in his voice. "I demand what is mine."

"I'm technically yours under our ancient Greek marriage rites. Are you demanding me?" I wiggled provocatively again, but got a sharp twist of pain in my wrists for my efforts. Rage inflated me and my face hardened. "Despite everything, Hades, I've never considered you morally bereft."

He had the grace to loosen his grip. Slightly.

"We are still married. We could never not be," I said, matching his low tone.

Hades' mouth was a straight line. "I consider myself a widower. The Persephone I thought I knew died so very long ago. If she ever existed at all."

I couldn't explain the punch to the gut. It was there, sharp and acrid, then gone, but the pain lingered. Of course he did. Of course he should.

It still pissed me off.

"You think you have a monopoly on hurt feelings?" I asked. Playtime was over. "You know nothing."

"I'm not here to argue about our marriage. Where is my Helm?" he demanded.

"You know, if we're going to be seeing more of each other, we really should number our arguments. There are so many. Take this one, for instance. Instead of demanding where I hid the part of your Helm I stole, you could simply say, 'Persephone, 561.' And I would immediately know what you were talking about. Then, I would say, 'oh yeah? Try 1002.' And you would know immediately that I was referring to the time you fucked Minthe after you made me turn her back into a nymph."

I could tell Hades wanted to rub the space between his eyes, the one that became painful when I talked this fast. Magically, he resisted. "I did not—stop. Just stop."

"See? The process works. Instead of denying it again, you would simply respond, '1002b' and I would know you were disputing the fact I saw you in her embrace mere hours after she was un-transformed from a mint plant. Which, I still maintain, was an upgrade. Where is that little nymph, anyway? I bet you let her adorn your bedroom without me around."

Hades' voice was ice in my veins. "Where is my Helm, Persephone?"

I looked down to the warmth between my legs. The heat pumping through my body was something I knew he could never resist. It was the antithesis to his ice.

Hades' eyes tracked with mine. Then they dilated, and I watched him swallow with some difficulty.

I lifted my chin, daring him to come closer. "Are you going to get it yourself?"

When he didn't answer, I said softly, "Ah. You'll pass it off to one of your generals. May I request Nyx? She has a softer touch than some of the others."

Hades gave me a long look, assessing me coolly. He pulled another bag from inside his jacket and dropped it on the floor. Without a word, he left the dungeon and shut the door. I heard the lock clink into place and the guards return.

Immediately, I rifled through the bag. My curiosity was much like a cat's, but this time, it made my eyebrow raise. Chitons. My old clothes. I pulled out a pale pink one, a midnight blue one, a black one edged in silver. It was probably the smell that made him decide to be kind. There was also a bar of lye soap.

"Hmmm," I said out loud. I truly couldn't decide who'd won that round. "We'll number that argument 10,881."

12

HADES

I eagerly counted down the seconds until I determined enough nectar had been drunk, enough squares of honeyed ambrosia consumed, enough oblivion obtained before I could risk sneaking away. One of these times, I should seriously consider bringing Hecate again, just to liven things up for once in a way that didn't make my eyeballs want to bleed.

Sadly for me and my eyeballs, we were right in the middle of the festivities when things escalated to a new level.

"Bring out the mortals silenced by the sirens," Zeus roared, nectar dripping down his beard onto his golden chiton.

I glanced around for Demeter and Persephone. Surely the girl's mother didn't want her to see this on her first visit to Olympus? I moved through the crowds, an indescribable feeling growing in the pit of my stomach. It was possible Demeter didn't remember what happened at Zeus' parties. She hadn't attended in gods-knew how long.

I searched frantically, but after a second loop, I still didn't see them. Perhaps they had left. Perhaps she did recall.

Hermes pushed a string of men onto the temple steps, once proud pirates, sailors, and fishermen, now shackled in death by their necks with chains made of corded lighting. They shuffled upwards, their heads down and their hair eternally wet. Their faces were frozen in a permanent expression of longing for whatever song the sirens sang. Hermes made them come to a shuddering halt at the top of the steps, a party for all to see.

As one, they bunched their chitons in their hands and lifted to expose aqua-toned skin courtesy of a death from the deep beneath.

In unison, a debaucherous orgy began, just as I spotted the little goddess behind a fern. Her mouth was slightly ajar as she watched the spectacle.

Within the space of a hummingbird's rotation, I was at her side.

"You don't want to see this," I promised, turning her sideways. I was big in her presence, taking up all the space available. I made it impossible to look at anything but me. She must not look at things obscene. I loathed it as it was. She must maintain her innocence.

"How do you know what I like?" Her eyes lifted immediately to meet mine in a translucent display of defiance.

I admit, I faltered. For a moment, I almost stepped aside at the complete change in the girl, but I wasn't cowed by her insolence, especially from one so naïve. With an extended arm, I ushered her around the growing crowd. Although I couldn't block the screams, only the view, I could distract her.

"Why did Demeter and Zeus finally decide you should visit Olympus?" I asked. "I must admit I am curious."

Her rosebud mouth pursed in delicious ways, and I wanted to grip the baby fat of her cheeks and kiss their corners. I wouldn't steal that first kiss. I could never. That would make me no better than my brothers, something I would always strive to fight against. Family was not destiny.

"Zeus has no say in my life."

I blinked at the venom in her voice. "I get that he is, at best, an absent father—"

Kore snorted in derision, and I broke off.

"Zeus isn't my father."

My world tilted once more. "What? But he told me…"

The corner of her mouth lifted in a sardonic smile.

"Lies," I finished, realizing I no longer had stable ground. "I see he told me lies." The urge to kiss her overwhelmed me, but I fought against it. I was a god and much older. I must model control, and I must not scare her. Never that. The poor thing was already frightened half to Hades.

"Can you keep a secret?" she asked. At my single nod, she beckoned me closer. I bent my ear to her mouth, feeling my body stir at her warm breath on my skin. It was the wonder at feeling actual warmth that almost made me miss the impact of her words.

As she whispered the truth, my body stiffened. Every molecule jolted in rage as if my very essence was recoiling at her words. It was all-consuming, blotting out all reasonable thought. Kore pulled back to watch my reaction with sad eyes, and I knew in that moment, I was doomed. I would do anything for her. I didn't even stop to think when she whispered in that broken voice, "Will you help me, Hades?"

13

PERSEPHONE

When my husband came to visit me next, I almost expected a conjugal visit. He wanted the missing piece of his Helm, and too bad for him, I'd hidden it where the sun didn't shine.

I felt him before the door swung open, that infinite darkness with a sultry center, like a salted caramel covered in dark chocolate. Hatred washed over me the moment we locked eyes. Except it wasn't pure, unadulterated hatred. I hated him for the way he made my core twist and tighten and my skin tingle in desire. I hated him for so many little things, but most importantly, I hated how I didn't hate him completely.

I could see in his eyes that he felt the same about me. I could always tell what he was thinking from just a look. For an immortal being, Hades tended to wear his heart on his sleeve. He hated wanting me still, after all this time, and my old clothes weren't helping. Our grudges were as ancient as us.

"Dear Husband, what brings you back so soon? I was

just getting comfortable with these cuffs still attached to my wrists."

False. It had taken me most of the day to wiggle out of my leather and into this chiton.

Hades waved a hand and they dissipated as if they never were. My wrists burst apart and hung limply at my sides.

I blinked. Well that was... easy.

Hades stalked closer, and for once, I couldn't fathom what he was thinking. Emotions raged across his face like ships searching for safe harbor, but I couldn't tell if he was the ship or the storm.

He threw a jewel-toned bag on the ground. Books, paper, a swan quill, and octopus ink tumbled from its mouth. I looked up, but Hades was already at my throat. His fingers slid down my neck and caressed the hollow.

"Hades?" I hated how fragile my voice sounded. How had he managed to surprise me? I couldn't recall a single time in our marriage... or was I being haughty and foolish? Surely he'd surprised me that day on the black sand beach. I still remember the dress I wore. Crimson and cadmium robes with flared sleeves and gold lattice work around the bodice. He'd given it to me after I'd admired a mortal queen for wearing one. He had ripped it right from her skin and presented it to me.

I wish I could say that I cringed. Or that I outright refused.

I didn't. I enjoyed the things he would do for me, so different from my previous, lonely existence with Demeter.

And now?

He bent his head near the corner of my mouth, exactly where he used to kiss me goodnight during the years I let my guard down. In those ancient days, he must have thought I was a tempest, as volatile as the weather, and I guess I was. My rage was an endless abyss in those years. But now? I didn't know this Hades at all.

He hovered, his mouth over mine, but he didn't move closer. My neck prickled at the touch that didn't come. His cold caressed me like a familiar lover in that space in between. He had clearly learned much in the interval from then to now.

Focus, I scolded myself. *You don't need to kiss him again to remember he tastes sweeter than strawberries. Sweeter than the stars.*

His hands were still gripping my jaw in an intoxicating way. With one wrist flick, he could break it. He owned me completely in that moment. I let my senses guide me to the object emanating death in his coat pocket. The skeleton key. It was a bit more literal than the human concept of a master key. I bit the inside of my cheek, trying to concentrate on not revealing that my powers worked despite his shields. Or that I wasn't getting aroused by his very presence.

I tilted my head to stare into his eyes. As much as he unnerved me right now, I knew it had to be infinitely and exquisitely worse for him.

I had picked my husband well.

Hades' breath was as cool on my cheek as his fingers were rough on my chin, just as they always were. His words, however, were new.

"I will uncover your game, Persephone. Know that."

My blood chilled as he moved away. "There is no game. I simply needed help, and you wouldn't respond. What else was I to do?"

Hades laughed softly, but it came out like a scoff. "Since when did you ever truly need help? No." He held up a hand. "Don't answer with some number. I'd rather not get into it." His eyes knitted together as he noticed the wetness surrounding the door. The Kako demons and their spit game were in tip top form.

"Ah," I shrugged. "I think I've offended your guards. They don't like it when I breathe."

His jaw ticked. "While you are my prisoner for the foreseeable future—indeed, the foreseeable eternity—I will not have the guards disrespect you."

My heart lifted, although I noticed he had returned to not meeting my eyes, as if I would turn all of his resolutions to dust the moment he let his guard down.

"No. If they think they can disrespect a goddess, even if it is my estranged wife, it is a small leap to disrespecting me."

My heart fell. So this was all about maintaining appearances and power. I bitterly turned my back on Hades and faced the far wall. I said nothing.

"You have your books and a journal. Would you like anything else?" Hades asked.

"A really expensive divorce lawyer?"

"I see you've come back from the mortal realm with a sense of humor. I'm sure the guards will enjoy your jokes. Without the Titans to goad anymore, they are quite dull."

"They always were."

"Don't let them hear you say that. Spittle will be the least of your problems."

"Why are you so talkative all of a sudden?" I snapped. "I liked it better when it was all, *silence*!" I mimicked his thunderous tone.

His right cheek quirked up. "Then I must continue if it annoys you so."

"Oh, I get it. You're trying to turn my strategy around on me." I folded my arms. "Bring it on, babe."

"Babe?"

"It's an Earth thing. You wouldn't understand."

"It appears not."

Hades left me clutching the soft fur of the blanket and staring lovingly at my old books. Even if this was bribery, it was damn good. It certainly didn't change the fact that I was going to burn it all down.

Burn, baby. Burn.

14

HADES

I hated how much I began looking forward to slipping away to see my estranged wife. Imagining her under my complete control was like an erotic conquest. The idea of her fingers skimming the bottom of her pale pink chiton, suggestively hitching it over her hip, led my thoughts down dark paths. Pressing my fingers into her soft skin and gripping her close, close enough to bite, to kiss, to expunge the bad memories from centuries of mutual abuse. It was about control, and I craved it like a flower craves sunshine. What can I say? The gods are as complicated as mortals.

The intense feeling of seeing her shackled and finally submissive in some small way was intoxicating—even more so was watching her fight back. She knocked me off-balance with a mere glance between her thighs. She wasn't lying. My Helm was there. Without that small piece, I couldn't properly use the whole thing, and my Helm of Invisibility would be quite useful in a war against a faceless enemy.

With it whole, I could wander freely to the far edges, be my own super-spy for once, not simply use it to hide what it now obscured. Unfortunately, hiding that from my wife was now as important as fighting my enemy. Just imagining Persephone's cryptically blank face put the coldest shivers down my spine.

Each time I went, I'd sit outside her cell without announcing my presence. I'd inhale her pomegranate and rose scent before finally stepping foot in the tunnels. I smelled it in my dreams and as I stalked the castle turrets, watching for my unnamed enemy. It was omnipresent. She was everywhere. There was only one way to stop this madness.

I had to stop seeing her. I refused to go and I succeeded.

For a month.

15

PERSEPHONE

Either Hades was busy or, more likely, busy fighting his attraction to me. He hadn't come for weeks. Perhaps a month. It was hard to tell with this eternal night. Rotting in some dank dungeon waiting for the years to pass didn't sound like my idea of an awesome time. He had left me to rot for longer. It was a good thing, then, that I had stolen his skeleton key.

It was so nice and short-sighted of Hades to unbind my hands. A little diversion, a little sleight of hand. He never even noticed. Now, I watched spits of green energy crackle between my fingers. I felt the two demons' death forces just outside, one on each side of the door. They stood mutely, never engaging in small talk to whittle away the hours.

Kako demons were basically sub-demons who fed off of misery. When I became queen, I let them roam through Tartarus and the Mourning Field as they pleased, but Elysium for heroes was off-limits as were the Asphodel Meadows where regular mortals of no consequence spent their eternity. It was one of the first laws that I enacted, which garnered me much adoration in the mortal realm, but let's just say a lot less among the Kako.

To be honest, I was impressed by their restraint. The fact that they hadn't tried to torture me for fun either spoke of their respect for Hades—or their fear.

I clung to the stone door and poked my mouth through the hole. "You know, I really think this place could use some sprucing up." I waited for a beat. "Get it? Spruce, like clean and like the tree? Because I'm a plant goddess? Oh never mind. If I have to explain the joke, it's not that funny."

The Kako demons resolutely ignored me. I poked my eye out next. From my small hole, I noticed an angry red mass of flesh on the nearest one's cheek. Hades had punished them. He hadn't flayed their skin or anything like that, but he had made clear what would happen if they continued their game.

Little tendrils of warmth spread through my core at the gesture, making me remember that one time he'd licked my bicep and underarm against the wall of his library. He'd gone further, his tongue moving in concert with my body. We'd—no. I shook myself free. *Focus. Torture of rude guards notwithstanding, Hades is your enemy. Although that was an oddly specific memory. A gift. Yet Hades did punish them. For you. No! He is nothing more than your enemy. He wishes to imprison you. Keep steady. Take courage and drink it with both hands.*

"So," I said conversationally, ripping the images from my thoughts. "If you had to choose, would you rather be a vegetable plant or a pretty plant? If you had to. No specific reason. Just passing the time."

Neither of my resolute guards, upstanding specimens of their species, answered.

"Don't say I didn't ask," I called cheerfully before slamming the skeleton key into the shadow lock and blasting it off its hinges.

My burgeoning magic, growing with each day spent in the Underworld, wrapped green vines with prickling thorns into the unprotected flesh between their helmets' eyepieces and over the backs of their hands. I twisted my wrist and watched grimly as the thorns drove into their flesh and lifted their feet off the ground. They didn't even have time to scream before the vines gagged their mouths and held them steady.

I went to inspect them. "Was that a vegetable or a flower?"

Their black, soulless eyes glittered between the thorns. I couldn't tell if they were afraid. I tended to think they didn't have a higher functioning brain.

"Let's see. Eenie, meenie, miney, mo. Catch a demon by the throat. If he hollers, let him mope. Eenie. Meenie. Miney. Smote!"

I tapped demon number one on the nose and smiled as he became a beautiful, sunshine daisy that dropped to the stone floor. I winked at demon number two and paused, my finger an inch from his nose. "Vegetable? Or flower?"

His face stretched and twisted as I waved my finger back and forth.

"What? Vines got your tongue? Okay, I'll choose. Vegetable it is!" and tapped his nose. A cucumber dropped to the ground.

"So nutritious," I lamented, stooping to pick up my two former guards. I twirled the daisy behind my ear and took a bite of the cucumber in one loud crunch.

Humming another little Earth rhyme about ashes and falling down, I pocketed the skeleton key and made my escape. Psycho ex-wives are severely underrated.

16

PERSEPHONE

My heart pounded as I creaked open the iron gates at the end of the tunnel, but all was silent as I crept through the endless night.

Hades must have hidden me somewhere near the Pool of Memory. That was entirely too close to his castle. I wondered why he didn't just bury me on the outer edges of his domain or throw me in Tartarus. That meant something. That meant something was wrong. Perhaps, he'd lost Tartarus. That was the only explanation. He was losing this war. And what sort of war was it? Surely not the old gods. They were all defeated and locked on Olympus.

So who, or what, was fighting him?

The tug in my belly pulled me one way, but I didn't follow it. I paused, staring at my old home. Things were happening here that I didn't understand. Like why Hades was trying to hide this war from me.

With one foot on the ledge of the bridge, I thought about dropping again to test my wings. The old Persephone would not have hesitated. The new, older, and wiser me pulled my foot back from the edge and thought it'd be better to find somewhere a little less fatal to practice. There were spiky things at the bottom of this ravine.

Having learned my lesson once already, I cloaked myself with the slight protection my piece of Helm offered. Guards were posted at the entrance to the castle, but if I moved quick enough, I appeared as a whisper on the wind. The Kako demons exchanged a glance before shifting their weight. Neither were bright enough to ask the other if they'd seen something.

There was a hidden door to the inner sanctuary. I had drilled it myself sometime in the third century. I couldn't quite recall if it was BCE or CE, but I remembered it had a three in it. Maybe two threes. It was before the Demon War, so probably BCE.

My knees sank between the reeds and rushes of the river's edge, but I barely paid attention to their gentle swishing. I closed my eyes and felt for the little spark of life, letting my senses guide my hands. That was the problem with everyone here. They never felt for life. It was too alien. They never understood the delicate balance between the two and the parts both sides must play in this great game.

Ah! There. I pressed my magic deeper into the little crevasse, igniting the life within. They were nothing more than three lentils, but they were still viable. I had left these little seeds to lie dormant years ago, like an eyelash in a coded envelope, a marker only I would know.

I hadn't even needed to glamor them, which was good. Hecate could have sniffed that out rather easily. Magic like that always leaves an uncanny stench to the trained nose.

When my magic touched them, sprouts erupted from their centers, breaking the seed apart and unfurling faster and faster. I could feel their pure, pulsing joy at this second chance at life. They curled into the brickwork, crumbling it to dust so that we both might have a second chance.

And I would not use mine lightly.

I let the lentils continue to sprout as I crawled into the tunnel they had exposed. My hands and knees hit puddles every few feet, but there wasn't much I could do about that. Water was also life.

My shins scraped against dry brick as the tunnel surged upwards. I'd dug these secret passages myself over the years. If anyone had helped me, I would have had to obliterate their soul, and while the Underworld is a good place to hide the dead, I still had some restraint.

These were completely my own. Sad. They were perhaps the only thing that was completely my own. I could have had a sprout, a garden, a purpose. A star. But I had this tunnel, and yet it was enough.

Soon, I reached the soaring, fan-vaulted ceiling carved in glittering tourmaline. Every lacy edge sparkled in a different shade depending on which direction I looked. Red and yellow, a carnelian rainbow. Surely there was a metaphor in Hades' ceiling.

It was exquisite, as if the hall waited. It waited for its queen. The entire portmanteau made me pause, and I berated myself. Fuck! Was it for me? Or was it a trick? That was the problem with our relationship. Every gesture of goodwill eventually collapsed into the question: does it benefit? (It sounds better in Greek.)

Was this a gesture of goodwill? *Come home, my love. I will strive to be better.* Or was it a threat? *Come home, my love. I will strive to be better.*

It's all in the unspoken tone.

Soon, too soon, the carved entablature turned into the familiar. Hades' rooms were ahead. A soaring library of shelves with a painted ceiling of constellations. Jewel-toned books of goatskin parchment, all filed neatly away on the shelves. I looked over my shoulder before pressing forward.

Quietly, I found his door and slipped inside. In the few seconds it took my eyes to adjust, I knew it was a mistake to come.

I knew, because he was in bed, alone.

His diamond plated armor stood at attention on the white Elmwood rack. It glittered in the dark of the forever night. His chambers were exactly as I remembered, down to the pale narcissus flowers in a small vase by his bed, and for a moment, my breath caught in my throat. Those were for me. Those were always for me.

His arm was thrown over his head and his cheek pressed to silken pillows. The matching red sheet had slipped down to his hips. I could chisel a statue of us with the rigid lines of his abdomen. My heart sped up, and I would be a fool to think it was because he was my enemy and not once my savior, too.

Damn!

I wanted, needed, to be closer. I needed to look at him without the veil of hate distorting his features. I wanted to remember the singular times he looked at me with no guile, no agenda. Had anyone else ever looked at me like that? No, not even Demeter.

I took a step.

Dark waves of hair framed his stony face and illuminated the paleness of his skin. His thick eyelashes blanketed his eyes. In sleep, he could almost appear innocent, our past misdeeds scrubbed clean by Hypnos. Every ripple of muscle threw shadows like mountain peaks. He was the same, but not. His eyelashes fluttered. His lips were the dregs of wine. I wanted them between my own, but—I knew what that meant.

New scars lined his jaw and etched their jagged edges into his chest. This war must be fierce for Hades to resume hand-to-hand combat. Although he preferred not to, he fought well. I recalled how he roared when blades hit his back, and the way he twirled and allowed the moonlight to pierce his enemies.

The last time he fought like that, it was for me.

It was a battle so terrible that not even the mortals dared to talk of it. They sang no songs and wrote no epics. Hurriedly, they hoped to forget.

I saw what they called Lichtenberg figures streaking across his side. If I rolled him over, the tree-like branches would cover more than a third of his back. I remembered the day he got them and how I traced the angry, gilded lines, thick with his ichor, willing softness to take away his pain.

Zeus has never fought fair.

I would kill him for it.

Men always lie. Women are hardly better. But listen thus. I will kill you, lord of light, lord of gods, lord of nothing. I will end you.

17

HADES

The rumbling of my night-swept horses as I emerged from the deep would burst the eardrums of any mortals in the vicinity. The frothing lips and red eyes of my steeds reduced the remaining animals into comatose objects that wearily laid their noses on their paws.

"Goddess of spring, it is the appointed hour," I boomed, pulling taut the demonskin reins. The field before me was silent save for a cool breeze that whistled through the green buds and danced beneath petals of yellow and white narcissus flowers. I whipped them again, crushing the delicate green stems beneath my wheels as I made a circle. Something did not feel right.

"Little Kore, where are you?" I whispered.

A shift in the wild saffron caught my attention. Jumping from the chariot, my sandals hit the ground with hardened thumps. Dormice lay dazed at the surface, unaware they should be scurrying to their holes at my approach. Darkness swirled in gray and black around my legs.

And Zeus asked me why I didn't get out more. I wanted to rip him open, from his scrotum to the empty space that supposedly held his critical thinking skills. I wanted to tie him to this very chariot and drag his halves behind me for eternity. When I wasn't so very angry, I was sure I could think of other, more fitting punishments, but the blind rage was just that. Blinding me. I was consumed by anger, and saving Kore was the only way to calm it.

"Kore?" I called softly. Despite my mood, I did not want to frighten her. The last thing she needed was another vengeful god taking something from her.

When the girl stepped out from the craggily mountain face, my skin crawled in delicious anticipation. With her shy eyes darting around the meadow and the pale pink of her chiton matching her flushed cheeks, she was the very image of a goddess to be worshipped. Orchids dripped down her crown, and her feet were bare. She kept rocking on her toes in the dirt, back and forth, back and forth.

"Did you ask him?" she whispered, flinching at the echo of her voice in the valley of the spring mountain.

I nodded, unable to answer without my voice betraying me. I had proceeded to wait out the rest of the party on Olympus until Zeus was roaringly drunk. I whispered that I needed to take a wife, and he obliged with a hearty yes. It had been done according to the laws of the land, and I washed myself clean of any treachery.

I reached out, and she took my hand willingly, the gold-lined hem showing me a flash of curled hair between her legs and I fought against every instinct demanding I press her against the seat of my chariot. Take her. Fill her, *my body commanded.* Rip the fabric and claim her body as one with your own. She is your wife now. *Only her downturned eyes forced me to whip the reins and open the maw of the earth.*

Finally, I asked gruffly to mask my intense desire, "Are you ready, Kore?"

"Call me Persephone."

I paused a beat, glancing at the small figure, trembling already at the frothing mouths of my black horses. Sometimes, it was hard to reconcile the girl who stared and the girl who didn't. The girl who couldn't.

"Of course. Are you ready, Persephone?"

She sat straight, an odd gleam in her eyes. "I am."

The moment the ground broke in two, she grabbed my thigh. Her nails dug welts with their ferocity, but almost as quickly, she released me.

"It's alright, Persephone. I won't let anything happen to you."

"I am not afraid."

I smiled as I urged the horses deeper. Persephone was silent as we rumbled into the abyss of the deep and transversed the realms. The air chilled.

It must have been nerves. She was scared to leave the only home she'd known with a god she'd only heard horrible stories about. How could I comfort her?

"There are so many things to show you, but it will be overwhelming. Even for a goddess. Is there something you'd like to see first? Something you may have heard of, anything spoken in whispers that made you fear me or my realm? I can show you the truth. Tell me and I will show you wonders."

My little wife shook her head, her bright hair curtaining across her face. I reached out to sweep it from her eyes, so I could understand her better, but she flinched. I curled my fingers, making half-moon crescents in my palms.

"Sorry," I began. Then stopped. I didn't want to start our life together like this at all. "I know we didn't get a chance to talk long, but I swear you will be happy with me. I will do everything in my power to deserve you. I will love you with my whole heart."

Persephone's entire face wilted, like a flower hidden from the sun. When she spoke, her tone made doom wish to run, to hide, to die.

"Hades, I never said I would love you. Only that I would marry you."

18

HADES

I stopped the rise and fall of my breath for a full five minutes after the door had shut. Why, if I was so powerful, could I not understand this woman at all? The mere girl she was so long ago was lost forever, and yet she almost appeared, if just for a moment, a girl once again. There was even a flower twirled in her hair. A yellow daisy. Perhaps that explained her clumsy attempts to sneak into the castle, to visit me in my chambers, as if I wouldn't have noticed her presence.

I rose dressing quickly so that I could follow her intoxicating scent. It left a tell-tale trail down the corridor, swerving left and then up a spiraling set of turret stairs. She made no noise, but I would always be able to follow. It was our bond—and our curse.

She had gotten soft on earth. I'd felt her hesitant powers searching for the skeleton key in my pocket, and I must admit I was curious. So I let her have it.

But that didn't solve the persistent, nagging question. What was she up to? Clearly, she wasn't escaping, and she didn't come to my chambers to stare. So what was her goal?

Looking for something, if I were to guess, and unfortunately I had a pretty good idea what she sought. For the good of everyone, I would have to keep them hidden in the safest spot I knew now that she was here.

The trail of sweet fruit lured me through the twisted stairs and past oil paintings of still life. Fruit bowls and *trompe l'oeils* passed in a blur. Together, yet corridors apart, we wended through my castle.

The only thing I knew in this moment was how stupid I was acting. A phantom war waged outside my castle walls, yet I had led a dangerous enemy right inside the gates. And I had kept a dangerous enemy a secret from my war council, letting her slip into my thoughts and haunt my waking hours. For my stupidity, I was the real danger to my kingdom, and yet, I couldn't help myself. I had to know exactly why Persephone had suddenly appeared in this realm.

Worse, I imagined ripping the strands out of that ridiculous, leather corset that hugged her womanly curves and flinging the contraption into the moat. I thought that seeing her in her old chitons would've reminded me who she truly was. Unfortunately, they did exactly that.

It hadn't escaped my notice that Persephone chose to keep her more matronly form over the one of her youth. She'd chosen her widened hips and fuller breasts that she acquired thanks to the birth of our daughter.

Melinoë, *I still hear you laugh. Don't leave me! I will die without you. I promise I will.*

Sometimes, the only thing that kept me going through the centuries was knowing there was someone out there who held the same sweet memories of our child. Someone else who kept the flame of Melinoë alive in their heart.

Gone was the slim, slip of a girl with dark hair to her belly button that hid most of her face. Persephone had used it as a shield, as if she were hiding from the world. Now, she was constantly tossing it, daring the world to look upon her vengeful face. Losing Melinoë had pushed her over the edge.

Suddenly, her scent veered into an abandoned ballroom. Persephone held a few fetes during her reign as my queen, but once she left, I refused to re-open the rooms or put them to use in any way. They sat collecting dust and memories as I resolutely ignored this wing. If I paused and listened hard enough, I could still hear the tinkle of crystal champagne glasses and light laughter, or smell the elderflowers and persimmons.

For a moment, I stood outside the onyx door, waiting. Just there, she must be crouched in hiding. I could keep walking. Pretend this wasn't happening. Instead, I crept inside. Oddly, I didn't feel her beating little heart, but that didn't mean much. Who knew what sort of tricks she'd picked up over the centuries. Dampening her heartbeat would be a minor feat. I waited for her to reveal the big ones, like if this was some planned invasion. Oh yes, that's exactly what this had to be. Persephone did not call on me for help. Not anymore. She was trying to undo me. She was trying to bring war to my doorstep.

Too late, my dear. That deed is done.

Silently, I took in the room. The damask curtains were merely decorative in a world with no sun, and the sparse furniture unused. I noted a lump on a winterized chair, and my fingers tingled as I imagined wrapping them around her neck as I dragged her back to the dungeons, the look of horror on her face. No longer was she the sly one, the one who managed to trick every mortal into thinking she was benevolent or that she cared. No, she was just a goddess. Nothing more or less.

I yanked back the blanket, practically salivating at the picture of a cowering Persephone with her pale, rosy-flushed skin, so it took a moment to realize what I was actually staring at—a marble statue of a seated woman, curvy and beautiful.

For a second, white hot rage filled me like molten metal pouring into a crucible. I felt it from my toes to the tip of my dark hair. A splintering sound shook me out of it, followed by a moment of pain.

Golden ichor welled up in my hand from where I'd shattered the statue with my grip. A single drop of it landed on the statue's eye and ran down her pristine cheek like a tear.

Wouldn't that be a feat? To see the real Persephone show emotion.

I began to laugh softly while inside I raged at allowing myself to be tricked so easily. Another familiar feeling, exhilaration, coiled around my anger.

Ah, Persephone. I have missed this.

I have missed you.

19

PERSEPHONE

Hades' footfalls led away, and I sagged in relief. It'd been too easy getting the skeleton key. I had a feeling he'd known. That laugh though... Was he unhinged? Surely I wasn't amusing to him. I was a terrifying goddess who'd tricked him twice now.

Quickly, quietly, I went back the way I came. Now, it was a race. Who could get there first? Hades might have thought he knew where I was headed, but he really didn't know me at all. Maybe I wouldn't need to hurry.

But I did.

We had been with each too long not to at least suspect what the other would do. While I desperately wanted to know more about the war being waged against him and to find my old implements of power, this was a long game. Immortals are well-suited to the long con.

My feet barely touched the ground as I headed into the unruly mess of our hedgerow maze. The roses clamored for inclusion. They desired to be noticed and admired. In my absence, they had gone wild, begging for attention. Roses are high maintenance that way.

I had to ignore them as I cut through the shaggy undergrowth with the bone-handled dagger I'd swiped off of Hades' nightstand, since he'd taken my infernal pink one. While I knew it'd find its way back to me eventually, I also knew that it could take a while. In the meantime, this rather boring bone one would have to do.

Behind the horrendous undergrowth and rioting vines, a small path led to a trellised archway, crumbling and decayed. My fingers itched to touch it. To heal it. I needed my full powers back more than I ever needed sunlight or rain. Giving them up to get into Earth felt supremely foolish in hindsight, but I didn't care to dwell on my past mistakes. The future was now.

I continued cutting through the tangle for a few more feet. Foxgloves had bravely staked a space near a left turn, but their tubular petals shriveled before my eyes. I went still, quieting my breath and sniffing the wind. The stink of a powerful being wafted through the maze. It was the smell of fermenting fruit and iron. It was the smell of death, and it was coming closer.

Shit. He was quick.

I threw the bone dagger under a tangled bush and sprinted into the cell. The half-eaten cucumber was still on the ground, leaking an unappetizing goo from its edges. I'd lost the daisy stuck behind my ear during my mad dash back to the prison. No big loss there. Not to me, at least.

I kicked the cucumber into the shadows and pounded into my cell. With a flick of my hand, I fluffed my hair and arranged myself as casually as possible with my heart pumping wildly. I even rested an arm over my brow and tilted my head back. I was ready for my closeup. Time to shine.

The door to my cell banged open a few seconds later,

and I peeked from under my arm to see Hades, barely breathing despite the chase. His dark magic skimmed the ground, and his wings reared out, as if he were prepared for a fight.

"Oh, my dear Husband. There you are! I have missed you."

"What did you do to the guards?" he asked.

I smiled sweetly and nodded my head toward the door. "I think they got scared."

See? That wasn't even a lie. They were certainly scared at the end.

"Scared." Hades repeated, grunting the word.

"Yep, I'm fearsome. Would you like to call more guards? I'll wait." I crossed my arms and gave him a congenial smile. I knew it was driving him mad, but really it was too much fun. I was starting to wonder why I hadn't trekked back to the Underworld more regularly. Imagine, popping in on Hades while he was at his war council. *Hello, dear. I think you've opened your left flank to attack.* Or walking through the courtyard. I was sure I could get a vein to pop out of his head if I timed it right. Or I could scare him in the shower. While he was lathering his abs with frothy soap and sudsing every part of his hard body after a long day wielding a sword. And maybe touching himself as he leaned one bicep against the stone of the shower while the water sluiced down his back—okay. That felt a little off-track. I yanked myself back to the present where Hades was staring at me with a suspicious frown.

"Persephone?"

"Don't mind me. Just thinking of... stuff. So are you going to call more guards? Should I tie myself up to the wall and torture myself for a few hours while I wait or do you want to do that part? I'm sure that belt could double as a whip."

"Why did you escape only to come back?"

I opened my mouth and closed it. I tried again, clearing my throat. Nothing came out. Both of my hands went to my throat. I massaged it and tried to tell my lie again.

Hades' frown had become a grim smile.

Icy fingers of fear grappled at my body. If Hades was enjoying this, whatever was happening wasn't good. I felt his intoxicating magic probing, rushing around me like a jet stream. Thanks to my prolonged trip to the mortal realm and the effects on my physical body, I wouldn't be able to withstand it for long.

"What are you—wait. I can't talk," I garbled, a fire blooming down my neck. I tried telling a lie again, only to have the fire assault me once more. I gave up on that and sang a quick Do-Re-Mi-Fa-So-La-Ti-Do. Totally fine. A sick feeling rushed down my chest and pooled in my stomach. Here I thought I was the great, stalking cat, playing with my mouse. I hadn't known anything, but I did now. I knew exactly what he'd done. Just not how.

"What was it?" I asked, my voice as low as a snake's belly to the ground. "What did you enchant?"

Hades' smile had widened. "It feels like you don't trust me, wife. Which is odd. I never betrayed us."

"No, that distinction would have only gone to me, eh? Come now. At least tell me what you put the spell on."

Hades glanced around my small cell. "I don't see my bone dagger."

Ah. Of course.

"You knew I would escape at some point, didn't you? You knew I wouldn't be able to resist seeing you because I missed you," I accused him, practically covering my mouth as the words slipped out. Anger coursed through my body at his tricks. I was never very good at controlling my temper. "So you left something I'd be sure to pick up in your room. How wonderful. What a conqueror you are!"

Hades' eyes hardened. "Tell me why you came back here."

I turned my back to him. "Leave me alone."

"Persephone."

"Now. Leave now." I wanted to scream. I wanted to roar. I wanted to smite things and dance in their ashes. Because now we both knew the truth. My lips and tongue were incapable of telling lies after holding the bone dagger. The truth serum would wear off after a few hours, but now we both knew.

His voice was quiet. "Persephone, I didn't ask you to tell me that you missed me. I didn't trick you into revealing anything."

I stiffened. I would rather have his scorn than his pity. "Leave. Me. Alone."

I still felt Hades' presence. It was large and commanding, even without seeing him. After a few minutes, I heard him sigh, felt a whisper of his scent at my neck, and I was alone.

How could I have let that slip? His eyebrow had gone up and he was intrigued. Now, he knew I missed him—and worse? It hadn't been a lie.

20

HADES

As one might imagine, our first dinner was quiet.

After her pronouncement, I spun around my team of horses, prepared to return little Kore immediately to the field. No one had to know what had happened. Only the bees and flowers had seen us together.

I whipped the reins as we began our ascent. We had not gone far, and it took but a moment. Yet the sunshine barely broke through the dirt before Persephone threw herself at the demon-spawn horses, tears streaking down her dirty face.

"Please, don't take me back!" she pleaded, as the horses reared to a halt, whinnying in dismay.

"Whoa, Alastor, whoa," I soothed my lead horse.

"How did you do that?" I demanded, taking back control of the horses. They were beyond spooked, but Alastor slowed his frenetic braying at my touch and the others followed his lead.

Persephone bit her lower lip. "I think I accidentally startled them."

My incredulous look said it all. To settle them, I let the horses nibble carrot snacks from the palm of my hands. Then I climbed back in the chariot.

I couldn't meet her eyes.

"You do not wish to be married. That is fine. If it is truly how you feel, I refuse to keep you here. Go. Run back to your mother. Hide under her robes and tell her the truth. I don't want a woman who merely tolerates me. I have the dead for that."

Persephone, as she so desperately wanted to be called, widened her eyes with each pronouncement. I almost felt bad for hurting her, and I desperately wanted to reach out to stroke that warm cheek and wipe away the rivulet of tears. But I had standards. No living woman would be kept in my Underworld against her will.

"Please, Hades. Take me to the Underworld. If you don't, I'll arrive through the more traditional route, although I must admit I am scared to do that."

"Don't force my hand," I said sharply. "Threats will not work on me, goddess of spring."

"Flowers die and are reborn. I am not so afraid. Only a little afraid."

"You should be very afraid."

Persephone clung to me at that, her eyes round circles that looked, in that moment, guileless. She was truly frightened of something greater than dying. She said nothing, and unspoken minutes passed before I angrily whipped the reins and returned to our descent.

Dinner was a quiet affair. I believe I had fresh figs dipped in honey and rolled in pistachios. There were carrots. And pomegranates. Persephone was allowed no food or drink. If she was hungry, there was always her home with Demeter and supper on their hearth.

Blindly, I pushed food around my plate. I only knew one thing. She could not stay.

I cleared my throat. "I have considered your request, goddess, but I am afraid I cannot accommodate you. No one stays in the Underworld that is not dead or a deity of death."

"But—"

I stayed her protest with a hand. "You will return in the morning. I will concoct some story of how you were lost and beset upon by hounds. Your fleeing soul woke me in the Underworld and I saved you. You recovered quickly under the care of Hecate before I returned you to your mother."

She leaned back and crossed her arms. "How gallant."

My head snapped up, assessing her. There it was again. The Persephone that felt much older than she let on.

"Yes, well." I cut into a roasted carrot and sprinkled pomegranate seeds on top. It tasted like sawdust. "We all have parts to play."

For a moment, her eyes met mine, as if begging silently. She moved an inch closer, her eyes tracking over my shoulder. I frowned in confusion as she lunged, snatching six blood red seeds off of a silver platter and swallowing them in one motion.

I grabbed her wrist and shook her arm, her whole body stiff with the power of defiance. Her hair swung about her face as I held her in my rage. "Do you know what you have done?"

Her chin jutted up, her mouth a straight line. "What I must."

"Then so must I." I snapped my fingers, summoning a Kako demon to my side. "Put my wife in her quarters. No one is to bring her any aid or comfort. No food. No drink. No one in or out. Understood?"

With that, I stalked off, waves of death roiling off of my body, only to be swallowed by the infinite night.

21

HADES

I watched her every day. Every day, she did nothing.

I watched her every night. Every night, she did something.

She thought I didn't understand her game, that I didn't understand her, but a pattern emerged. I lost a pair of demon guards each night in increasingly imaginative ways. One night, she created a shower of rose petals from their bodies. Another, they drifted in dandelion puffs across the dungeon floor. Tonight, she arranged their bodies into vines that spelled out the words, "I loathe you."

Then, she roamed the Underworld. First, she would search for something. She always returned to the same area, the area I knew well because I had searched there first. Each night, her searches grew more frantic.

When she inevitably failed to uncover her prize, she turned to playing politics to demons, before slipping back in her cell before morning. Her false modesty was as obvious to me as the sun, but it was clearly working. Her visits were calculated and political. Under-served villages, mourning siren mothers. She kissed babies and hugged demons caught in the middle of my war like she was campaigning for queen.

Once she visited Virgil. I'm sure that time was purely revenge. She'd always detested the poet, which might have been why I enjoyed his company so much. I didn't care to psychoanalyze myself, though.

Another night, she went to the edge of the human shade field, the Asphodel Meadows. She watched from afar for many hours, and I wondered why she was seeking out a shade or who she might have cared about. But those moments were rare. Most nights, she waged her silent war against me, forcing me to fight on two fronts, and this war, I had to fight alone. Hecate was already suspicious, even though I hadn't done anything out of the ordinary. I altered no routine and changed no steps, except for when I slipped away to watch my wife's movements. Somehow, Hecate could look at me and see my soul. I wondered if that was a thing. Maybe she actually could; she was a Titan, after all, and there were still plenty of secrets in my realm. I knew I was but its temporary caretaker, and the Underworld would never give up its secrets so easily.

Tonight, after her search, Persephone went back to the river's edge where siren mothers gathered water among the rushes, hauling it on their sloped shoulders to trudge back to their huts. Little demon babies clung to their backs, their eyes round and unblinking as Persephone wove silently between the people. I heard them murmuring, "my queen" under their bowed heads.

She would respond, "Shh. I'm not your queen anymore. I'm just like you. A mother grieving. Hush now, I will fix it. Stay strong."

I gritted my teeth, but I didn't stop her. How could I? If this was a propaganda war, beautiful Persephone would win every time. I would be the snarling ogre come to break up her crusading cause, and she would bat her eyes demurely and dip her head at me, a proper Greek wife under a stolen veil.

I watched as Persephone gripped the shoulders of a siren mother, their foreheads touching. Despite the duplicity of her actions, my chest warmed. See, she even managed to dupe me despite my awareness. A dangerous foe indeed!

That's when the hairs on my neck bristled. The air had gone silent. It was stale. It was wrong. Tiny insects that drank demon blood along the banks ceased their droning. The meadows looked as if they tottered on the precipice of a great pause. The gray sky wavered, illuminated from below by some lamplight—or fire.

I was already in the air when the first horde of demons rushed over the hill and slaughtered down its side. Screams erupted in the village. Baby sirens can't wail—a great paradox of their species—but their mouths opened in silent terror. Mothers refused to change their form to escape under the waters since it meant abandoning their babies, so they stood, clutching their children to their breasts and searching for a savior.

Persephone swung her head around. Her eyes narrowed when she saw me swooping through the air, but with a swift nod, we prepared for battle. We were allies, for now.

From a hidden pocket under her chiton, she revealed her pink dagger. Clearly, she must have put a spell on it to make it return. Again, I'd underestimated her. Again, it warmed my core.

"So the great Hades goes to battle," Persephone said, twirling it threateningly.

"It appears so." I plucked my own bident from the ether,

pulling straight down and stabbing under the hard shell of a beetle demon. I thought about using my hellfire, but that would devastate the entire village. Nothing would be left, and this wasn't total war. Not yet, at least.

Persephone ducked under the claw of one monstrosity and stabbed up at its belly. Her black hair swung wildly in her rhythm, and I caught myself watching. "Be careful," I bellowed.

Persephone yelped as a pincer swung down hard at her head. My face glowed oil black in rage, and I unleashed on the horde. By the time I had finished, they were decimated.

Persephone had clustered the siren mothers together in a circle against a hut and was trying to protect their front as a circle of traitorous demons collapsed in on them. They must have been contracted, swayed to my enemy's side. If only I knew who my enemy was.

She fought back, throwing little seeds in her wake that immediately dug under the surface to take root, their unfurling green vines snaking around scaled legs and tails, holding the attackers long enough for her to stab them through the heart with that infernal pink dagger of hers. I almost rolled my eyes. Of course she'd hidden more weapons. Seeds would have gone unnoticed, burrowing under the earth to lay dormant for as long as she needed them. I bet she had them strewn throughout my Underworld.

Still, more demons came. A new wave crested the hill beyond the village with venom in their eyes and on their tongues. They looked like angry yellow jackets, winging from their nest to attack in droves. The unnatural bent to their joints made even me pause.

Yet they kept their distance from me, choosing to attack Persephone instead. They must have heard stories of her.

Her ferociousness. Perhaps they could sense she wasn't quite the same.

Fuck. I rubbed the space between my eyes, the spot that tended to become painful in Persephone's presence. If I wanted to strangle her myself, I would now have to save her. Eventually, though, I would get around to the strangling.

Swiftly, I spread my wings and prepared to defend this insidious goddess—until the one being I absolutely did not want to see right now strode into view. It didn't take a god's intellect to know that Hecate looked pissed. She stood wreathed in green fire, her magic spitting as her pinched face glared at me.

"Who's good and prudent now?" I declared as I slammed into a demon. Offense was always better than defense with Hecate, the dark witch.

She rolled her eyes, crossing two swords off her back and lopping a demon in two. "Oh yes, this is much better, Basileus."

22

PERSEPHONE

Hecate blasted green fire at the last surviving beetle demon. It disintegrated with a shriek that sent goosebumps rippling across my near-mortal skin. Between the three of us, we made quick work and left no survivors. There would be more later. There always were.

With no demons left to occupy her, the goddess of magic turned to face us, the green fire from her hands matched in her eyes. She was pissed. I hoped it was at the situation and not necessarily at me, but we'd never gotten along. It was probably me. I'd better get down on my knees.

I more or less fell to the ground, my breath hard and heavy. With my body practically in a mortal state, humility was a necessity around Hecate if I wanted to survive the next five minutes. I wasn't used to exerting this much magic. Finding and calling my little seed warriors had worn me out. Worse, my wings still didn't work, no matter how hard I begged.

"Thank you for saving me," I gasped and held up a finger. "Quick question. Why did you save me?"

Hecate looked down the tip of her nose. "I thought that was obvious. So I could kill you myself."

I was afraid of that. I guess I wasn't going to get out of defending myself. "Look, I can explain—" I began, stalling for time. Coming up with a plan.

"I don't want to hear it, you treacherous traitor."

Okay, so supplication wasn't going to work. "Fine," I said, giving up the act and standing up straight. "You know what, I really don't care. You are the one who betrayed me first. You got what was coming to you and more."

Hecate's long face went from middle-aged to an old crone before settling on the little girl, her eeriest form. She stared up at me from blank eyes, her long, cinnamon hair parted down the middle. Imagine the little girl from the *Ring* standing at the foot of your bed at night with those creepy, dead kid eyes, and you get the general idea.

I crossed my arms and scowled. "Fine. Be mad. Go ahead, both of you. I can hold grudges, too."

Hecate conjured an equally creepy baby doll, a jagged line of red thread for her mouth and glassy, blank stones for eyes. She made it speak in her child-voice. "Want to play?"

I shivered involuntarily. "You know I hate when you do that."

"I'll let you brush my hair."

Shivers coursed through my body, making child-Hecate smile. Her mini-me doll cocked its head.

"I promise it will be fun."

"Hecate, I know we've never been friendly, but we've always understood and respected the other. I don't see why that has to change."

Hecate's voice deepened in the doll's mouth and it screamed blackness at me. I ducked, my hands over my head, as her doll burned green fire and launched itself at me.

I leapt to the side and brandished my knife to hold it at bay. The fire scorched my skin, but when I tried to stab it, there was nothing there.

Hades' bident had speared the doll like meat on a spit. "Enough," he said, swishing Hecate's magic away with his own. Nothing could counter Hades' magic in the Underworld. Except for mine, once upon a time.

Hecate, still a creepy-ass child, pulled down her reed torches from the ether, and we watched as they ignited in her death fire, green and sparking as if sprinkled with potassium nitrate. She twirled them in arcs, flames spitting off of them, flare-ups forming where the grasses were driest.

"Not this time, Basileus. I should have known or maybe guessed. I knew it had something to do with her, but to keep this a secret from me? I could have helped you. I could have skewered her and saved you from yourself." Her beautiful face twisted, and her green eyes glowed the same shade as her fire. Hecate did not forgive.

Hades' face remained impassive. His high cheekbones were like marble, and his glossy black hair fell in thick waves over his forehead.

"There's nothing to save," he said. "Persephone is not the cause of this."

"She's always wanted to burn your kingdom down. Not in so many words, but look at her!" Hecate thrust her reed torches at me and I flinched—for good measure. Flinching made one look innocent and unaware. Also, Hecate could seriously harm me in my current state.

"Me?"

"Quiet, Kore," Hecate jeered.

That pissed me off. She knew how I felt about that

name. Over the centuries, the sharp edges of it had been honed to a point. If she thought they'd grown smooth, like a buffed river stone, she was wrong.

Despite our past, even Hades abhorred that name on my behalf. And that was saying something. He didn't give her a warning, and the clang of their onslaught rattled my bones. They'd always practiced so viciously, yet were still able to laugh and share a drink after first blood.

Hmmm. Maybe I could take advantage of the situation. My eyes sharpened, searching for a good escape route as they threw themselves completely into their fight.

I had barely made it two steps before something caught me by the chiton, holding me fast, twisting like a worm on a hook. "Hey! I just got this back," I cried, turning to see Hades' bident stabbing through the gauzy fabric.

"Stop running away, goddess. It's very tiring."

"I was simply checking out that flower over there."

"I'm sure."

"I can't help it. I'm the goddess of spring."

Hecate sighed, morphing back into her middle-age form. Two bands of black paint drew a sinister line starting at her forehead, running over each eyelid, all the way down to her chin. "I do not offer my compliance, Basileus, but I will offer my silence. For now."

"On what terms?" Hades asked. His bident disappeared back into the ether without warning, and I tumbled to the ground. The death gods barely paid me attention now. I thought about running again, but figured I'd save my energy. For all that I was, stupid wasn't one of them. Although the way Hecate was staring at me now made me reconsider.

"Simple. I bind Persephone to you. She doesn't take a piss without you knowing about it."

23

HADES

I spent my days pacing my chambers and my nights swooping large arcs in the black sky. Hecate wouldn't stop heckling me. As if her love life were any better. Her excuse for only teaching women the dark arts of her magic was as thin as silk and just as porous. In the laws of Zeus, she would never be able to act on her desires, and Artemis had made plain her disgust for female sexual encounters of any kind. Thus, Hecate was stuck at her crossroads.

The last time I teased her about it found me with goat ears, horns, and cloven hooves for five hundred years, so I tended to keep those jokes to myself now. The imagery had even found its way into the human collective consciousness after a few mortals managed to escape their deathly chains and return to Earth for one more chance at life. It was rare, but I couldn't say it never happened.

And so was the balance of power between us. She could joke. I could stare broodily. Hecate was a little frightening.

I stood on the balcony looking over the village beneath my castle. Triangular flags snapped in the breeze, and the smell of market days swirled through the currents. Fresh fruit from the volcanic soils of the far western edge were my personal favorite, as they could only be harvested once a century with Stygian water shovels. For all of my own troubles, at least the Underworld was thriving. It was more than I could say for my brothers, who were constantly finding themselves in conflicts.

Hecate billowed in, her black robes like spilled ink in her wake, her neon green eyes and cinnamon hair offset by the black bands she painted down each eye. A little polecat played on her shoulder, yowling when she dared pet it. Much like Hecate herself.

"How's married life?" Hecate smirked. "Happy wife, happy life, eh?"

I didn't answer. Everyone knew what my little wife had done by binding herself to the Underworld with those six seeds. They whispered behind their hands as I stalked past them, my teeth gritted while I listened to their gossip. Most of the gossip was wrong, but enough of the tidbits were close to the mark.

"Happy enough."

"You know I would do anything for you."

"Would you?"

Hecate slipped into formal, Homeric Greek. "Basileus, tell me what you desire. I shall make it so."

We watched the hive of activity below for a few minutes. "Zeus has been down twice, once shame-faced and once belligerent. Demeter is beside herself, he tells me. She wants her daughter back and is threatening to blanket the earth with her grief. She will blight crops and kill them all for the girl."

"What will Zeus do?"

I snorted. "Nothing. He will defer to Demeter in everything." I held back my wife's secret, even from my most trusted general. That Zeus was not her father and clearly Demeter was blackmailing him. He dared defy me rather than her.

"And what would you have me do?" she asked.

I resumed staring into the distance. "Persephone will be picking flowers near the Asphodel Meadows this afternoon."

Hecate needed no more instruction. She saluted and turned to do my bidding.

A part of me wished I could say goodbye, perhaps only to give the goddess an opportunity to change her mind. To decide to give me a chance at being a good husband. To beg me, for once, instead of the utter quiet she deployed now. Perhaps I wanted to look into her eyes and understand why she did this. Why stay? Why torture me?

Instead, I slowly put on my diamond plated armor and went to the tiltyard. Goodbye, goddess of spring. Your mother misses you. And you will not miss me.

24

HADES

I would have preferred the silent treatment. Instead, I got Hecate. While I usually enjoyed Hecate's inability to mince her words, I preferred when it was turned against others.

"I knew that goddess was your one weakness, but to keep her a secret from me?"

The space under my collarbone still stung from her witchcraft in the binding, an image of a bident entangled by thorned vines. "Ah, so you have hurt feelings because I didn't confide in you."

Hecate slammed her Stygian bladed boot onto my toes, and I jabbed my elbow into her back. She gritted her teeth, and we resumed our pace back to the castle. We had left Persephone in her cell. No guards this time. I couldn't afford to keep going through them at this pace. I needed them at the front, and she was bound to my will for now. That would be enough to keep her from sneaking out and getting caught in a war. It was disorientating how very vulnerable she was after her stint on Earth.

"I am the revenant witch. I don't get hurt feelings."

"That sounds exactly like something that someone with hurt feelings would say."

Hecate whirled to face me, her eyes in angry slopes. "What the hell is with you? Has Persephone invaded your mind? Are you actually *smiling*?"

"I don't smile."

Hecate sniffed and I held still. She never pulled punches, even in practice, and certainly not when she was mad. Keeping Persephone a secret? I'd be surprised if Hecate didn't stop trying to maim me for at least a century.

"I know you're worried about her effect on me and what it means for the war. Trust me, I've beaten myself up more than you ever could over this. Hey, why are you snorting? I have."

Hecate's eyes made a wide tour of her socket, and we continued our breakneck pace back to the castle.

"She's not responsible. She's weak. You saw her with those abominations. All she had were seeds to sprout at them. Against you and me? Her honeyed tongue. That's it. That's all she's got. She's been stuck on Earth for years, and it seeped away her magic."

"I presume she's here to find more?"

"A good presumption."

"So kick her out. If you think she's innocent, send her on her way. We have no use for her." She waited for a beat, but I said nothing. "The only reasons I can see for letting her stay is that you know she's not innocent and you're waiting to make your move. Or you've once again been blinded by the goddess of spring. I'll let you guess which one I think is the truth."

"I don't think she's magically changed in fifteen hundred years. Persephone isn't capable of change," I said.

Hecate threw up her arms, terrifying amounts of power

rippling along her leather arm guards and making the eyes of her silver fox epaulets glow green. "Then what, Hades? What the actual fuck? You just can't get enough—"

"No. Of course not. I'm simply curious what her game is."

"You are delusional. The only other time I saw you this delusional was when Persephone became our queen."

"I have something she desperately wants. Something she searches for."

Hecate cocked her head, her eyes narrowed. "Love and acceptance?"

"No one could truly offer her those things," I said, shaking my head. "No. I have these."

From under my breastplate, I pulled out a little bag I'd fashioned from a piece of my Helm and dropped six seeds into my palm, each one still red and plump with tangy juice. Hecate's face was illuminated by their glow or by her own hunger staring at them.

"I'm sure you have a few questions," I said.

Hecate licked her lips and blinked, as if to consciously break the seeds' power over her.

"Where did you… no. Why does she not… wow."

Pleased, I put them back in my Helm. Not many could make Hecate speechless, including me. I relished the rarity of the moment.

"I don't know why she shed them," I admitted. "Or how. Only that I found them. Maybe a hundred years ago at most. It must be why she can't get her wings to work and why she remains quite powerless except with her trinkets."

"Do you know what this means?" Hecate whispered.

"That it's not an act. She truly is low on power."

Hecate waved that away. "That Persephone has been here before without our knowledge. She had to have been, for she was still a goddess in full control of her power when she last left."

"I know. I know. I don't understand how she did it, either. Something made her expel these, though, and hide them here."

Hecate shot me a critical look. "You aren't going to tell her you have them, are you?"

I snarled and Hecate lifted her palms. "I had to ask. She'll gut you like a guppy if she finds out."

"She'd have to swallow them to do that."

Hecate snorted. "She'd probably bite your fingers off to get at them."

I summoned an appropriate sized smile, although her comment made me think of the other times Persephone had bitten me. One in particular was memorable where she'd—I shook myself. I could not dwell on those precious few times I held Persephone in my arms. More importantly, I could not let Persephone know I had her pomegranate seeds. She could search to her heart's content for her lentil and sunflower seeds, her roses and daisies and all other manners of vegetation.

These, however, were much too dangerous.

25

HADES

The volcanic fruit tasted bitter in my mouth. One of my few pleasures, ruined by Persephone. I tossed the brilliant verdigris melon back at the vendor and continued walking the agora.

The market grounds had been rebuilt twice over the last hundred year's war, and innumerable times before. No matter what, my demons rose where they could. Some I would mourn forever. The Furies were the first to go, those beings of vengeance. While hardly responsible for a shade's miserable afterlife, they were a convenient scapegoat, so the rising shades and demons captured them to protest their agony at the Furies' claws.

All around us, the double row of drab stalls disappeared into one another, a crooked tableau of gray and black sheets. While most products here were harmless, including food that was magicked to taste real and snake oil potions that promised to let its buyer feel pain or pleasure, some were decidedly more dangerous. I knew there was a brisk black market trade in ampoules of water from the River Lethe, River Mnemosyne, River Cocytus, and even the River Styx.

It was better to let it occur rather than risk open rebellion. At least, it had been. While most attacks were still coming from outside of the city proper, I was under no illusion that spies didn't operate everywhere. Even within my own ranks.

The agora was more crowded than usual. Hawking and shouting between vendors and customers rang loudly, and there were no instruments or musician stalls set up. It was not a content sort of cacophony.

Near a stall of caged fire lizards, I saw something odd, a creature I was unfamiliar with. I nudged Hecate and motioned with my head. "What do you think?"

Green sparks sizzled on her arm, disturbing the polecat curled on her shoulders. So, she was still upset with me. I could tell, though, that sharing the secret of Persephone's seeds helped a little. Besides conveying that I trusted her, it also showed that I wasn't completely blinded by Persephone. Not anymore.

Her eyes narrowed at the creature. "I've never seen his kind before. When was the last time demons bred something new?"

"I put a moratorium on that a few centuries ago. No cross-breeding. It was too dangerous."

"Perhaps they have stopped fearing you."

I sniffed the air, trying to figure this creature out. I studied its build and its snout, like one would look at a mutt and try to guess its parenthood. "No... something doesn't seem right. This doesn't feel like a simple star-crossed demons incident."

"Well, the last time was certainly memorable enough to dissuade future fools," Hecate snorted, referring to the time I put two demon lovers on an icy wheel to spin for a decade on opposite ends of my realm. "Come, let's follow it."

We stalked through the shadows of the stalls following

the demon with its oddly spiked head. At times it strode with purpose before dropping back into a meander, as if he momentarily forgot he was supposed to be nonchalant. Or maybe it was the other way around, and he merely forgot where he was supposed to be going.

We cloaked ourselves to avoid detection, even distorting our voices, and Hecate took the opportunity to question me further. I would expect no less from my dogged general.

"If not to destroy you, why do you think Blossom is here?"

"You know she dislikes that name as much as Kore."

"All the more reason to use it. Odd thing that is. I mean to get so upset over a name. There are many other things to be upset about. War. Plague. Torture. Dismemberment. Marriage. I'm sure there are others."

I found myself wanting to defend my ex-wife for a moment. Of all the gods and goddesses, Persephone had suffered the most. Not even Hera had so little power or suffered so much humiliation. All the others could come and go where they pleased. Persephone had been chained to the Underworld and then Earth for her six months with no recourse. Hecate would not see it that way, however, so I said nothing.

Quickly, I curved around the edge of a stall selling memories of loved ones and watched as the unnatural demon paused longer than usual. Did that mean he had memories he wanted to access? If so, I needed to see them.

The wind shifted, and I caught a noseful of the demon's scent. I almost swore aloud at his stench. Stygian. If he was crafted and not born... I couldn't decide which was worse.

As if sensing our presence, the demon suddenly grabbed the vendor by its poisonous tail and ripped it out, leaving the manticore thrashing back and forth on his table.

Hecate and I threw off our distortions. Shouts rang out in surprise at our sudden appearance. Some demons dropped to their knees for mercy, while others fled as fast as their tentacles would take them. Hecate pulled her reed torches from the ether to create a perimeter, while I called down my bident and grabbed the demon by his neck.

His abnormal face twisted beneath mine, but he showed no panic at his near-obliteration. He even attempted to stab me with the oozing manticore tail. I hooked his wrist and dislodged the weapon, tossing it some feet behind us.

"Where did you come from?" I demanded.

"That is not the question."

I resisted the desire to strangle him. "Fine. What is the question?"

"Where am I going?"

I waited for him to respond. The demon sort of smiled, and it creeped me out. I decided to play along. He would deliver his message at any rate.

"Fine. Where are you going?"

"Your castle. You will fall and then it will belong to us, its true guardians," he rasped.

"Well, you got one thing right," I said, squeezing his neck tighter, determined to take him somewhere where I could question him in private. "You are going back to my castle, but not as a conqueror."

"This piece of me is irrelevant."

The demon laughed at my confusion, a wet, bubbling sound as if he were liquefying from the inside out. His face distorted, like a wax figure exposed to heat. A demon with a self-destruct button was new indeed.

"Hecate," I commanded forcefully, driving the whole agora to silence by my voice. "Put a binding spell on his life force." But it was too late. The demon was dead before I finished my sentence.

With disgust, I stabbed my bident into his grotesque body and held it at arm's length. Hecate's eyes were troubled as she let her green magic pour over the dead demon in order to preserve his body long enough to study it back at the castle. What we would learn, however, from a glob of slime, I didn't know.

A scream rent the air, high-pitched and piercing. The first bomb was distant, like it had occurred underwater. The vibrations made the ground tremble and waver. The second one exploded on its heels, and the third was there and gone before the ringing in my ears had time to dissipate.

For the second time in minutes, Hecate and I snapped to attention, searching for the source of the disturbance. To my left, a stall flipped over. Jars smashed one after another, glowing with potions and scenting the air with their noxious gases. More screams filled the agora as the potions wound through the crowd of shades, tilting their bodies.

More explosions roiled across the landscape, leaving a thick smoke of saltpeter. We winged up the ramparts, taking in the destruction. Demons ran wild-eyed toward the rivers, anything to escape the fiery ruin, risking even the oblivion of the River Styx or the quiet embrace of forgetfulness in the waves of the River Lethe. It really wouldn't be the worst way to go.

The smoke was thick enough to chew as it rolled gray across the town beneath the keep. Chaos had come for the castle.

I began barking orders at the nearest guards. They didn't move. Fury filled my chest at their insolence. Then, as one, the Kako looked at me. Dread pounded in my chest. The Kako had gone rogue.

26

PERSEPHONE

The first explosion wasn't much, but the tenth one made me start to wonder if I should worry about my situation.

I paced. My legs and arms were jelly after the battle at the siren village, and my stock of seeds had dwindled. In this part of the Underworld, at least. I'd squirreled away more across the land, but they were farther out. If a few rogue demons wanted to take revenge on their ancient queen, now would be quite the time.

When I first heard the clicking of pincers and hard shells on stone, I figured it was Hades' ranks going to war. Yet, the noise grew louder, moving in an unnatural rhythm, until it stopped outside my door. It seemed I would have to fight my way out.

I gripped my dagger, threw open the door, and smiled widely. "Welcome!"

The Kako demons all stood at attention. One of them had to be in charge, probably the one who had managed to somehow find his head not connected to his ass. If I could slay him with my dagger, the rest would fall like sheaves of wheat under my blade.

But which one?

Mixed with the Kako were rows of demons in glittering black armor, only their wrists and noses exposed. These were not around when I was queen. They didn't look natural, either. They looked reptilian, each one a perfect copy of the other. Their black eyes glittered between their bronze nose pieces, and the smell of rotting fish emanated from their pores.

Diplomacy might work, I decided. Anyway, there was always a first time for everything. I cleared my throat. "I get it. This might be the only time you have to take on the Dread Queen."

I thought I heard a snicker in the crowd, but my ears were still ringing from the explosions. Surely they weren't laughing at my title.

"But as much as you hate me, think hard about the consequences of your actions. Hades is a good and prudent ruler, but he'll be royally pissed when he finds out you are here, which will be soon. Hecate bound us."

They spoke as one, their voices gravel to my ears. *Hush, little baby, don't say a word.*

Okay. That was unexpected, and it sent an icicle down my spine. No, that was an understatement. It made my whole body convulse with the creeps. "Have it your way," I said, taking a step back into my prison, creating a bottleneck at the door that would force them to attack me one at a time. If I was going to survive this, I would need every advantage I could get.

The mass of bristly boar snouts and horned noses, some helmeted, others just out for bloodlust, advanced. I destroyed the first five before they even made it through the threshold, but more crowded behind them, overwhelming my position.

I screamed a random Amazonian war cry and vaulted off of a kneeling demon, knowing that would hurt in the morning. But that was a problem for the morning, assuming I made it past the next ten minutes.

I swung and made contact with a demon's unprotected wrist, slashing down before stabbing him in the eye. Two more fell like knuckle bones, but it wasn't enough. Hundreds more crowded outside my cell doors, all there, all aware I was vulnerable.

A demon bellowed out a command, and they took a moment to regroup. A single bead of perspiration drizzled down my temple. So much for never letting them see you sweat. I watched as they pulled whips from their belts and marched in unison one step forward, their braided tails snaking along the ground.

Despite my rage, I could hardly project enough power to turn them all into flowers. A dozen or two at most, and that would take time and energy.

They had a faint, rasping sound in place of breathing, which I found odd. Even demons needed to breathe. Their synchronous laughter made my skin itch. It was metallic and left a sour tang in my mouth.

"What are you?" I demanded, wondering about the rules of Hecate's spell. Would Hades sense my trouble and come? What if he felt it and chose not to care? I could hardly bear that. "Where did you come from?"

My questions went unanswered. One demon cracked his whip. It went sailing over my head, a warning shot, or perhaps he was simply testing the waters. Surely they could sense my lack of power, but to what extent?

I bit my lip. I hated begging. I mean, I did what I had to do to survive, as I was first and foremost a survivor, but begging was my least favorite tactic. Desperately, I pictured

Hades and his firepower. When he was in full battle lust, his eyes blazed like an oil slick that could burn for millennia.

I wondered if he'd actually come when I cried this time. The scream bubbled up and ripped out of my very essence, slashing the night air.

"Help me, Hades!"

27

HADES

I ducked as another wheel of Greek fire rolled across the moat and through the leaded window panes, exploding shards of glass in a deadly spray that shattered the cloisonné enamel work. Damn, that had taken centuries to perfect.

As the goddess of ghosts and necromancy, Hecate battled the cyanotic blue shades. She glowed in her tri-parte form, but even I could see her power waning slightly. For every shade she turned back into a compliant ghost, five more vaulted to overwhelm her. They moved like flood waters, pulling all resistance into their revolving mass.

Whereas intimidation had always worked and small uprisings were quickly quelled, this was the first major offensive that ground us down, forcing us to rethink battles and siege. It was disconcerting. Whoever was behind this war knew me well.

I roared, twisting down and spearing up as the hordes descended. I could do nothing against the shades, but the demons were dead if they reached me. As they departed, each one evaporated into their purest essence.

It wasn't until I'd killed a few hundred that I took a

breath to think about what that meant, the battle lulling long enough for me to rub the demon dust between my fingers. Immediately, my nose wrinkled.

Chthonic.

Dark.

Ancient, even to me.

Did these demons come from the depths of Tartarus? Were they created down there? A cold fear passed the length of my neck. I had never trekked farther than where we had built the prison for Kronos and his ilk. It always made my stomach turn and my lip curl. I did not care to see any farther. Perhaps I was afraid.

A screech high above me made me pause. Scally, my loyal commander, glided on the air in his owl form. An impressive sight, except for one thing. He should be on the rampart defending the castle.

I slammed my bident into the ground and energy exploded all around me, clearing the field of demons for hundreds of yards. A second later, Scally landed with a run, transforming into a soldier in mid-flight. "The castle is breached, Basileus," he said breathlessly. "It's not just thrown fire. There are reports of those odd demons crossing the moat and battering down the grates under the River Styx."

"You've seen this with your own eyes?" I barked. I refused to make a battle strategy on "reports".

"No, but I trust the intel. Whoever it is has released all of Tartarus. Virgil has taken over command of the shades, while these new demons have control of the Kako. We still don't believe the Kako kin are responsible, however."

I held up a hand. "I get it. The shades are merely opportunistic while the Kako can barely wipe their asses on their own. Someone else is at the core of this fight."

He nodded, grim. "Precisely."

"Begin the emergency evacuation procedure. Thanatos, Nyx, and Hecate should know where to go. May the gods better than me be with you."

Scally saluted and turned on his heel. In the next blink, he was gone, skating silently on owl wings as he soared to relay my orders. He would stay behind to spy. I needed more good and loyal soldiers like Scally. Instead, I was stuck with—

Damn. Persephone. I shouldn't worry about her. I should let her rot in that cell. If the truth serum on the dagger had proved anything, it was that lies spilled from her lips like water.

Except, I couldn't.

She had been pathetic when it came to fighting me. She easily dispensed with the Kako demons by the twos, but she hadn't stood a chance against me or Hecate. Whatever was attacking my castle would easily throttle her and leave her for the carrion.

That was my job.

I wanted to swear, but I didn't. Persephone would laugh at me. She'd always called me emotionless, the Bare King. She'd say it was unnatural to never show emotion, not even anger. That I was passionless. Now? She would mock me for changing.

I would show her true apathy, but first I had to save her.

28

PERSEPHONE

"Bow before your new masters, Olympian-vermin," the Kako said in unison. If it wasn't so creepy, I'd have laughed at the rehearsed nature of it all. Unless it wasn't rehearsed and something controlled them. The thought made my laughter die in my throat. Much like I was about to do.

"You know I'm not technically an Olympian, right? That would be Demeter and Zeus. Or, you know. Your boss."

The demons showed no reaction.

"Remember him? Hades. Lord of the Underworld. The Deathless God. He Who Attracts All. None of those names ring any bells for you? He rivals Zeus for ultimate power as all life ends with him?"

Not even a blink at the name. So perhaps it wasn't Zeus. My little dig did nothing to upset them. I thought it was a bit of a stretch to think Zeus had secretly figured out how to get across the barrier and escape Olympus. Even more of a stretch to think he might have the foresight to plan a chthonic uprising against his dark rival.

"No spoilers about who made you little cuties?" I asked, temptingly.

They cracked their whips in unison, the demonskin leather hitting the stone floor with a sickening snap. The few dead ones suddenly sat up. The wounds on their arms and faces zipped up, jagged lines of thickening black blood crusting over grotesquely.

"The Titans?" I guessed. "No?"

The demons cracked their whips, two hitting me at once. I couldn't help but cry out as their stings registered. *Crack*, again and again.

"What do you want from me then?" I shouted.

In response, the roof of the dungeon flew open, revealing the endless night ablaze with hellfire. I ducked as stones rained down on us, and demons screeched death knells, but my heart swelled. He'd come for me.

Hades' expression was a sublime mixture of anger and destruction He blazed above me, smiting demons who were too stupid to run, and my stomach swooped remembering times before. He raised one Kako demon to the level of the roof and tore his chest open with a flash of his hand.

This version of Hades was the reason his brothers feared him. The eldest son of Kronos and the true heir of his powers was formidable, and the Titan war would have been lost if not for him. Another demon's heart burst from his chest, and I winced as his eyes burned black. Two more had their spleens eviscerated with a simple command from the deathless god.

Sure, he'd only come back because of the binding spell, but I'd never felt more elated to see his eyes blaze in anger. For once, it wasn't because of me. I should mark that down, but I was too busy jumping into his arms for my getaway.

And then I felt shock. The look on his face... It was only there for a second, but I saw it. Relief. He was relieved to see me.

Death rippled off him in crests and waves, making vibrations run down the length of my body. My nipples hardened at the sensation, forcing me to cross my arms. Hades did not need to know that. It was fine for him to accidentally show his hand and his relief, but the knowledge of missing him was more than enough ammunition in our cold war.

"I assume you still have no wings?" he grunted as he speared another unnatural demon with his bident. It went down with a scream that ended in a wet gurgle.

"Nothing."

"Hang on then. I'd hate to drop you."

"That wouldn't break Hecate's binding spell. And then, you'd probably get seven years' bad luck, but it'd be worse because you'd be stuck dragging a corpse around for eternity," I said.

"Are you sure about that?"

He laughed softly when my only response was to cling tighter to his chest. The hard edges of his shoulders were the softest thing on him when he wore his diamond breastplate, so I hooked my wrists under his arms and closed my eyes. Mortality really took the bravado out of me.

"Took you long enough," I scolded him. "I was making small talk. Small talk! With my wannabe murderers."

"No one could murder you. You'd find a way to hang onto every last scrap of life, just to spite me."

"And don't you forget it, just in case you get any big ideas. What is your plan, anyway?" I asked, as my chiton ruffled in the freezing night. Every so often, we flew through puffs of heated air from flames of Greek fire below, but goosebumps still peppered my flesh. Yes. It was definitely from the chill. "Why aren't we going to the castle?"

"The castle has been breached. It may soon be lost."

"Lost? How does one lose a castle? Last time I checked, it didn't have wings or legs."

Hades didn't reply. He swooped over the crag of a hill. Dark shadows trekked through the valley below. An icy breeze came off the rivers that smelled of musk and death. The serpentine river wasn't as peaceful as I used to find it. Instead, it was crawling with the new demon soldiers.

They marched in eerie alignment with the traitorous Kako, their bronze helmets glinting in the torch light. As demons drowned, more used the floating bodies to cross, jumping on them like bobbing, stepping stones.

"Who do you think created them?" I whispered. It'd been a good long while since new demons had hit the Underworld.

"You're going to help me find out, after we save the castle."

"After we what?"

Hades' only answer was to soar into the dark sky, the burning fire of defeat the only light around.

I gasped at the sudden altitude, but Hades paid me no attention. How he kept so calm at this proximity was beyond me. Personally, being so close to such power, more than I'd felt in centuries, was threatening to make me lose control. I wanted to devour it. It was insanely addictive, and I was already shuddering, my eyes rolling in the back of my head. Where his hands gripped, hoarfrost followed in lacy patterns that burned as hotly as a blaze.

Surely he could feel my pulse racing. Whereas he had the benefit of immortality to keep him cool, I was constantly aware of how very human I was right now. My delicate, pulsing veins beating against his chest must seem grotesque to him. Unlike the gods above who occasionally had contact with mortals, the only ones Hades saw were dead.

I felt a thud reverberate through my body as Hades jerked forward. He barely blinked, but I saw two feet of spear piercing his wing, pinioning him to his own body where the bronze tip had embedded in his hip. We were falling—fast. Air whistled by as Hades tried to rip his wings free.

In an instant, I realized we weren't going to land gracefully. I screamed, only for it to be swallowed by Hades' wings as he wrapped me like a cocoon and cushioned our inevitable crash. I felt it only through the jostling of his semi-controlled tumble as we hit hard packed earth.

As we struggled to our feet, Hades didn't make a sound. His face was a mask, but he was in pain. I saw it in the tenseness of his shoulders and a million other little tells. This was not what I wanted. Not today, not a thousand years ago, not a thousand years in the future. I needed Hades. Alive and well.

"What do I do?" I asked frantically. "You'll heal, right?"

"Just pull it out, flower goddess." His eyes boiled blue lava, already focused over my shoulder at the demons pouring through the black gates.

"Oh sure," I muttered, gripping the thick, wooden spear. "Just pull it out. I'm trained for that. The once-queen of the Underworld is really good at keeping people *alive*."

"Indulge where you can," he grunted, spearing any demons who got too close.

Even gods felt pleasure and pain, greed and gluttony, benevolence and brutality. In fact, the full range of human emotions sprouted in us first. Zeus and Hera used to argue over who derived more pleasure from sex: a male or a female. We even felt compassion. Most of us, anyway. So to have to take out a spear from the side of his hip where it had grazed bone was unfortunate for me, to say the least.

Hades didn't react, but I saw his pupils dilate as I tore a tip of his wing. My yank was, perhaps, a bit too vigorous. It was the adrenaline; I couldn't help it.

As soon as it was free, he was a blur. The only way I could track him was by the streams of gold that flew from his wounds in a spray of droplets. They were as brilliant as the explosions against the inky sky.

Hades was fighting hand to hand now on the castle steps, ripping Kako in half and beating others with their limbs. It was a glorious sight. I could have sat and watched it all day, perhaps waving a foam finger with a #1 printed on it. Hades wouldn't get it, but that was okay. It was more fun that way.

I felt something skitter closer, reeking of death, its life force non-existent. I jumped backwards as one of the new demons came snarling closer. Fabricated. It had to be. And with a whiff of chthonic mists, which could only mean Tartarus. My body thrummed. I couldn't wait to tell Hades. If I was right, he might trust me enough to give me what I wanted. A way to find my seeds unimpeded.

The thrumming got stronger. I was practically vibrating. Power pulsed all around me—Hades must be near. His presence was a balm and an addiction all at once.

"If you have any power left in that body, goddess, now would be the time to use it." Hades had on his general voice, the voice that won wars against Titans and corralled the dead. He was ordering me, and I was powerless to resist.

"I don't know. I don't think so, but being here has helped." I swallowed. "Watch my back," I finally said.

I held out my hands, pushing as much of the chaos and sounds of battle away from me as I could. For this, I needed to feel. More of my tiny seed warriors were nestled in hibernation beneath the ground, warm and waiting for my commands.

Hades was to my left, although I didn't know that from sight, only a feeling as I gathered my forces. I heard the clashing of his weapons on hardened demonskin and the strangled gurgles of their deaths. I wiggled my fingers and lifted my hands, calling forth my little warriors. They were ancient, moldy, forgotten. Stuck in a weakened state, I couldn't seem to give them more life. I turned to Hades, panic in my face as I stepped closer to him and—there! I stepped again and the power cranked up another notch. It was as if every step I made to him amplified what little powers I had left. I fed them into the earth in a continual loop as I ran to his arms, determined to juice this connection for all it was worth.

"Hades, hold me."

He obeyed without question.

"I'm more powerful with you," I murmured, closing my eyes again, knowing he would watch over me.

It was a dark power that surged and it was all mine. I relished in the force of seeds blooming to life, swelling and crawling up, rushing across the ground as they grew and entangled anything standing in the way. Shades and demons alike were no match, but as long as the gods of the dead were fast enough in flight, they would be fine. Hades snatched me at the last moment, although my seeds and their vines would not have harmed me. They fed from me, and I fed from them. My old power sang in my veins and made me flush, hot to the touch. I needed more. More of everything.

For a moment, I let everything else fall away except how delicious this felt. I clung to Hades, kissing his lips and ripping at his armor as the cold air of the Underworld whipped past us and we spiraled up, up, up in dizzying heights as his immortal wing had already healed itself.

My mouth was making animal noises that I couldn't control, and so were my hands. I was quenching that thirst that lived in the back of my throat, that ache that couldn't be sated except with Hades, but then, something peeled me away and there was a coldness where before there was heat.

"It's over, Persephone. It's all over. You can stop now."

Hades' voice was soft, but it went straight through my heart. He didn't need to tell me he meant both the battle and us. I already knew.

My fire of want quickly turned to a fire of shame in my chest. I turned my cheek and let the air ice a traitorous tear before he could see. This feeling of rejection was easily the coldest thing in all the land.

29

PERSEPHONE

We spent our days apart and our nights even further, as if we lived separate lifetimes. By the very act of taking me with Zeus' permission, who was my father in the eyes of the gods, we were married in accordance to our ancient laws. Vows did not have to be said. Virginity was unoffered. Hades knew that. Taking a bride was considered enough. I had merely made it more official in the eyes of the ancients by swallowing the seeds. I would be his queen, not only by law, but by something much more ancient. By the very food of the dead that bound me to this place.

It was for a very good reason. Eventually, I would have to tell Hades the truth. But not yet. Already, I had had to beg for my life when his pet witch, Hecate, kidnapped me and brought me back to Demeter. They finally struck a deal. After my six months were complete here, I would be forced to ascend for another six and spend them with my mother.

I knew something they did not, however.

Sighing, I slid from under the soft, gray fur covers and wiggled my toes into the slippers I kept near my fire. Servants had already been by to stir the embers and begin the sunless day. The hexagonal pattern of the onyx tile floor pleased my need for patterns. I loved the symmetry of flowers in the spring and the tessellations of nature during my time with Demeter. I adored the open throats of lavender foxgloves, searching for the sun. Little white crocuses made me laugh at their adulations of the early rains.

Hades had barely blinked when I asked him at our weekly dinners.

His fork and knife scraped together over the spiced walnut and pomegranate molasses stew. He ate it with chickpeas and unrisen bread. He refused to eat meat.

"I can redecorate my quarters?" I asked. "I can plant seeds?"

"Whatever my wife wants is hers, of course."

And the next day, workers entered and began taking measurements, asking if I preferred metallics or pastels. They weren't sure, you see, because Hades was the god of precious metal, but I was a goddess of spring.

I missed how the moon seemed to emerge from a secret pocket in the dark sky to light up the night. I missed the pricking of the stars through the soft velvet of the sky. I even missed the sun and its insistent desire to be admired. Though, not as much as I thought I would, I must admit. I embraced the night.

The workers must have mentioned something to Hades, however, because the next day, a string of moons hung shimmering across the black sky. Their beauty made my throat lump painfully. Hades wasn't going to make this easy on me.

He meant to torture me with his kindness, but I saw it for what it was. A manipulation.

30

HADES

"So, we live to fight another day." Hecate had her boots on the map table as she picked her teeth with a bone. The black war paint that hooked over each eye to her chin was smudged from the battle. I didn't realize it could be smudged. Her polecat balanced on her shoulders as she stood up quickly. "I think we have two strategies. First option. Publicly kill a demon a day until we find out who is behind the new monstrosities."

"If I shall not be loved, I shall be feared?" I asked dryly.

"Second option," she barreled ahead, really in a mood. "Sacrifice our dearly returned queen to the greater gods and hope they're merciful."

Thanatos held up a fist. He wore a full ceremonial robe of hummingbird feathers, one of the fiercest birds in existence. They glittered menacingly in the candlelight. "I vote number two."

Only Nyx looked thoughtful. "Our ex-queen is settled in her old chambers, I suppose?" she asked. "Best keep the key yourself, Basileus."

"I bound them," Hecate interjected. "We'll know if she

tries to escape."

"She'll try, but it isn't her escaping I'm worried about. It's what happens when the nymphs find out she's escaping that I worry about," Nyx countered.

"I have it under control," I said, standing. "Now, we must focus on the new breed of demons. As I took Persephone to her room, she mentioned that she smelled chthonic mists on them."

"Tartarus?" Thanatos asked, but Hecate laughed.

"I didn't smell that. And why would she be so keen to help us? She betrays us even quicker every time."

"You fought shades, not demons, and I smelled it too," I said.

"Then we capture one of them and do our own experiments," Nyx said, still defending and deflecting for Persephone for some reason.

"Are they not vanquished? The Dread Queen's little... trick... was rather effective. As much as it pains me to admit," said Thanatos. "Everything looked bleak there for a moment."

"They'll be back. I have a hard time believing that was their entire force. Some factory in Tartarus is certainly churning them out. I want guards posted at all entrances and spies in every village stall. Scally?"

My messenger lieutenant saluted. "Yes, Basileus?"

"See to it."

He launched himself out of the nearest window, his owl wings silent on the air. The rest of us turned back to the map and began making more detailed preparations for every known entrance between Tartarus and my realm. Officially, there was only one. Unofficially, I knew there were several weak points. It wasn't easy to access any of them, as I supposedly held the only skeleton key as the warden of the immortal prison, but copies had been known to be made—and stolen.

Hecate, however, was still hung up on Persephone. "You cannot possibly think you have everything under control where that girl is concerned. This binding is deep, but it won't stop her from walking around, exploring; it will only give you a head's up. What if she..."

"She won't."

Hecate grunted in reply. Even she had to admit the Helm dampened all traces of my queen's six pomegranate seeds. "You won't get any peace so long as she stays. Why don't you throw her to the dogs of Tartarus and let those demons take care of her for you? Or better yet, if you really want to punish her, make her walk back to Earth exactly the way she came. How she managed that feat is really something you should let me question her about. Alone."

"I'm sure that would be cathartic for you, if not fatal for her."

"I know she's weak. I wouldn't kill her, but I'd reserve the right to maim her a little. For the greater good."

"She's basically mortal right now. You might get carried away. Mortals really are fragile little things. Look at some the wrong way and their heart practically explodes," Nyx pointed out.

Hecate paused at the threshold of the door, as if itching to race out and torture Persephone. Her face was sour and pinched. "Fine. I'll wait until she wreaks more havoc. Then you'll be begging me to interrogate her."

"I like your optimism," I noted. "Get some rest, everyone. Heal. The only thing we know for certain these days is that the demons will be back. The war is not—" Then, the bident and briar tattoo binding on my shoulder twinged, and I was unable to hide it, least of all from Hecate.

31

PERSEPHONE

A knock resounded on the door. That was odd. The servants bustled in to stoke my fire and empty the bedchamber pot. They didn't knock to warn the scorned queen.

The knock came again as I pondered. "Coming, coming," I called. "Give me a moment." The onyx floor felt cold where my bare feet touched, so I slipped on my rabbit fur slippers. I found my silk robe and tied it gently around my middle.

As if my words hadn't registered, the knock came again, insistent and loud. I swung open the door to see Hades. He looked... disheveled. He kept running his fingers through his hair, making the dark locks stand on end. A warm buzzing began at the pit of my stomach. What was he doing here? In my quarters?

Seeing me in my nightgown must have triggered something primal in Hades. His eyes were hooded and he licked his lips, resolutely keeping his gaze on my eyes. How noble of him. "Come with me," he said hoarsely.

"Can I get dressed first?"

"What?" he jumped. "Yes, yes. Gather your things. I'll wait outside."

I closed the door, my mind jackrabbiting through the possibil-

ities. Whatever he had in mind did not bode well for me. I hardly expected it from the good and prudent god, but perhaps I should have unbarred my door at night, taken him into a proper marriage chamber, even if only once. Perhaps I should try now. Anything to stay.

I refused to gather my things. I was not leaving. Instead, I gathered my thoughts as I drew on a dark blue chiton studded with diamonds that Hades had pulled from the ground.

Hades didn't look at me when I opened the door. "Are you ready?"

"No."

"Well, this way regardless," he gestured vaguely toward a region of the Underworld I'd never seen before. It grew lusher as we walked, but I could barely appreciate the beauty of the succulents embedded in sandy dunes or the velvety blackness of the sky. My stomach dropped the further we trudged.

"Where are you taking me?" I asked, but there was no reply.

I grew more frantic.

"Where are you taking me?" I demanded, louder, trying desperately to pull away from his iron fingers. He held me fast, and the bile began to rise in my throat. I remembered his brother, heavy on top of me, and I began to breathe faster, more frantic. "Stop, please! Wait."

Hades paused, and my panic surged at once. I bit his fingers and ran as his grip slipped for a fraction of a second. I ran like a terrified rabbit flees a predator, but Hades was no ordinary predator. He caught me before I had taken more than two steps, his eyes glowing blue with hellfire.

Apparently that day of truth-telling was today.

"You can't renege on our marriage."

Hades' grip didn't break this time, but his eyes narrowed.

"Oh yes," I said, my words biting as deeply as his three-headed dog. "That's the only thing it could be. You want to break

our vows and send me above. I know you think your magicks down here will break them. Well you can't."

"And why is that, little Kore?" he asked with that detestable name. It was the name the king of the gods grunted as he filled me.

"Because I am with child."

32

PERSEPHONE

My first order of business now that I was back in the castle was to leave the castle. Obviously.

The only problem was my welcome home gift from Hecate. I ran my fingers along the hard ridge of Hecate's binding spell just under my collarbone. Once I'd gotten a moment, I'd seen she'd bound us with a tattoo of a bident entangled by briars, as if I were choking Hades. I appreciated the symbolism if not the sentiment.

While there was definite death magic involved, I could have sworn there was earth magic in the binding as well. The only way I'd be able to break it was to know exactly what it contained. And I intended on breaking it one way or another.

My bronze and lapis-studded hand mirror sat on my vanity carved of a single tusk of ivory. Etched on the back was a pomegranate tree in intricate detail with carnelian stones representing the juicy fruit. I paused, my hand hovering over the mirror.

It was beautiful. It was also strange that it was here. I glanced around. Actually, everything was in its rightful place. It was as if I'd never left. There was even the crystal decanter and matching glasses by my bedside that I'd requested from a mortal, medieval queen once upon a time. She had been full of self-righteous indignation, but Hades still plucked it from her hands to give to me.

I ran my finger along the rim, a smile tugging at my mouth when the beautiful vibrations sang in the quiet of the room. Inspecting my finger, I found there wasn't even a speck of dust.

The onyx floor in hexagonal patterns still shimmered in the candlelight. Near my bed of ox-blood damask covers, a golden hook in the shape of an elegant swan's neck held my silk robe. My rabbit fur slippers sat beneath them, as if waiting for me to get out of bed and slip into them while drawing tight my robe. Honestly, the whole room was like a creepy shrine to me. The only thing missing was an oil painting of myself in some fabulous pose. Maybe with a dagger or a vial of poison in my hands and a Mona Lisa smile on my face.

Yet, warmth flattered me. I was moved. Hades had kept all of this for me, knowing I would never be able to return. At least, that was what he sincerely believed. Maybe this plan would be easier than I thought. Hades' soft spot for me was well known. I was banking on it still being there, dormant, somewhere.

As for me, being this close to Hades again was immensely harder than I thought it would be. I missed the space of the dungeon. It made it easier to make logical decisions when I was surrounded by stinking, wet stone floors rather than my old life. Everywhere I turned lurked a memory. My face flushed as ghosts of our former selves glided across the room, loving each other, arguing with each other. Spending lifetimes with each other.

When we were at our best, we moved through the castle as heads bowed in deference. At our worst, they still bowed, but in fear. Maybe I was craven to admit I liked both.

I had told Hades some of my deepest secrets in this very room, and he had shared his hopes and dreams. We had also screamed and fought and flung things and kissed and made up. It was all so... normal.

If I wasn't careful, I might overlook a detail I had so painstakingly put together. Hades was clouding my mind and my judgement. Here in the Underworld, powerless, I had no room to make mistakes. One misstep could destroy everything. I would forget something crucial because I was busy imagining running my fingers through his hair or the feel of his tongue on my neck. I wondered if it would be weird to request the dungeon accommodations, again. It wasn't in my plan, but neither was the desire that coursed through my body. Perhaps it was a hate thing. Like hate-fucking. Sometimes it was beneficial to work out those mutual hate-love feelings and purge them in order to go back to neutral.

I snorted, once, and then louder. I was seriously about to talk myself into sleeping with my ex-husband "to purge" lustful feelings. Right. Good one, Persephone. Clearly, I'd have to begin to test the limits of this binding to get some much needed space.

My room sat in one of the taller spires. The slick black obsidian wouldn't make climbing down possible. I stuck my head out of the window and breathed in the Underworld. That familiar scent of loam and decay was there, but saltpeter and soot overpowered it. War. It was covering up the things I loved most about this place.

While most feared death and decay, that was what made the best life. Like a fallen log in the woods, it housed the most beautiful insects and toadstools. It created the richest fertilizer, and from its death, it grew the brightest flowers and most nutritious crops. Death was life. Death had been my life for so long.

Gods, I needed to get out.

I toyed with my piece of Hades' Helm, shivering at the warmth my fingers encountered and the pleasure of picturing his angry face when he'd realized I possessed this morsel of his invisibility. He'd wanted it, badly. Only his honor kept him from plucking it out of me himself in that dungeon.

Quickly, before I went too far down that train of thought, I cloaked myself and slipped out of the front door, blowing kisses to the posted guards as I went, leaving only traces of a shimmer that made their eyes cross. With the Kako gone over to the dark side, there were only shades left to guard the castle, and they were easier to manipulate than dirt.

Earth to earth. Ashes to ashes. Brains to dust.

33

HADES

A tug alerted me that Persephone had left the premises. I resisted an eye roll and checked the clock over the roaring fire instead. She'd lasted all of twenty-six minutes and twenty-three seconds before breaking the rules. An admirable feat.

Of course Hecate noticed whatever small reaction I'd made when the binding twinged on my shoulder. Or perhaps that was part of her spell. Either way, her gaze jumped to it as she was leaving the war room. She hardly needed to ask what had happened before changing course.

"Shall I follow her, Basileus?"

I wanted to resist. My body ached to go myself and catch my wife in the act of disobedience. I felt unrestrained passions when I pictured present-day Persephone. Her curves and dimple fat on her thighs, the fullness of her cheeks where there used to be dark hollows. She was much more beautiful as a woman than a girl.

And that sudden burst of power. Had she somehow tapped into the seeds hidden deep within my Helm? Or was it merely being back in the Underworld? Or were there more lies I had yet to peel away from her, strip by strip?

She was a fantastically delicious story. Always had been. How had she done such magic? I should have questioned her more closely, but I didn't trust myself then, either.

The history between us only made it harder. I knew how she felt, and like an addict, I wanted more. I felt depravity in my veins and I couldn't trust myself to be responsible around her.

"Basileus?"

Nyx was watching me with concern.

I pulled my attention to Hecate who was scowling as if she knew exactly what was running through my mind. Or who. "Yes. Go now and report back once she's safely ensconced in her room."

Hecate whirled on her heel, too much glee in her body. My wife really should learn to follow the rules. Nyx was right; it wasn't just Hecate who hated the Dread Queen for what she'd done. This was for her own good.

34

PERSEPHONE

Hecate did her best to track me. She really did. It wasn't her fault I was wily. So far, I'd been able to slip in and out of the castle a few times without getting caught. I only gloated a little when Hecate would come baring her teeth into my room in the middle of the night to catch me in the act... of sleeping. As if she really thought I was sneaking out then, like a thief in the night.

No, I strutted out in broad daylight. She posted her polecat as my guard, but animals, even magical ones, were easy enough to subvert. They always had been for me. Watching Hecate's mounting frustration was a pleasant diversion from my situation. Soon, I had the feeling she would resort to sleeping at the foot of my bed to find out how I was leaving the castle, which, admittedly, would be trickier, but not impossible to get around.

Fine. I gloated. Because I, too, was soon going to go crazy if I didn't put the rest of my plan into motion. There was a woman I wished to find. Her name was Josephine, and she'd had the world at her fingertips. She could have chosen divinity. She could have been made a god. She could have lived forever.

She chose not.

I set aside my pink dagger and let the Helm's invisibility powers glimmer over me before sticking my head out of my room and tiptoeing past the posted shades. Without the will to live, being dead and all, they really were poor guards.

It was nothing to trace my steps through the castle, draperies rustling in what looked like a phantom wind behind me as I passed. But then, one rustled in front of me. I paused my stride. A being swathed in back shadows was silently stalking me.

I turned fast, looking for safety in my room, but there she was, in the flesh. The goddess of night. And she was blocking my exit.

Nyx leaned back against the black column with its striking gold veins, looking very unhurried. She crossed her arms and took me in from top to bottom while my heart pounded against my ribcage. "I think your invisibility spell is wearing thin."

Sheepishly, I dampened the small square of Helm I held. Nyx raised an eyebrow. "Does Hades know you have that?"

"Actually, he does, if you'd believe it."

Nyx was silent for a few blessed moments. Her scrutiny was sweeping, a colonoscopy of a gaze meant to see all of my dark parts. Eventually she nodded. "Actually, I do. If you'd believe it."

I laughed. "You'd be the only one. Well, I was just getting some fresh air, but I think I've gotten all my lungs can bear. I'll just be on my way."

"What's the rush?" Nyx asked, and I couldn't help but feel a bit like a prey animal. "We never got to talk after the Demon War."

"Right. Well, different realms and all that. Is there something you need? Are you the one that's supposed to be taking me back to my rooms since Hecate can't seem to catch me? If so, I'll go willingly with you. It's more about the principal with her, you know." I held my wrists out together.

But Nyx didn't seem interested in dragging me by my hair back to my room. Instead, she was roving my face with her eyes, some unspeakable tragedy in her look. Was that because she felt it her duty to gut me on behalf of the whole Underworld? Did I need to get down on my knees and plead, or just throw the kitchen sink, aka my weak magic, at her and sprint for the other side? I flinched when she opened her mouth, but my own mouth dropped open at her next words.

"I'm sorry about Melinoë. I know it sounds worthless, and it's hundreds of years too late, but I was shocked when I heard she died. And then Hermes died and Athena, and it was every goddess for herself. After the surrender of Zeus I figured..." the goddess of night trailed off.

I put my hand on her arm, mortal warmth to her frigid chill. "It's not your fault. I left the Underworld and you never got the chance."

"Still. There are ways to get messages across the realms. They say you sent Hades a spirit note. Without your powers."

I gave her a wry smile. "They?"

"Fine. Scally. He says Hades acted like it was nothing."

"The deathless king doesn't have emotions, Nyx. You know that."

"And we both know that's not entirely true. Otherwise you wouldn't be in your old room with all of your old stuff perfectly preserved, eh?"

I didn't have to pretend to be affected by that. The

emotions of seeing it all were real enough. "I did spend a stint in a dungeon," I said lamely.

"So how did you do it? Send the note, I mean."

I smiled. "Never count out the weaklings. We have more fight in us."

Nyx returned the grin. "I never did. I'll pretend I didn't see you scoping out escape routes if you pretend you didn't see me when you inevitably get caught."

I winked as I repeated myself. "Never count out the weaklings, Nyx. Ever."

* * *

I WANTED to scream into the void, except the entire Underworld was the damn void and then Hecate would be here to gleefully tie me to her waist and yank me back in shame. No, I had to go quietly, but everywhere I turned, I was met with resistance.

I tried combing through the Asphodel Meadows where surely the mortal I searched for idled her eternity away. She certainly would not have been deemed a hero. For one, she was a woman. That right there would discount her from hero-status. For two, she destroyed the world as everyone knew it, and she did it without fanfare. Not even mortals knew her name, so she died without hymns in her honor or waxing poems. She really should have seen to her own afterlife.

Still, I tried the Elysian Fields anyway and had a rather pleasant encounter with Odysseus. I left him cowering in fear that I might come back and torture him for a few more centuries. The pompous ass.

Next, I wandered the outer rings of the Meadows and the banks of the rivers, where the shades gathered who hadn't been able to pay the boatman's fee. She could have been there, as I doubted anyone in the chaos at the end of the war thought to properly bury her body.

But she wasn't.

I got the feeling that the shades were actively hiding this mortal woman from me. What I would give to have a taste of my old powers back! I would see them crawl on broken knees to explain themselves to me.

Well, I hardly needed her anymore, so I turned around and returned to my room. At least I didn't have to contend with spitting Kako demons. At least it wasn't the dungeon. Clearly, Hades was okay with letting me wander, secure in Hecate's binding magic. Their mistake.

On my way back, a polecat yowled in the distance. Shivers cascaded down my body, and so I ran. Very, very fast.

I waited an entire day before I tried again, and this time, I went a tad better prepared. I'd finally found another hidden cache of magical items I could suck dry, including an enchanted rose that I once gave to a French king who had no respect for women. Most say a witch turned him into a beast, but this was not true. I merely revealed his true nature. Which just so happened to be full of bad body odor and shaggy hair and a truly appalling and savage personality.

I also dug up a few more lentil seeds, my preference due to their incredible sprouting ability, and a dragon's tooth. It was one of the teeth sown by Cadmus and could regenerate into a battle-ready warrior if I needed assistance.

Fully armed to the literal teeth, I slipped unseen past my guards, not even bothering to kill any on the way out. Then, as stealthily as a jaguar, I hopped over the low stone boundary lines—and was smacked down by a spell stronger than I'd encountered in a long time. It was no normal slap on the wrist or magical "electric fence" type spell. It was one meant to wound emotionally, tie up a prisoner mentally so they couldn't move or breathe, without pain.

It was an assault of memories.

A high-pitched scream tore from my throat, but that only seemed to feed the boundary and make the images come faster. The memories brought me to my very knees, two dull thuds in the earth as I tore at my hair and scratched my cheeks in our ancient mourning traditions.

My body revolted, but I was frozen by the pain of these memories. I felt myself being ripped in two, wanting to see them and wanting to get away from the horror of them. Blood ran down my face as I fought to break out of the grip of the spell. It was so strong, so insistent. Soon, I was crying, the salt of my tears burning the cuts on my cheeks. There was only one witch who could put this much power, this much brutality, into her spells. Hecate wanted me to suffer.

I scraped and crawled on my hands and feet to pull myself free like a fly in amber. A minute? A year? It was hard to tell with so much compressed into every unit of time. Finally, with a loud squelch, I broke across the boundary line and felt the release.

I didn't hesitate; I was a coward, fleeing as fast as I could back to my room as the sound of laughter haunted me.

* * *

THE KNOCK on the door could only be two beings. Nyx or Hades. Anyone else would barge in without asking or glide through my door. Nyx had already said her piece, so it had to be Hades.

I let my anger rile through my body, igniting my fighting spirit. He had to have known about the barrier. He had almost certainly given the order. Now, he was coming to see his pet witch's handiwork. Not today, Satan. Not today.

I rolled back my shoulders and marched to my door, throwing it open with a flourish. I opened my mouth, but stuttered for a moment. Hades stood holding a cloche. Perhaps some kind of dinner. Before he had time to unveil it and derail me, I launched into my questioning. "What was that... that sorcery?" I demanded.

Hades looked shockingly different, a pair of earth-bound blue jeans and a light gray t-shirt molded to his body. He didn't wear shoes, but really, he had no need. He didn't feel the ice of the Underworld. It'd be weird to wear shoes.

He raised an eyebrow. "Did you stray from your room again? This time, you must have gone too far from the castle grounds. I did warn you not to do that."

"We're bound," I retorted. "You know exactly where I go."

"Yes, which is why I had Hecate erect a proper boundary. As I've said time and again, you're not safe on your own without your powers."

Inside, I was seething. I was a ball of heat and fire, and I wanted something to smite. Especially Hades and his stupid indifference. That coldness that told me he cared not at all.

"Did you know what that boundary was?" I asked carefully.

Hades tilted his head, clearly unsure. That was something.

"I delegate. I don't need specifics when I trust my generals—"

"Memories, Hades." My voice was low. The emotion clutching at my throat was no act, and it made my voice as thick as syrup. Hades met my eyes, and I detected fear in them. Or perhaps pity.

"If she forced you to re-live the moment you forsook us, I hardly see how that's my concern. I am shocked it affected you so after all these years. Being mortal has made you weak."

"Memories of our children," I hissed. "I saw Zagreus suckling at my breast and Melinoë twirling in a field of nightshade. I watched the life drain away from her. I witnessed the burial rites of them both. Did you know that? Did you know Hecate's boundaries weren't physical but emotional? Would you like me to paint more pictures? Of our young daughter reciting odes and poems in front of an audience of attentive death gods and shades, because you threatened physical violence if they didn't pay attention? Or when—"

Hades stood quickly. "This meeting is over."

I stood, too, the blood pounding to my head and making me dizzy. "I haven't finished!"

But he was already gone.

35

HADES

She was pregnant. Of course.

The pieces clicked together perfectly as I lost my nerve to rid myself of this girl who wanted nothing to do with me. The lack of shock at the Olympus party, the fear in her eyes when she begged me to save her. She was no maiden, but I was still a fool.

However, there were a few flaws to her story. When would Demeter have let the girl out of her sight? Who would have been so trusted by the goddess to allow them time alone with her precious virgin daughter?

"Zeus." The name came out of my mouth like a stranglehold, fighting me the entire way.

She met my eyes fiercely. "Did you expect any less?"

"Demeter is no great friend to Zeus. Besides, the official story is that he is your father. For all of his many flaws, he has never slept with his own children."

"Please. Continue to believe your brother." She looked away. The rigidity of her lines told me she was hiding something. Or was I just being paranoid?

"Why don't we take a breath and you tell me your side," I said, guiding her gently to a rough-hewn bench in the maze. A

canopy of flowers bloomed where she sat as if to shade her from the sky of nothingness. My servants told me she feared it, but I wondered if she feared anything anymore.

Her fingers played with her diamond chiton, winding and unwinding the same crease as I waited as patiently as I could bear. When she spoke, her voice had an ethereal quality to it, like a cobweb spun in dewdrops.

"I was picking flowers. Demeter and I had recently had an argument, and I needed some space. Please don't ask me what it was about. I don't want to recall two traumas today."

I put my hand over her nervous ones, interlacing her fingers with mine. I didn't say a word.

She took another sharp breath. "I still remember the smell. It was sweet but slightly acrid on my nostrils."

"Ozone," I supplied softly. "From his bolts." A fitting metaphor for Zeus if there ever was one.

She nodded. "Lightning struck just before I saw him. It was his herald, and I think he was trying to impress me."

"Had you met before?"

She nodded once, slowly, then again. "Yes. He had seen me from the sky and came down to question my relationship to Demeter. I think it annoyed him that she never mentioned me before."

"So he truly isn't your father?"

"Truly."

My jaw muscles ticked. "Go on."

Persephone stood suddenly, upsetting a little clutch of cooing birds. She began to pace, wearing treads in the dirt. "He took my elbow and led me to a shaded oak tree. My heart was pounding and he sensed it, because he said in this delighted voice, 'Are you afraid of me, Kore?' I didn't respond, but his smile widened."

And now I knew why she didn't like the name Kore. Shame burned through me like a wildfire for hurling it at her.

"He pulled his fingers through my hair and seemed to grow at will. He towered over me, and my feet lifted off the ground as still he held me. I—" She broke off and wheeled around to meet my face. *"I don't want to tell anymore. You know what happens next. What gods and men do in the dark."* She put her hands protectively over a tiny bump on her stomach. I wouldn't have noticed it if I weren't looking. *"I don't want Zeus to ever know about this child. He doesn't deserve that. He deserves nothing."*

I kneeled instead of standing. I refused to tower over her in this vulnerable moment. "I will call him out if you wish, or I will keep your secret, wife. Tell me your will."

She bowed her head at that word, and her dark eyes shined with unshed tears when she looked back up. "You would raise the babe as your own?"

"I would."

"Even though I can't promise my love?"

Despite my hope to hide it, I winced at that. "Even so."

"Then let it be done. This is between us, husband."

I feared for my sanity, even more than when I thought I knew the truth on Olympus. This feeling of her in my arms, truly open and vulnerable, was intoxicating. The smooth texture of her skin, her smell of goldenrods in spring, and even the wetness of her tears intensified the protectiveness coursing through my body. We were in this together.

Life has shifts you can reflect on later. Some you recognize in their big moments for what they are. This was one. Except, not for the reasons I thought at the time.

36

HADES

Whether Hecate realized it or not, her little trick had stirred emotions in both Persephone and me. On this, we were united. A true first. Except, for only the fourth time in my existence, I was livid. Our children were off limits.

My voice, however, was calm when I found her. "Your boundary was a success, witch general."

Hecate narrowed her eyes, and I lunged. I grabbed her throat, and her polecat yowled and fled in terror. "Tell me the unbinding. I want to know it, in case anything should happen to you."

Hecate gurgled as if she couldn't speak with my fingers around her throat, but I refused to lessen my grip. Finally, she ground out, "Surely that's not a threat, Basileus."

"Then you would be mistaken."

Hecate hissed, her fangs bared. It was just a reflex in self-defense when faced with my death waves, but I could tell she wanted to transform into her tri-parte form and challenge me. Only her honor kept her from doing so.

"I did it to protect you, my king. Where is my thanks? Where is my pious anger?"

"You think this is pious?" I threw her away from me. Her long nails scratched across the stone ground as she slowed herself to a stop. Instantly, she jumped to her feet, her fingers itching to reach for her reed torches. She knew better than that, at least.

"I think it is blindness," she said. "So I lit your way. That is my purpose."

"If you honestly believe that you don't have blinders when it comes to the former queen, then you're as delusional as you think I am."

"Perhaps I do," she allowed, bowing her head finally. "But what I do is for the safety of our kingdom. We have too many fronts going on to fight one within, Basileus."

"Agreed, but don't you dare think of using my children again. However you wish to punish the Dread Queen is fine, but don't overstep." I towered over her, and she hardly dared move or breathe.

Death rippling off of me, I stalked back to the castle.

My thoughts tumbled as wildly as a snowball coalescing into an avalanche. The crash at the bottom of the mountain was inevitable, and I couldn't fault Hecate for wanting to diminish the impact, just not like that.

Now, I thought of my daughter, of my infant son. I remembered the life I used to have before it all fell apart, and I missed it. Imagine that. The king of the dead mourning the dead. Perhaps Hecate hadn't meant to do that, but it was happening all the same.

37

PERSEPHONE

I waited a day to leave my room again. I would've waited a month, but I had to keep up appearances. Cautiously, I threw a rock at the boundary lines I'd so stupidly missed. The rock tumbled a few feet under a bush. I threw a few more. None hit any resistance.

Gone?

The boundary was gone. I stood very still, feeling for any death magic around the premises. Had Hades truly gone to my defense? Was I free to roam again?

The thought comforted me, yet, for some reason, I didn't feel like wandering or testing Hecate's patience today. Instead, I wanted to sit under the blinding light of the white elm tree of False Dreams. It had been my ritual, something to ground me. Usually, I kept all of the dead's secrets, so I loved getting lost in fiction, as mortals today would get lost in a book. It was comforting, a nice break from the harsh reality of the world.

I gave one last look at the land beyond the boundary and turned around. Even if my old memories of my children wouldn't haunt me again, their resonance did. I felt a sad prickling between my eyes. I thought I could do this. I thought I could be here in the Underworld, do what I needed to do, and keep myself emotionally distant. But maybe I couldn't. Being here dredged up all sorts of emotions I thought I'd packed away, and now I realized I'd been punishing myself for such a long time. Punishing Hades, too.

Maybe I didn't have to go through with it.

I settled under the branches of False Dreams, the leaves fluttering in the wind. The kaleidoscope of images soothed me with their escape, until something small fell to my left. My head snapped to the sound, but it was just a pebble. I flicked it away when another fell, *clink*, to my right. This time, I shot up, my nerves bristling.

An eerie whistling noise flickered through the branches. Someone—or something—was here for me. Only, it was impossible to know which of my enemies it was. A giggle almost escaped my mouth. Wouldn't it be a sight if all of them banded together to torture me? Hating me was probably the only thing that threaded together so many of the creatures in this castle.

I recalled the things that could be done to mortals in this realm, the things that I had done to them. Then, I did my best to forget. Fear wouldn't help me now.

A gust of fetid air blew through the courtyard. A branch creaked overhead, but I didn't dare look up. I knew it was a distraction, yet everywhere I turned, there was nothing. Only the sounds of the white elm tree, groaning in the thickening wind. Quietly, I backed away from the tree. Climbing fast would do me little good against the things that lived here.

It was possible I was overreacting. This all might be calculated merely to scare me. If that were the case, I was absolutely going to roll over and show my belly. If I acted pathetic enough, they might grow disgusted and leave me alone before I was forced to use any more of my precious reserves of magic. What fun was there in kicking an enemy who was so wretched as to be contemptible? Indeed, what fun was there in kicking an enemy so far down to the ground, they were practically worms, twisting through a skull?

None. I hoped.

I also hoped they'd show themselves so I could remember their cruelty. Grudges die hard in the Underworld, and I would certainly make them pay when the time came.

I didn't have to wait long. A moment later, I caught sight of a nymph's ankle, nimble, green-tinged, as it turned the corner. Minthe.

She stood before me now, no longer hiding. I had to give it to her. She was really leaning into the green thing. She embraced what I had made of her. Where before she draped herself in expensive baubles taken from graves and roped herself with bits of stolen seaweed from above—she was, after all, a water nymph—now, that girl was gone. She wore a slink, kale green evening gown that left nothing to the imagination. Her bright hair flowed effortless in ringlets over her shoulders and just seeing her celadon eyes made a tiny flicker of jealousy flare, no matter how quickly I attempted to dampen it.

When I first came to Hades' court, Minthe had become my instant enemy. She had attempted to make me feel ugly by pointing out my plain features, common black hair and dark eyes. Was I even a goddess she wondered? Most goddesses had more lustrous locks and beguiling eyes. Mine were deadened. Obviously, she didn't realize it was because I felt dead inside when I arrived in Hades' realm. Obviously, she didn't care to know.

The desire to crush her like a weed overwhelmed—No! *Act simple. Play dead. Show your belly.*

All around her, shades began to populate. They winked into existence, their essence darkening into something of substance. I quickly realized I was ringed in. Just as quickly, I wondered if I should rethink my playing possum strategy. Damn, I hated when Hades was right. I plastered a smile on my face. "Minthe. Your coloring is magnificent. It really suits you."

Minthe laughed softly, dragging a mint leaf over my cheek, down my throat, and between my breasts. She must have felt really triumphant, like it was some great irony to have the pleasure to gag me with a mint leaf. Surely that was the plan. If I were her, it would absolutely be my plan.

"Can't turn me into a plant now, can you?" she goaded. "I can feel it. You're neutered."

Coolly, I replied, "Pretty sure last time I checked, I was neither a male, nor a dog."

"No, you're just a bitch. A cowardly, spayed bitch who abandoned her people. There. Is that more accurate?"

"Yeah, I guess that about fits it."

My tormentor paused, her head cocked at how agreeable I was being. Then she scoffed. Minthe was used to my performances. "Hades hasn't been with anyone since you left. You ruined him. You took a virile god who shone above the others and you made him weak. You broke him like he was one of your toys, and then you threw away the parts before putting him back together."

"That's not true," I said, although I almost didn't care what else she had to say. Hades hadn't slept with anyone since I left? Giddy little bubbles of effervescence tickled my insides. I, of course, could not forget that he slept with Minthe at multiple points after our marriage... but to learn he hadn't slept with anyone in fifteen hundred years... my bubbles quickly popped one by one. Had I broken him? I didn't want to break him. That wasn't in my plans at all.

The warm fizz faded into reality, which at this point, was a green-faced nymph. Literally. She was so jealous of me, I wondered if it was truly my magic or her own envy that had changed her skin. She was saying something about pulling out hearts and guzzling my warm blood, which was a bit off brand for the nymph species, but I think I'd also broken her. Maybe that was what I did. I broke things and didn't know how to put them back together.

"Well, this has been fun," I said. "Thanks for the stroll down memory lane. I'll just be on my way back to my personal hell of solitude, if you'll permit—hey!" I slapped away a shade's hand, then another. I was about to jam a lentil seed into their eye sockets and watch them twitch when ten green fingers locked around my throat.

The shades formed a wall, rising up into a dome from which I couldn't escape. Damn, I really, really hated it when Hades was right.

38

HADES

Something felt wrong. There was a thickening of shade activity nearby, although I couldn't tell what the disturbance was. Donning my diamond armor, I stopped mulling over Thanatos's and Hecate's competing plans for the Kako demons and went to investigate. The wrongness emanated near the white elm, but I moved slowly, loathe to go. I didn't want Persephone knowing I had taken up her habit of sitting under it after she left.

I didn't want to see her at all.

A lie, of course. I just didn't want her to see my own weakness dimpling the surface of my being. My feelings for her were like imperfections in a gemstone. So I went, slowly.

When I arrived, Minthe had her hands curled around Persephone's neck, a hoard of shades behind her for support. I felt a deep, wellspring of rage at the interaction, but before I had time to intervene, Persephone pulled something out from beneath her robes.

I blinked, refocusing on the object.

A single rose, dried and shriveled, exploded. It dusted all within its radius with toxic spores. Minthe screamed and ducked, but caught a face full of them. Shades touched by them began to sizzle and melt, leaving only puddles behind. Where the fuck did Persephone keep finding these things?

Immediately, I swung into the air and landed between the two of them. Minthe was still screaming, alternating between clawing at her face and the air. I enveloped her in a sheet of protective fog as she clung to me, her screams now punctuated with sobs. Persephone looked defiant, although perhaps a bit fearful.

Of me.

I tried not to relish it as I ordered the remaining shades to escort Minthe to a healer inside the castle. As she stumbled up the steps, still sobbing, I surreptitiously checked Persephone to see if any of the spores had touched her by accident. "Are you hurt?" I asked.

She shook her head, dark eyes wide as we took in the devastation of the courtyard. The only thing still standing was the white elm of False Dreams. A flood of goo marked the spots where the shades had turned to mush. My eyes swept down to her legs where pale skin peeked out of the tear in her chiton. I forced myself to only give it a glimpse before pinning her with my arm and marching her up the castle steps. "Good."

Persephone tripped, crying out. "Slow down, I'm not as fast as you anymore."

I forced myself to take the steps slower, although my grip on her arm did not lesson. Nor my interrogation. What I had witnessed shouldn't be possible. "Where is this magic coming from, Dread Queen?"

"How should I know? I simply use the magic of other things now."

"So you insist on playing dumb?"

"It's hardly playing if I really am dumb."

"You are a lot of things, goddess, but dumb is not one of them." I sighed heavily. "I already know the answer, anyway, so against my better judgement, I'm going to take you back to your quarters. Really, you would have been safer in the dungeons, but I think that's out of the question now that everyone knows you're here."

"Magnanimous gesture, Basileus."

I winced at the title, hiding it by jerking her through the obsidian gates. "Maybe the best option would be to force you back to Earth," I mused, more for her benefit. "While you won't tell me how you got here, perhaps there are ways to shove you through to the other side. You did manage to get here, at least. There must be a way back."

Her eyelids fluttered in what I took to be a small sign of panic.

"Stop worrying. I don't want anyone else thinking there's an easy entrance to my realm. That means you're here. For now."

We arrived at her room, and I pushed her inside before turning to leave. Persephone protested in a squeak. "You're leaving so soon? I haven't thanked you."

"Stay in your room, Persephone. That will be thanks enough."

"I get bored."

"Only boring people get bored."

She raised a shoulder and let it drop. "Then I'm the most boring creature that ever existed."

I waved a hand and spiced wine filled itself into the crystal decanter, brimming with dark liquid that was scented with cloves and cinnamon. Her favorite.

"Amuse yourself with this, why don't you? For once, you might try taking my advice and confining yourself to your room. I doubt you will, but there's always the chance you'll prove me wrong. You do so love to do that. Actually, this might be fun to watch. What is more important to you? Defying me or proving me wrong?" I let my eyes gleam as Persephone squared off in front of me, her shoulders back and her chin up.

My back stiffened as she inched closer, although stalked closer would be a more appropriate description for the way she moved. Uncomfortable prickles of longing sparked up my belly. I hated how she still had the power to make me want to dominate her. Without her around, I had easily been able to keep any lustful thoughts tucked deep down— the Bare King, emotionless to the end. Not anymore. Not with her standing in front of me.

I spun around, but she caught my wrist, grazing the inside of it with her nail. Immediately, I threw her off, perhaps a bit too forcefully, and she staggered back, toppling into the ebony-carved bedpost.

"Don't touch me, daughter of Demeter. We are no longer bound by marriage."

She laughed softly as she pulled herself to her feet, wincing a bit at the impact and rubbing her back. Her chiton had hitched up to the apex of her thighs, but I averted my gaze.

"Aren't we bound? Our ancient marriage rites cannot so easily be put asunder."

"You were quick to pretend they did not mean anything to you for fifteen hundred years. I'm not sure why that has to change now."

"And that was a mistake. I'll admit I made a mistake. There. Does that make you happy?" She chanced a step closer and I let her. By all the stars and heavens, gods-forbid me, I let her. Her voice lowered. "I'm here now, Hades. Don't pretend your heart doesn't pump faster at the sight of me.

You already know, thanks to your truth serum, that I missed you."

Acting by instinct, I hooked my hands under her arms and brought this small, mortal thing within an inch. I meant to intimidate, and it seemed to work. Her breath hitched, and I could feel the heat of her skin. Indeed, it steamed where I touched bare flesh.

She spoke first. "Do you want to feel my heart pumping a thousand beats?" She guided my hand to her breast. "Here, touch me. Feel my truth for once."

"You're flushed," I said, jerking my hand back. "Exertion from the adrenaline of a battle is dilating your blood vessels."

"It's not from battle." Her hands reached up to cup my face as the longing of ten thousand lifetimes pounded through me. My whole being strained to let loose and take back what was once mine. Even if for one night. Then, she leaned her head back, exposing a pulsing vein in her swan-like neck, so very mortal and forbidden, and yet, so familiar.

I reached out—and touched.

39
PERSEPHONE

Heat bloomed up my legs and pooled between my thighs at his touch. Torturous. Traitorous. Exquisite. My heart had begun to churn, and I was powerless to hide my desire. Hades would recognize the truth immediately.

This time? I wanted him to. I needed him out of control. If I were to lose some of my own control in order to savor this last moment with him, then so be it. This was raw power and I craved it. I was desperate for it.

My breast was heavy in his palm, and the sounds low in the back of my throat. I groaned when he dragged his tongue up my torso to my neck and kissed my mouth. Hades went colder, but that just meant it was working.

His magic rippled over me like a dark wave, and I was left gasping for oxygen. It felt delicious and dangerous. Shadows of black and mist of darkness swelled around us, obscuring our bodies as the temptation reached a climax. Yet I wasn't ready to descend.

It wasn't that I'd never wanted my husband or denied him out of indifference; it was that certain things had to be abstained from in order to capture the grander prize. But shouldn't I enjoy this? Shouldn't I lower his inhibitions? If I enjoyed it too, well, that didn't affect anything.

I sucked in air, panting as my breasts rose and fell, almost obscenely. Neither of us would ever admit how much we wanted the other, but it didn't matter. Any words spoken would just be lost in this moment. The old power connecting me to him turned electric. If he touched me, I would scream. Hopefully, no one would come running for a good long while.

Groans escaped without prompting, and I knew I was no longer in control. Had I lost myself? Because I wanted this more than anything. I wanted to forget all of the history between us and strike the numbers of our arguments from my mind. I wanted to indulge.

"Your body is weak. I would hurt you, Persephone. Stop now," he warned, although his voice sounded like he was really warning himself. I put the hem of my torn chiton in his hand and yanked down. The rip startled us both, but I pressed my nakedness to his hard, diamond armor, shivering at the pleasure of the chill.

"Aren't you enjoying having me in your grasp, though?" I whispered, guiding his fingers to where the pain of emptiness stretched between my legs. I needed pressure there. I wanted it to be him.

"No."

"Liar." I laughed low. "I'm enjoying it. Here, feel me." He let me continue to guide his fingers to feel the wetness seeping from inside of me. I felt rage pouring off of him as he took in my desire and rubbed it between his thumb and forefinger.

Hellfire snapped, and just as suddenly, I found myself shivering from the cold and sprawled on my bed. At least he hadn't thrown me to the floor.

"Enough, Persephone. I told you not to cross that line. I meant it. It's too dangerous."

I didn't bother covering up with a blanket or rummaging for my ruined dress. Hades knew every inch of me. "What do you want me to say? I'm sorry? Because I'm not."

"No, that would be a feat, wouldn't it? I'd rather you—get down."

I raised an eyebrow. "Get down? Sort of sending mixed messages, aren't you?" Then I squawked indignantly as he threw me behind him and flung open the window. An arrow sliced into my room, spearing the damask drapery and embedding itself in the bedpost. All protests died on my tongue. I dropped to my belly feeling especially vulnerable as Hades' enormous body filled the frame of the window, torches reflecting brilliantly off of his armor.

"Hurry, Persephone. Get dressed."

"Did you really mean it?" I asked, hustling into a new chiton, suddenly wishing he had updated my wardrobe.

Hades didn't spare me a look. He continued concentrating on the scene below, probably forming a thousand battle plan scenarios. "What?"

"That you never want me to cross the line. Because never is a very long time."

"Yes. You're nothing but a dangerous distraction. I can count on two hands how many times you've almost caused disaster since you've arrived, including three seconds ago. We would have been impaled if I'd let you continue down that route. Those arrows pierce glass."

"Oh yes, it's all my fault. Tell me this. Do you recall me saving the castle from destruction a few days ago?"

"Go ahead," he snarled. "Show me again how useful you are. Save your people. Look at it this way; it's not as if you could make them hate you more, so feel free to fail."

My mouth moved up and down, but nothing came out. It was whiplash, and the rejection stung even deeper than before.

"What?" he taunted. "Suddenly you have no words?"

"You assho—" I stopped, insight zinging through me. I saw what this was. Hades was so laughably see-through, so guileless and transparent. Then again, he didn't need guile in the Underworld. His control over it was absolute. Until now. This whole alpha-act was designed to push me away because I unsettled him. I took some of that absolute control away, and as Basileus, he couldn't have that. He'd almost given into me this time. I could feel it. On the flip side, I was also letting him get to me. I almost believed him!

Maybe he was right. We were nothing but a dangerous distraction to each other.

Hades barely spared me another glance before he leapt to the window and flew over the battlements, his wings glinting in the light of the white elm tree. I ran to the window and looked down, my wing buds refusing to sprout without my seeds. The magic of the Underworld was potent and powerful, adding to my small stores of lentil seeds and my infernal dagger, allowing me to transform mindless Kako and scare the already terrified Minthe, but without true power, I couldn't possibly hope to fly, to soar, to reign.

Except for that moment with Hades when we'd fed each other strength and dark magic. Either he wasn't telling me something, or we had truly been magical together. It was possible I had tapped into something bigger than us and it had saved us both.

For now, I frantically packed my things, strapping my dagger to my thigh and checking my last magical stores. Dragon's tooth, lentil seeds... it wasn't much but hopefully I wouldn't need to use any of it.

Moving toward the door, a locket caught my attention. The ivory and onyx cameo swung on a delicate chain, the image of a rose carved between the black and white, set in a filigree gold base. I paused as the sounds of roaring animals got closer. Time was of the essence if I wanted to escape, but my fingers itched to hold it. With a furtive glance to the window, I slipped the locket down my chiton and covered my head with a traveling veil.

The fuzzy outlines of shades riding elephants trampled the walls. The elephants decaying armor and bejeweled trunks told me this was Hannibal, come to take revenge for Carthage. From the south, Dante led another legion of shades. Gods, I hated that man. I didn't see any souls from Elysium. At least they were smart enough to cower in their blessed eternity.

Screams rent the air, demons in the agora raced to take cover. The night was fire and ash as Thanatos and Hecate worked their death magic together. I saw the green aftermath of their spells like a contrail in the sky. The pulsing of it pounded in my veins, a singular drumbeat with no end.

I bolted past room after room, the battle rattling my bones. My binding to Hades sizzled on my skin. I let out a yelp, covering the barbed bident with my hand. Surely he was fine. He was the deathless god.

I heard footsteps in the stairwell, blocking my exit, so I raced across the ballroom, slaloming through the abandoned furniture and sheets. Without my seeds, I wasn't much good against an entire Underworld of pissed off shades. Hades could have taken me with him, but he didn't. He didn't want me around him, clouding his mind and all that.

I cried out when my tattoo blazed again. For a moment, it felt as if smoke were filling my lungs and choking me. I fell to my knees, clutching my chest and rubbing oxygen back into them.

This was ridiculous. I hated being so powerless, and it made me miss my seeds more than ever. If Hades had hidden them, then we truly were bound. If he died, I would never find my seeds again. Cursing his stupid pride, I staggered to my feet and launched toward the battle. I couldn't let Hades die. And the funniest lie I told myself? That it was only about the seeds.

40

PERSEPHONE

It had been almost six months since I told Hades the truth, and I was nearing my time to ascend to Earth and my time to whelp. My bump felt bigger than me. I didn't like to stroke it most days, but some days I did. It made no sense and all the sense in the world. I knew it was a little girl. I could feel her heart beating in rhythm with mine. When she stretched, I could feel all of her toes and wondered if it was her little magic sensing mine, reaching out to let me know she was there. And there she wanted to stay.

Lazily, I rose from my bed and warmed my hands by the fire. My maid had left my tea and ginger biscuit on the platter like usual, her little touch of neon green ferns in a vase always welcome. The stones she put hot in my bed at night to curl around were cold now. It was less pleasant to wake to them than it was to fall asleep. For some reason, I didn't think Hades would be terrible to wake next to. He'd be stone cold, too, but it was the fire that burned in his eyes that would keep me warm.

Except, recently, he seemed preoccupied.

Last night, he'd been especially distant at dinner. There was no banter or story-sharing. He barely reacted when I told him about a funny little bird I'd seen in the maze. It had a sharp beak, iridescent gray feathers, and intelligent beady eyes. When we parted ways for the evening, he didn't brush a kiss to my forehead like usual or bid me protection from my nightmares.

This wasn't what we agreed to. This wasn't Hades. After I told him my secret, he told me we could be friends, and I believed him. Now? I felt more lonely than ever.

Hades wasn't in his chambers and the maid hadn't seen him. I wandered out in the hallway, absently noticing details I had skimmed over when I arrived. The stone corridor was simply decorated with a few carpets and oil paintings, but a marble table held the most gorgeous contraption. There were silver dials and gears and etched markings that must have told him some information. A giant sea serpent had been carved at the base, and constellations decorated its face. A sad little vase of flowers drooped next to it. I took their faces in my hands as if to smell them and breathed into their petals, lavishing them with my love. They perked up at my touch, and I put them back with a satisfied smile. If only everything could be solved so easily.

A shade floated by, and I asked if it knew Hades' whereabouts, but it drifted away, a dazed expression on its translucent face. Worry beat a drumbeat in my chest at its silence. As if it were bound by Hades not to speak.

I began to run. Hecate wouldn't lie to me. She was gruff but guileless. When she brought Demeter to me in the field, she lit the way with her reed torches and told me she had no choice. She had to obey her king. And so my rage turned back to Hades, although she, too, deserved retribution for betraying me.

The witch was at her bath, two women kissing her breasts and running their fingers through her red hair as it floated on top of the water. Her tub was made of hammered gold, and black narcissus blossoms floated on the surface as long tapered candles filled the stone niches. The floor had been decorated with rich mosaics of women dancing, women writhing, women enjoying themselves.

Suddenly, I found Hecate positively fascinating. I would not have guessed she was into women.

She half-rose at the sight of me, water dripping from her toned skin like droplets off a duck. "My queen?"

Ah, so now we were back to honorifics. Well, it would be good to reinforce that imagery. "Where is my husband, the king?"

Hecate sank back down, more concerned with her concubines than me. "He's handling something."

"What?"

Hecate's eyes tracked to my stomach. I found myself cradling it protectively and angling away from her. Her eyes snapped back to mine.

"King things, I would suppose. I wouldn't worry, my queen."

"And if I do?" I snapped.

She shrugged. "Then you worry."

Her girls tittered in the water, and I flicked my finger at one. A black blossom immediately lifted from the water and stuffed itself down her throat. She began to gag as her eyes bulged. She tried scraping it out of her mouth, but I pressed it deeper. The other girl began to scream until she thought better of it and covered her mouth with both hands, her eyes racing back and forth, left and right, frozen in her fear.

"Where is my husband?" I asked again.

Hecate hadn't moved. She watched me impassively for a few moments as the girl continued to choke. Continued to die.

"He went to his lover."

I flicked my finger again and released the sobbing girl, although something had twisted deeply inside of my gut, and I felt the urge to choke them all. Instead, I managed to say, "That wasn't so hard."

Hecate sank back among the flowers, her body creating little eddies that swirled gently. Her hands were crossed behind her head as she studied me. The two girls quietly comforted each other.

"No. But it doesn't really matter to me if you go. You won't, if you're smart. Or kind. A god like Hades needs someone to attend to his desires, not just cater to yours."

"Don't worry about that. Smart is not something I've been accused of yet—ahh!"

Hecate rose fully at my animalistic screech. "Persephone?"

I was hunched, clutching my stomach. Bands of pain had rippled across it, gone as quickly as it had come.

"You're going into labor. I will call a shade midwife if you'd like."

"No," I said, bracing for the next one. "I don't need help. I need Hades."

I flew from the chamber, my wings beating for release on my back, praying I wouldn't fall out of the sky when the next wave of pain consumed me.

41

HADES

An inferno consumed the narrow market streets. I winged over them, pulling out screaming demons and tossing them free of the blaze. Their skin and scales were blackened and charred beneath my touch.

Nyx soared over the white elm tree, bringing darkness with her. We hoped to confuse and confound the enemy. The elephants would rampage and trample themselves. We gods of death were not so easily frightened as Roman legionaries.

Smoke filled my lungs and seared my throat. I soared up, searching for the enemy commander. Surely something had to be directing these souls. If I could find them, I would rip their heads from their bodies and death-wheel the remaining traitors. These shades would easily become compliant again under Hecate's ministrations. The Kako as well, but these new demons would suffer my wrath.

As I searched, a familiar pale leg flashed a hundred feet beneath me.

Persephone.

Did she have a death wish? Her eyes were on the sky

instead of in front of her where demons lie in wait. A monster in concealing armor jumped on her back and yanked her to the ground. I arrowed myself at them, pulling him off of her with my fists and leaving a hole where his heart should have been, if he weren't fabricated.

Behind me, Persephone flung her pink dagger, but it was deflected and sent spinning into the flames. She gulped and I saw her throat working up and down in terror. The new demons sauntered closer, but it barely had time to lick its lips with a forked, serpentine tongue before I tore their bodies in two and grabbed Persephone by her waist. For a moment, we looked exactly as the frescoes and mosaics depicting her "abduction" showed us. It had only been thousands of years in the making.

"Hades," she gasped. "The castle—I don't have any more warrior seeds to call up."

"The castle is lost for good this time. Or for now, at least," I told her. Scally had orders to gather the commanders and wait for me, but first, I had to follow a hunch.

"You're retreating?" she gasped, clinging tighter as we ripped across the black sky.

"We're regrouping."

"What about Nyx and Scally? Or the shades in the castle? The demons?"

"Remember how you wondered who, or what, created those new demons?" I asked instead, alighting near the entrance to Tartarus. The bronze walls rose into the smoky sky, cool to the touch. I ran my hand along its seamless metal.

Persephone backed away, already not liking my tone. "No. Nope. I don't remember any curiosity. None. They say it kills cats and you know what? I'm a cat person. A serious cat lady. I had at least three strays on Earth that followed me for scraps. Blinky, Winky, and Tinky. No, that's not right. Blitzen, Comet, and Cupid maybe? Well anyway, I'm a cat person."

I let her run out of steam before lamenting, "That's too bad. Because we're going to find out exactly who did. Find the creator, find the source."

"We?" she squeaked. "I can barely feel death anymore and it's all around. I can barely make a flower bloom. I can barely—"

"I get it," I interrupted. "You're weak, I should definitely underestimate you."

She balked at the darkness I made snap in my eyes and her voice twinged with nerves. "So what are you going to do?"

"Not fall for your performance."

"And do what instead?"

"And take you with me to the depths of Tartarus, dear wife. You're the one who speculated it was chthonic mists."

"What? No. I have no idea. Anyway, I didn't mean us. I meant someone else. Someone like you or Hecate. Basically anybody but me."

"Staying together now that the castle has fallen is your safest bet, and besides, Hecate's binding spell requires us to stay close. Where I go, you go, and that's Tartarus."

42

PERSEPHONE

I snorted once. Hades said nothing, just waited expectantly. I snorted again. Still nothing. I threw up my hands and began to pace.

"So your grand plan is to drag me along on some crusade to save the Underworld, even though I'm practically mortal at this point—"

"Shh," Hades hushed me.

Then, right in front of Hades, my pink dagger reappeared, shimmering on my leg.

Shit.

His eyes narrowed. "Is that...?"

Obviously, using my dagger again so soon wasn't the best idea, but going on a sight-seeing tour of the Underworld for evil sounded worse. It was an easy choice, really. Before Hades could rip away my new accessory, I yanked it out of my thigh holder and pressed the tip of the blade to my shoulder where I felt Hecate's binding spell pulsing. "Don't come any closer," I warned.

Hades blinked.

A bead of ichor appeared, faint and thin. Without my power, most of the golden color had been leached away, giving it an anemic appearance. It made the briar vines look like they were weeping.

Before I could press deeper, Hades smacked my hand away, sending the dagger skittering to the ground. I really had no strength, speed, or stamina in this state.

"Why did you do that?" I demanded. "Don't you want to be free from this curse? Here, if you wanted to go first, you masochist, all you had to do was ask."

But Hades was staring at the smear of ichor.

I wiped it away. "It's not polite to stare," I said, my voice tight. It was embarrassing for him to see the truth of my weakness. "Fine," I snapped. "I'll do yours first. Say no more."

I leapt on Hades, violence in my veins, but he easily pushed me away, and as I fell, I heard a sickening snap. We both stared in wonder at my dislocated shoulder.

"Persephone?"

Desperately, I tried working it back into its socket. I swore a few times while staggering around, something about mothers' whores and other curses I'd picked up at the Black Sea clubs. Some were for the dramatics, but not all. He'd overpowered me quickly and aggressively, remembering our old battles. It was probably a reflex to him. Another gentle shove out of the way that completely knocked the breath out of me.

"How long were you on Earth?" he asked. "Your body is like a twig. Like a diseased twig. A really brittle, sickly, diseased twig."

"Long enough, clearly. Are you going to help me here?" I nodded toward my dangling arm.

"Tell me what you did to your dagger," he demanded, as he pulled down the strap of my chiton, his fingers cool on my inflamed skin.

"May your guts become as liquid as water," I swore, as his strong hands gripped me. "May your insides liquify and be swallowed by mites, may—" *CRACK*. The rest of the curse died in my throat at the instant relief. My shoulder was sore, but manageable.

"Better?" he asked dryly. "Good. Now tell me what you did before I un-fix you."

"That is highly unethical," I complained, wheeling my arm backwards and forwards.

Hades lifted an eyebrow. "You clearly did dark magic. No retracing spell works so well, and the fact that you are still pathetically weak here is odd. So I'll ask you again, Persephone. What did you do to your dagger? What is preventing you from regaining your powers?"

I tried not to show my emotions, although they were roiling. *No*. The trust would slowly need to be rebuilt, and I couldn't seem too eager, as if I were offering it too easily. Hades would see through that.

"You don't want to know," I finally settled on saying. I missed the feeling of true power. The loss of my seeds had devastated me, but it was the only way. I felt their loss every second of my existence. For a moment, I almost bent over with want. It physically hurt to remember how it felt to wield them. The loss of death magic felt like a death itself, and I cried myself to sleep more nights than I wished to count.

Hades began walking. "Keep your dagger and your secrets. You could slit my throat, but it wouldn't matter. I can't die in that way. You, on the other hand…"

"Yeah, yeah, I could die," I said bitterly. "You know, if you let me do things my own way I could end this war."

I looked up from the rocky path just in time to see Hades cloak himself in mist and lunge for my throat.

43

HADES

Persephone's pomegranate-red lips were still babbling, but I heard nothing. She knew. She always knew more than she shared. I barely processed moving before her little body was pinned under mine, my fingers finally, so deliciously, around her throat.

I squeezed.

"Who is it?" I growled, intimately aware of the times when I held her like this, my teeth grazing and growling at her throat, but the words were different. The dance was hedonic.

Her dark eyes were large and frightened. She always tried to sway me in that manner, calling on my protective nature. Her fingers grappled at mine to pry them loose, but I clenched tighter. Long ago, she had promised to bring me down, and she was excellent at the long game. Nearly two-thousand years and a literal war between gods and demons? An excellent long game, indeed. I snarled as the thought of her brilliance made my veins bubble with heat, and my armor tighten uncomfortably.

"I don't know who it is! All I meant was that I know a way to find out. Let go of me, you maniac!"

We stared for a few heartbeats. I hated how little time it took for me to uncurl my fingers and how less time it took my heart to twist in shame at the marks on her throat. Her look of defiance was so familiar, it pricked at my exterior, shame wedging a hole and doing the rest. "Persephone..."

"I'm going to let that one go, because of that one time I... Well, you remember."

Yes, I did remember. I still had the scars.

She pointed a finger between my eyes. "But now we're even. Clean slate. If we're going to work together, no more tit for tat."

"I'm not agreeing to that."

"If I tell you something about my weakness, will you trust me?"

"It rather depends on what it is."

Her voice was so soft, I thought I misheard.

"What?" I barked. "What did you say?"

"I lost my seeds!" she shouted. "They're gone, and I can't find them."

"I thought you were smart, Persephone. These vapid lies don't suit you." I kept my face blank as her seeds burned a hole in my conscience.

Her hair sheeted behind her, rising with her anger in electric bolts. "I am pouring my truths out. I don't have magic. I had to strangle a freaking octopus with my bare hands to get here and who do I run into? You! And you threw me in a dungeon for a month. And refused to visit. Now you're scoffing at me when I reveal I don't have my pomegranate seeds anymore."

"And my Kako guards from the dungeon? They just

magically vanished every evening? That little trick with the seeds to save the castle? A lucky coincidence?"

Her wolfish blink was enough. "Fine. I have a little magic, but I truly don't have my pomegranate seeds. Help me find them and I will save us both," she insisted.

"Absolutely not."

Her voice was as brittle as bismuth and just as intricate. "So you will never trust me as long as we survive this world?"

"Never."

"What about mutual mistrust? Will that work?"

The weight of my secret pulled on me like an albatross. I promised Hecate I wouldn't reveal it to Persephone, but that was before my castle was breached and shades rose up as one and swallowed Thanatos. But then, Persephone was speaking and the words weren't making sense. When I heard them again, they fit together like a language I'd only just figured out.

"With my seeds, I can transverse the realms. I always have since the beginning of the Accords. I don't know of any other being that can, except for me. I can go to Olympus and drag the truth from Zeus' lips myself. See who's making creepy demon babies. All I need is for you to help me find my seeds."

44

PERSEPHONE

My heart was a wild thing as I winged through the gray sky. Of course he should be with someone else. Of course, of course, of course. Another wave crashed across my belly and my flight faltered. I righted myself and kept going.

Why did I not expect it? Even mortal men have needs. A god's needs must be extravagant. If only I hadn't cringed at the thought. If only I hadn't been so frightened.

If only's bought me nothing, though. I gritted my teeth and tore through the clouds that had settled like bricks over the city.

There was a nymph. She was brazen in her disdain for me. I hadn't paid her much attention at first. Everyone was full of scorn for their queen who snubbed their king. Eventually, however, she stuck out as particularly confident.

Once at a full court dinner, she had curled one of my black ringlets around her finger and giggled. I said nothing, realizing she must feel very secure in her role at Hades' court to be so bold. "You're not as pretty as they say," she finally said.

I nodded appreciatively. Where others only whispered behind their fingers, she dared speak aloud. "What do they know of beauty, right?"

"Exactly. I had to see for myself."

"And you found me lacking?"

She nodded savagely.

"And I have heard staring at the white elm tree of False Dreams will blind anyone. Even nymphs."

Minthe raised an eyebrow. She had not expected boldness to match her own. "Be careful, little queen. Hades has not always wanted a wife. He might yet go back to that position." She cocked her head to the left as she watched me. "I wonder, how did Hades come to want a wife?"

"I guess his last lover did not suit him."

Without another word, Minthe straightened and turned on her heel. I knew then that there was something more than a jealous flirtation.

Desperately, I winged downwards. Minthe lived somewhere near the River Cocytus. It was fitting that she came from the waters of misery. Demons below covered their eyes with their hands to glance upwards at the dark blot in their sky, but I barely cared. I had to find Hades. Despite our recent distance, I did not want to give birth alone like some animal in the woods.

As I neared the river's banks, cries of misery flowed from the waters. There were pleas for mercy and mumblings of wrongs they wished right. But mostly, I heard weeping. Ignoring it by focusing on the pain of another contraction, I made my way to the lavishly decorated cove at the bend in the river.

A single Kako demon guarded the door of driftwood. He was drawing indecent pictures in the dirt with the tip of his spear. I could hear ecstasy in the voices behind him. A moan chased another one, growing exponentially on itself. I knew they must be coupling, and I did not care.

"Let me through," I commanded.

The guard fell away at the force in my words, my nails scarring the wooden door as I shoved it open. It was almost comical to watch their surprise, yet I couldn't stop taking in the details. The greenish sweat along her toned arms. The way she clung to his body. How his large shoulders covered the bed completely.

"Persephone, what are you doing here?"

"The baby is coming."

Hades rolled himself off of Minthe, wrapping her bedsheets around his waist and handing her another one. She didn't take it, preferring to let me see her hardened nipples instead. When I met her eyes, she was glaring. But it was a triumphal glare. Did she even care about him or was this about making me jealous? I had usurped her without even knowing it and that was what stung her. "My queen," she said with a sneer.

"Are you sure?" Hades asked. "Have you spoken to Hecate? She can find you a midwife." His eyebrows were furrowed as if he weren't quite sure why I was changing the rules of the game.

I wanted to scream at him. You've changed the rules! You don't talk to me like you used to! Instead, I said, "I wanted you."

He shifted his weight, but it was Minthe's tinkling laugh that set my teeth grinding. "A god? You want a god to watch you give birth like some animal?"

"Preferably."

"We all know you are not fit to be queen. I'm sure that's why you don't act like a queen. Because you know you are not. Now get out, little Kore. Let a woman do her work. Hades will attend to you later as is proper."

I vaguely heard Hades reprimand her as my insides curled, like a piece of parchment sent to flame. Blackened and hot. I snapped. The pain of labor and the anger at that name were twin cyclones of rage, bubbling up and over, a great force of energy I barely understood, but yearned for all the same. That was the scariest part. The yearning was incalculably more immense than the pain. It overwhelmed everything. I screamed as the twin desires mingled together and thrust it toward the nymph.

She was there and then not.

Hades abruptly let his sheet drop, and I did not avert my eyes at his manhood, still hard for the nymph. Besides the brief encounter with Zeus, I had never seen a naked man, let alone examined one at this range for this length of time.

"What did you do?" he whispered.

I pulled my eyes from him. I had done real magic. It must have been the pomegranate seeds I'd consumed. I bent to examine the little green plant leafing up from a crack between the stone tiles in the floor. It had a sweet, earthy smell, growing vibrant and dainty, just like Minthe herself. If anything, I'd improved her, although I could hardly put into words what I'd done.

Another wave of pain washed over me, and I bent over the plant, one hand bracing myself on the ground. For some reason, the smell took away some of the pain and nausea. It was as if my magic knew exactly the type of herb to conjure in order to help.

Hades was at my side immediately as I staggered to my knees, my hands cupping my belly. I could feel the ripples of the contractions through the silk of my chiton.

My eyes were wide and every nerve sizzled. I felt frantic, pawing at his bare chest as another wave came.

"Don't tell Zeus. Don't tell Demeter. You promised."

45

HADES

My wife had this uncanny ability to say and do things that knocked me off my orbit. I think she reveled in it.

That was a lie.

She absolutely reveled in it.

She could realm hop. From the beginning. Of course she could. It was how she got around all this time after the Accords. How she did it hardly mattered. All I could think was one thought: *she could've come back at any time, but she didn't. At least, not to see me.*

Words were still spilling from her lips.

"I can travel the realms. Me alone. Your body will probably condense and then all your juices will ooze out. It wouldn't be pretty, but I'll just skip over and see if any Olympian or Titan is ordering the attacks and creating new demons. All you have to do is—"

"Trust you," I interrupted.

She pinned me with a spiky gaze. "Yes. Simple, really."

I waited. "That's it? I'm supposed to be overwhelmed by your honesty and let you go off to Olympus with your dagger and all your mysterious power coursing through your body?"

"Did it work?"

"No."

"Hades, I know we've had our past, but I'm your only hope right now. All you have to do is take that leap of faith. You know in your heart that I love the Underworld as well as you do, and I can't stand to see it burn. If you don't trust me, at least trust that."

"Elegantly said, goddess."

Her face shone with triumph for a moment, until I turned and began walking toward Tartarus. We'd have to sneak in and my Helm wouldn't be much help since it was currently hiding my secret. Persephone still had a piece, although just thinking about that piece made it difficult to swallow.

She must have used my Helm to sneak into the Underworld, shed her seeds, hide them, and leave a hundred years ago. That's why I didn't sense her presence. This time, she was using the Helm to hide her dagger, so I sensed her immediately, meaning she had wanted me to catch her. I rubbed that space between my eyes. The pieces were there, but the picture was elusive.

Persephone was waving her arms as she talked rapidly. "I'm not going to argue with you about this. For one, we didn't assign this argument a number. For two, we don't have time. I have to get to Olympus."

"Actually, we have to get to Tartarus," I corrected.

Persephone stopped moving altogether. "You're out of your mind. Do you even know what is in the depths? No, you don't. There are things down there that would frighten even you, deathless god. They would sense you and your power immediately! They'll—"

"I guess you'll have to give me that piece of my Helm, then, so they can't."

"Now you want me to give up my only bargaining chip? You're worse than out of your mind, you're... you're..."

"What?" I called back as her shouts faltered.

"Insufferable."

"I like the sound of that."

Persephone's mouth resembled a razor, straight and sharp, as she jogged back to my side. It had been worth a try, getting that piece of Helm from her. I didn't like the idea of her sneaking around without my knowledge.

I prepared myself for her trickery, but she didn't try anything. She didn't try anything obvious, at least.

"Are you serious about Tartarus?" she asked.

"I don't trust you on your own, and to be quite frank, you're not safe on your own. You have too many enemies. Where I go, you go, and currently, that's Tartarus."

"What about my seeds?"

"I assume you went looking for them already and didn't find them."

She lifted her chin, defiant, without even the grace to look ashamed.

"I'll take that as a yes. Why do you think we'd be able to find them now? Isn't it more likely that some creature stumbled across them in the last few decades and took them for themselves?"

"No," Persephone hissed. "I would have felt it if someone consumed my seeds. I would know."

"Would you?"

"I would know it in my bones."

"Okay," I shrugged. "If you say so.

46

PERSEPHONE

There had to be a word for that feeling one got when they desperately hated and admired someone in equal measure. Hades toed that line as if it were his day job. Annoyingly stubborn and noble—how it tormented me! His hair was wild in that windswept way, fluttering around his face, which was currently scowling at me.

"So your plan is to simply stroll into Tartarus even though you've never been farther than Kronos' kingdom of the damned?"

"Basically," he said.

"Oh this will be fun to watch. I need snacks." At Hades' bland, emotionless face, I added, "I should at least get a reaction when I say funny things."

"And you'll have it when that occurs. I might even crack a smile."

I gaped at him. Since when did my husband find his sense of humor? Someone must have stabbed him with a funny bone. I wondered if it left a mark.

"What are you looking at?" he asked.

I held up my hands. "Nothing."

Hades had a long look on his face. His muscles tensed as if preparing for battle, but he always did that when deep in thought, like he was preparing to go to war against another's mind.

I interrupted. "We really should go to Olympus. The Titans are there and your brothers. If it's not one, it's the other."

Hades didn't respond. Instead, he asked, "Do you know who ruled the Underworld before the Titans?"

"What?"

"I don't know who, but there was something before us and something before the Titans."

"What are you saying, Hades?"

"Forget Olympus. We need to go to Tartarus. I think I can manage it well enough without ripping realms and all that rot."

Every fiber of my being strained to slay him right then and there. My alarm rose like geese off of a lake, flapping and honking as they took flight at once, the clamoring louder than my thoughts. No. No. No. Not Tartarus. Never there. I would not go back.

Hades was watching me closely, though, so I met his gaze impassively. "'Look on my works ye mighty and despair! Nothing else remains.'"

"Precisely. Ozymandias syndrome. We may forget, but there was always something before us. And there will be something after."

"Whatever happened to Percy Bysshe Shelley?" I asked, struggling to find an alternative. I wasn't ready to go to Tartarus. Not yet.

"Funny you should ask," Hades said, as if we were enjoying a conversation on our obsidian thrones. "I thought Dante's idea about those violent winds always buffeting adulterers about was pretty good. I put Shelley in charge of that."

"Oh yeah. It was fairly good. I'm glad Dante was worth something."

"He wasn't that bad. Some writers are way worse."

"Most writers are way worse."

There was a moment of silent, shared existence. We had gone through so very much together.

Suddenly, I narrowed my eyes. He was holding something. Something he was twisting, his knuckles white with effort. "Hades, what are you—no!"

There was a ripping noise as he rammed the skeleton key into the space his powers had created. A space that wasn't there a moment ago. Then he hooked his arm in mine and pulled me straight into a deep pit, my mouth full of curses. My scrabbling grip met nothing but air, as dark shadows slid past me, coating me in condensation as we plummeted.

47

HADES

Persephone's moans were so very different from the pleasurable ones I had just coaxed out of Minthe moments before. No, these moans were like wild animals tearing at each other's throat. I could hear the eerily similar moans from the River Cocytus through the doorway. There was no time to call a shade midwife.

Already, golden sweat sheened Persephone's upper lip and drizzled from her temple. She clung to the bed frame, her knuckles white. Yet there was a blessing in our situation. Cloaked in our Underworld darkness, nobody knew of the child, so there was no god to make the baby's passage difficult. A vengeful god could make a goddess labor for weeks or even years. As it were, Persephone merely had to give one good push.

I caught the wet thing, slimy and unfit for the world, and held her to my chest. Before I gave her to Persephone, I tucked the babe under my chin, wrapped carefully in my arms, and I jogged around the small hearth in Minthe's room as was our custom. It was makeshift, but it would do. I wanted my wife to know I fully accepted the baby, just as we agreed. "She is perfect," I announced.

Persephone's eyes were wide and perhaps the most innocent I had ever seen when I finally handed her the babe. Mortals waited days before jogging around the hearth. They waited to see if the child survived first. In a matter of days, this little godling would be walking.

"Melinoë. She is Melinoë," she said. Her voice was rough, so I took a dipper of water and held it for my wife to drink. The water ran down her chin as she gulped until she was sated.

"Melinoë is the most beautiful creature I have ever seen," I marveled. I gave my wife a hard kiss on her forehead, and I could feel her positively buzzing. Maybe this child would settle her roiling spirit. She grew so angry at times, I feared for her sanity.

"So you're not angry?" she ventured, dragging a finger over the baby's stomach, counting every finger and toe. She didn't bend to kiss those fingertips, but I could see how she wanted to. She just needed time.

My glance was sidelong, preoccupied as I was by this marvel of life. How could something so perfect come from something so vile as my brother Zeus?

"Angry?"

"At me."

I stopped nuzzling the baby to give Persephone my full attention. "You shouldn't have done that to Minthe. They were just words, and I had no intention of letting you walk out alone to give birth on a dirt walkway."

She crossed her arms petulantly, and I was reminded again she was but a child compared to me. "So you are angry with me."

"I didn't say that. I am happy you did not kill a living thing, no matter how upset you were. Once you kill, it cannot be taken back. Even if that thing comes back to life, you would not be the same."

"Are you asking me to turn her back into a nymph or are you commanding me, my king?"

"I'm merely suggesting that it would be a good growth oppor-

tunity." I went back to cooing at Melinoë, blowing raspberries on her chubby, milk-drunk cheeks, and tickling her feet.

Persephone loosened her arms a bare bit. "She dishonored me."

"By all means. Make plants out of the whole lot of them."

"That is my point! Why do you never take offense? Demons whisper behind your back, too, you know."

I stopped adoring my daughter sincerely this time and gently gave her one last kiss. My wife's face was incredulous when I looked up. It got more so as I spoke.

"Persephone, are you serious? I have more important things to do with my time than to care what others whisper and think. I only care if those whispers have real teeth behind them. Of course my ex-lover was going to be jealous. Everyone thinks Melinoë is mine."

"Keep your voice down," *she hissed, covering the baby's stomach with a hand.* "And from what I saw, Minthe clearly wasn't your ex-lover."

"Fair enough," *I granted.* "But should we talk about why exactly she is and you aren't?"

Persephone turned her cheek to the pillow. "You speak in the present tense as if I might actually turn her back and you will continue to be lovers."

"As I said, it is merely a good growth opportunity." *I left the unsaid part hanging like a waxing moon between us. If Persephone were to accept me fully after this, perhaps things could be different. The question hung. The answer was all hers.*

48

PERSEPHONE

I was still screaming.

They say it took nine days to fall from Olympus to Earth and nine more to fall to Tartarus, but that was in mortal-time. I lived centuries on Olympus before I realized a day had passed. It was why I'd gotten confused after the Accords and didn't return to Earth until man had forgotten about the Greek gods. We had become mere characters in their paintings. Mankind was frescoing chapel walls in Rome and roaming across the oceans for the first time. I thought it'd been a tiny nap after the horror of the Demon War and my last betrayal of Hades, but it had been almost a thousand years in mortal time.

Essentially, my scream was short-lived, but it didn't make me any less livid. "How dare you—"

Hades' calloused hand clapped over my mouth, and I smelled pomegranates. My mind twisted for a moment, but it was my own breath. I exuded it, still. I always would.

Hades was still silent with a single finger to his lips. His eyes searched the perimeter, a true general in his element.

So far, there were no prisoners waiting to devour us after centuries of neglect in our dungeon basement.

Hades' voice was barely above the flutter of a moth's wings. "Tartarus is no longer under my control. As you said, there are things here that terrify even me, and they have overrun this section. So now, Persephone, will you hush?"

A sentient looking mist moved in to envelop us, and I flinched when it touched me. It curled through a plush carpet of springy moss and tickled my arms and the back of my knees like a thousand soft fingers stroking my skin. Sinisterly.

I'd forgotten that Tartarus was not for squishy lifeforms —like me. How the mist seemed to gasp and exhale, swirling around us and sniffing at our necks. It was taking our measure. If what Hades claimed were true, we would need to stay on guard.

I looked sideways at Hades. He hated it down here. I think it reminded him of the one thing gods truly fear: being forgotten. All of the other forgotten gods, disobedient mortals, and discarded heroes were sent here.

No empire can survive indefinitely, not even a godly one. They eventually cripple from within, reach for too much, and let greed gnaw them to the bone.

There were levels to Tartarus, deep and dark. I knew because I was one of the few to have traveled them. I was certain of that. Whenever I casually mentioned places or things, Hades never gave a sign he knew what I was talking about. I let him believe they were places on Earth where only nymphs visited or some other misdirection. I never let him know about my visits to the very bowels of Tartarus. No reason to start being honest now. It'd be weird.

Sadly, even I was too frightened of it to leave any weapons, like more lentil seeds or my precious pomegranate seeds, down here. They might be gobbled up by the very air, this miasma that cloaked and choked us. It felt like dipping into a salty pool, the mist clawing at my scratches and open wounds. Hades barely gave a sign it was affecting him, except his eyes were dilated in the near-darkness, as if to force the world into clarity.

He pointed to a path carved out of the ancient rock bed, and we trudged through the underbrush to reach it. This way led to Kronos and his kingdom of the damned. It was where Hades imprisoned them after the Titan War. I had only been here once and for a very good reason. Hades hadn't been back since the day he locked them in and threw away the key.

The key that I found.

If Hades ever suspected I had a hand in setting the Titans free during the subsequent Demon War, he kept it to himself, but I think he did not know. His rage would be unrivaled.

"What's your plan? I assume you have one," I said.

"No."

I stood still at the edge of a primeval lake bed. It had been carved by forces unknown even to the Titans before us. There were fossils of creatures entrenched under the ice that I had no names for.

"What do you mean 'no'? No plan? You pushed me into a pit of hell and you don't have a plan? I can't believe this. Oh wait. Yes, I can."

Hades put a finger to his lips and pointed, but it was too late. I stumbled over a particularly fierce skull with fangs the length of my femur bone. Hades grabbed me before I hit the ground, my chiton swirling up to my hips. He averted his eyes, and I couldn't help but taunt him.

"You gave me these clothes, yet you can't bear to look at

me? Earth has moved on, you know. Women wear pants now." Actually, that had sort of shocked me, too, although I didn't need to tell him that. Flying vehicles? Sure. The downfall of monarchies? Obvious. Women wearing pants? Yikes.

"And so have we. You didn't see Hecate wearing dresses. I just never expected to see you again, so there was little reason to update your wardrobe."

I mimed a stab to my heart. "Oh, good one, Hades. Point scored."

He said nothing in return, merely removing his hand from mine and barreling forward. His shoulders were hunched, but his face had an inner fire of conviction that took most aback when they saw it in person. It was exactly that look, which he wore so many years ago during our first meeting, that convinced me he was the Olympian brother I needed for my revenge on Zeus.

"What are you hoping to find in Tartarus? Whoever is behind this probably isn't leaving a breadcrumb trail for you to follow," I whispered as we neared a curved gate made of bones and ivory. Its creamy white light came alive in the stillness of Tartarus. Abandoned Tartarus, that is.

"You'd be surprised at the things creatures leave behind."

We ducked under white ash trees with little translucent mushrooms adorning their bases. The forest beyond the gates looked just as old as the lake bed and more menacing. Most believed Tartarus to be bleak, much like the rest of the Underworld, if not worse. It was a playground for punishment, after all, but Kronos' kingdom of the damned was not that. Not even a close. I'd always found it odd that their punishment was to be merely contained in Tartarus. Prometheus, a Titan who fought for Zeus, endured much worse for giving humans fire to keep their shriveled bodies warm at night. His liver was ripped from his body and eaten by an eagle every day and then regrown every night on the top of a mountain. But the Titans who tried to kill Zeus? Oh, just eternity in their own upside kingdom. Kronos even had a castle and miles of gardens and vineyards for his own winemaking. There was a village to rival ours, and plenty of demons to be bred as slaves for sex and labor. The Titans in exile wanted for nothing.

During the Demon War, I wanted Zeus dead. I unleashed the Titans to fight again, and my act had turned the tide. Zeus sued for peace. The Titans were allowed to live in Olympus, locked away with the Olympians. Now, Zeus spent his days fending off their attacks. While that made me smile, it was still a half-victory. I wanted him dead.

"After the Demon War, who moved into Tartarus?" I asked.

"I gave Kronos' castle to Thanatos."

"And now who lives there if you've lost control of Tartarus?"

"That's what we're going to find out."

"I don't like the sound of that."

"You're probably going to like the sound of this even less, then."

I whirled around, but it was too late. Hades loomed over me, a fierce burning in his eyes. "Tell me why you decided to go to Olympus after the Demon War," he demanded. "Why did you abandon your people?"

As he spoke, a chill blasted off of him that could sear flesh. I tried dodging it, but it was cold and my movements were jerky, halting and impossible. I couldn't even get my mouth to work. At least the truth serum had worn off. That was a hitch in my plans I hadn't calculated. "Why did you choose Olympus?" he repeated.

I fell to the ground, shaking. The cold abated a little, but only around my face. The rest of my body turned an unappealing blue color.

"You know why," I hissed, angry at his constant treachery. "We weren't in love, the children were dead, and I had work to do on Olympus. Someone had to exact revenge, and since you were too weak to move against your brother, it was up to me."

"You set Kronos free," he accused.

I continued to struggle against his cold, but he waited. Patient as always.

"What does it matter to you? Everyone knew you would be untouchable. Neither the Titans, nor the Olympians would have removed you from your throne. No Titan wanted the Underworld for themselves and no Olympian, either. I knew you would be unaffected."

"No, goddess, you did not. You just didn't care about anything other than hurting Zeus. That entire fiasco was because you wanted revenge on him. What I don't understand is why you didn't stay in the Underworld and rebuild with us once you got your heart's desire, once Zeus was imprisoned on Olympus with his mortal enemies. The Titans have been attacking Zeus for the last fifteen hundred years. Is that not enough revenge? And yet, when the time came to decide where to spend eternity, you chose Olympus. With him."

I closed my eyes, remembering the moment Hades held out his hand, waiting for me to take it. I never forgot the look on his face when I brushed a last kiss on his marmoreal cheek and slipped across the divide into Olympus. My betrayal had been infinite. It knew no depths, but that's what it takes to win a war against an immortal.

"Zeus still survives," I said.

Hades didn't move. "It's a half-life for him. He is no longer revered by mortals, and he is surrounded by enemies that would never miss an opportunity to torture him."

"You think that's good enough for him?" I shot back. "It's not. It's merely a prelude to what I want to do to him."

Gray smoke drifted off his body, obscuring his face. "Will anything be enough for you, goddess? Don't answer. I'd rather not listen to more lies pouring from your lips."

"Do you not care what he did?" I demanded, gesturing to the scars on his back.

"Not caring and not acting are two different things. I cared, Persephone. I still care. Deeply."

"Not enough, Hades. And not nearly as much as I do."

"And look where all your caring got the gods. Melinoë died because the Titans roamed free. She died because of them."

Hades didn't abandon his signature cold demeanor, even though his words were worse than ice since they were mostly true. *She didn't die because of the Titans, but she did die in the chaos they created. It made us all vulnerable.*

He left unsaid the second part. That Melinoë died because of me. The fact that he wasn't prepared to come out and say that hurt more than if he had. If he had accused me of killing our daughter—even unintentionally by setting loose the power of Tartarus—I could have defended myself and justified my anger toward him for suggesting such a thing. Never in my wildest dreams of revenge did I ever think that price would be acceptable.

Feebly, I offered up my only defense. "I didn't know that would happen. I would have never…"

"Oh yes. You're very good at keeping secrets. What a child you still are to need this revenge. It was never enough to mourn."

My face reddened as if he'd physically slapped me. Without waiting even a moment, I turned and stalked away. I couldn't bear to see his face. Not anymore. It wasn't his style to lash out so when he did, the pain weighed double. Hades *had* changed. At least, now I could justify what I'd do next.

"No, it wasn't enough to mourn," I called. "I will kill Zeus."

"Well you'll have to wait a little longer for your revenge, because we're stopping this infernal coup first. You will do penance for leaving the Underworld by saving it. Then I couldn't possibly care what you do with the rest of your eternity."

49

HADES

Statues erected to the Titans rose along the entryway like a grand processional. I knew it had been dangerous, allowing them to build statues to themselves, but Hecate thought it might give them a puffed sense of importance. They would betray themselves long before they betrayed me.

Instead, as Persephone just confirmed, it was my dear wife who betrayed me first by letting them loose. I wished I didn't know why. Her hatred would consume her completely, but she had lived long and hard. When I looked at the dark-eyed Persephone, I never saw that innocent girl from Olympus ever again. I didn't see anything young in her at all. There were centuries of pain, of seeking, of disappointment. She bore more than anyone of us immortals and still... and still. She could be witty and kind. She could love deeply and see pure hearts.

Yet above all, and I would do well to remember this, she had one purpose. Destroy Zeus, as painfully as possible. Everything she did was a stepping stone to that end. "I understand you don't want to be here—"

"Understatement of the century," Persephone muttered.

"But we are bound by Hecate's witchery. As soon as we end this war, we will have her undo what was done, and you can frolic over to Olympus as you wish."

"Frolic. Right."

"Those are my terms. If you don't like them, I will leave you tied to the pillory post over there and pick you up once I've destroyed the traitors on my own."

"Like you could."

"I intend to."

Persephone jerked forward, bunching her chiton in a fist as she maneuvered over a muddy puddle in the yard. "And give you the pleasure of tying me up again just to forget about me? I don't think so."

"I didn't leave you in my dungeon."

"You might as well have. This is worse torture than anything the Kako could've imagined."

"I really have missed our charming conversations, dear wife."

We walked through Kronos' abandoned castle in silence after that comment. For every step forward, there were always two steps backward for us.

Keeping my voice low, I nodded at the turrets jutting up from the crenellated wall. "I don't want to get caught inside if something is in there. Let's check the surrounding village first. Thanatos lived here long enough that most traces of the original Titans are gone. Anything still remaining will be a clue."

"How long ago did you abandon Tartarus?" she asked, her laser gaze as much an accusation as her words.

"I had no choice," I began, but she waved it away.

"I'm not saying you did. I'm just asking how long ago Thanatos left."

"Only a few days before you arrived. About six weeks ago."

She nodded, not meeting my eyes. We scanned the tiltyard and surrounding barns where my black horses were stabled when not pulling my chariot. They had been let loose some time ago by angry shades, and I hadn't seen Alastor, my lead horse, in months. Where he went, the other three followed. The demonspawn could certainly take care of themselves. However, I still missed the beast that had been my constant for thousands of years.

We walked through the abandoned castle yard and the surrounding fields. Old cobblestones and large pavers were cracked and blackened. None of it looked familiar anymore. Grime covered everything. I couldn't say if this was done before Thanatos took over or in the six weeks since we'd pulled out of Tartarus.

Something caught my eye, and I ran my finger along the base of the stable wall. The stone structure had a fair amount of black soot coating it. I brought my fingers to my nose and smelled the residue. Iron.

"What is it?" Persephone whispered, sniffing before recoiling. She'd clearly sensed it, too. "Someone is using Stygian water," she said in wonder.

As if on cue, a fog began to roll in, thicker and more oppressive than the mist. Bilge rose in my throat at the nature of it. This was a chthonic mist.

My voice was grim. "Of course," I said, as the temperature dropped and breathing became a chore.

"What?" Persephone furrowed her eyebrows.

"They're shielding their activities using a chthonic fog in order to make Stygian iron."

Even Persephone was aghast. "For weapons?"

"Or worse." I brushed the soot off. "Did you get a good look at the new demons when they attacked you?"

"Honestly? I tried not to."

I raised an eyebrow at her squeamishness. "Well, their skin... it was like a nightmare."

"You think they were forged," she said bluntly.

"I think it's a distinct possibility."

We moved deeper into the village, staying close to the walls, hopping from shadow to shadow. Occasionally, we saw other things scurrying in the shadows as well, but we both knew enough to know we didn't want to meet them. Soon, we found a stream and made our way towards the forge. As we approached, we heard a great clanging noise. Bursts of orange flames lit up the sky, and black smoke coiled, mingling with the clouds.

Despite the heat, a chill skittered down my spine, and Persephone and I caught each other's eye. The forge was on; that much was clear. But who was feeding it and why?

I pointed toward an outcropping of stone, and we crept closer. The smell was noxious at this range, and we were still a few hundred feet away. Persephone tied her long hair in a knot in front of her nose, but I didn't see what good that would do.

Suddenly, the noxious fog grew thicker, almost like a barrier. It coated everything in its toxic grip, and hid our feet from our eyes. Blinded, we crunched over the ground wherever we stepped. I paused and threw out an arm to stop Persephone. Her large, liquid eyes watched me accusingly. Yes, I had forced her here, but it was the only option. Before she took any more revenge or realm-hopped herself back to Olympus for the rest of eternity, she would help me discover who was waging this war.

After a moment, we pushed on, emerging on the other side of the dense fog to an explosion of color. Blooms of red dampened Persephone's cheeks and made my sword sweat condensation. Despite the noise of the forge, the rest of the castle grounds were eerily quiet. There was no hive of activity, no shades, no Thanatos. As if the entire Underworld had fled this land, which perhaps they had. They had poured into mine.

Hunching down, we crept silently along the rocky outcroppings toward the open oven. The mouth was the size of a cavern and just as deep. The ringing noise of something being forged blistered my ears. Surely anyone who worked it regularly would soon go deaf.

A large creature stood roaring in the middle of the billowing flames as if unaffected. It was naked from the waist up with only rough, homespun canvas pants to protect his body from the flames. I doubt he truly felt any heat however. Long, corded hair shook behind the mass of muscle as the creature's arms expertly pounded something in the fire of the forge. Protruding from his bare back were foot long spikes that oozed poison. Every few seconds, the creature reached around to prick his finger and pinch droplets of poisoned blood onto the weapon he was creating.

"Holy shit," Persophene whispered, "it's a Telechine. Aren't they supposed to be extinct?"

50

HADES

I frowned. "Zeus destroyed them all, but their essence dispersed to Tartarus. Clearly, they've reformed."

The Telechines had discovered the secret to mixing Stygian water with sulfur to create blades of immense power. They crafted the sickle wielded by Kronos to castrate his father, as well as Poseidon's trident and, my own, diamond bident. It was bound with Stygian iron at its core, an incredible conductor of magic. After the Titan War, Zeus struck the beasts down with his thunderbolts so they would never be able to make weapons for our rivals. Now, they were forging again. Only one question was left: on whose orders?

The one before us looked quite grizzled with a long scar that ran from his right temple across his nose and left cheek, ending in a circle around the nape of his neck. His skin had a grayish tint, and his nose bent at an unnatural angle. His face was a roadmap of where not to go in life—basically, anywhere near Tartarus, the Titans, or the Olympian gods.

"Any great ideas?" Persephone asked. "Besides sneak away, because that's my idea. It's already taken."

I grabbed her by the chiton. "Oh no, goddess. We're together or we're dead."

"I don't need the reminder," she said stiffly.

During the Demon War, a human and a demon working together had found the secret to killing immortals. No longer was the threat of eternal imprisonment in Tartarus the only thing to fear. Now, we had the threat of death hanging over us, and nobody understood how it worked. Was it a weapon forged by a Telechine?

Our daughter Melinoë was the first casualty in the war. This told me the weapon must have come from our realm and not Earth or Olympus. Despite centuries of searching, we still didn't know what caused it. Was it some spell or perhaps a potion? Did a demon dance under the naked moonlight and call upon the gods to kill themselves? What?

It hardly mattered now. Keen-sighted Hermes was next, followed by gray-eyed Athena. Zeus surrendered after that, his back broken at the death of his favorite daughter. If I had much pity left, I might have spared some for my brother, but I had none. I had a daughter to mourn and an infant son dead long before that. We never did figure out how the mortals and demons were able to kill an immortal being. We could no longer fight this phantom enemy that stole through the night, devouring gods, sucking their immortality dry.

"Plan?" Persephone mouthed.

I pointed her to stay down and out of sight. Killing Kako demons with whatever little magic she kept hidden—and I would figure that out—was a completely different beast than taking on a bloodied Telechine.

She shrugged and mouthed, "Your funeral," before crossing her arms and sitting down behind the rock. Her long, black hair had come unknotted, and she re-wrapped it around her nose to block the stench. I swallowed as I recalled the way it spooled heavily in my hand once upon a time, flowing through my fingers like water.

Without a word, I blurred my outline as best I could without my Helm at full capacity and crept closer to the Telechine. First, I wanted to know what he was creating. Then I would slay him.

The sulfuric scent buffeted me as I drew closer. From here, I could see black sweat dripping between the spines that dotted his back as he worked with meticulous care. He was absolutely creating something of equal power to the divine weapons of war. Of that, there was no question.

But for whom?

Something skittered at the corner of my senses. I turned to look for the disturbance. I saw nothing, but Persephone turned, too. And then she quickly slipped behind me.

Whatever was coming wouldn't matter, because the movement was enough to catch the Telechine's attention. And he didn't look pleased to have an audience.

51

PERSEPHONE

Screaming like a scorned siren, I launched myself at the demon that appeared through the fog. I had to. I'd stupidly let the Telechine know I was there with my jumpy nerves. Being mortal was the dregs. Better to fight the demon than the Telechine, though. I'd leave him to Hades.

Our bodies slammed into each other, and the impact made my stomach turn unpleasantly. Somehow, I didn't think throwing up on the demon would do much good. Instead, I flicked a lentil seed in his eye and willed it to grow.

While the tiny green tendrils sprouted through its brain and the demon dropped to the ground in agony, I spared a glance for Hades. He wasn't doing as well as me, but then again, not many could.

The Telechine snarled as he removed one of his spines like a thorn from a rose bush and brandished it as a deadly sword. Hades ducked and stabbed at the Telechine with his bident, which only made the Telechine more angry.

"I forged that weapon for you, deathless god!" he bellowed. "I have the right to take it back."

"Then come and get it," Hades taunted, spinning the bident once, twice in his hands. I rolled my eyes. At least he was annoying someone else for once.

With a low grow, the Telechine attacked, and the force of their clash almost toppled the forge itself. Sparks flew from where the rumbling earth split in two. Fingers gouged at eyeballs, and nails shattered against armored skin.

Below me, the demon still writhed on the ground as my lentil seed invaded his gray matter, replacing the folds with its roots. Good. I wasn't defenseless against this new breed, as long as I could cultivate more seeds. I kicked his twisting body out of the way and readied one more lentil seed for the monster roaring over Hades. I only had a couple more, but I couldn't say for sure if the Telechine would even be affected by it. They were ancient, powerful beings, here before the Olympians.

Still, Hades was a god for a reason. For every attack the Telechine unleashed, Hades parried his blows. Death poured off of him, blinding and bewildering the Telechine, making him vulnerable to Hades' own counter-attacks. I had never seen Hades move so fast or so powerfully. Ancient beings, apparently, brought out the sexy in him.

In seconds, the Telechine lay on his back with Hades' huge hand around his neck. The Telechine bared his fungus-slick teeth. "So, the great deathless god has been so kind to pay me a visit."

Hades raised his bident, threatening a final death blow. "Who do you work for?" he growled.

The monster laughed, a dull ringing noise that grated on the nerves. "I do not know, and I do not care. They do not like you and that is enough."

"Then what did they offer you?"

"Offer? Why, I'd kill Olympians for free. The pleasure of

watching eternity fade from your eyes is more than enough payment."

As he spoke, the Telechine searched frantically for an escape. He found it in the fire. There, glowing red, sat the weapon he had been forging. Even half finished, it gleamed with power.

His hand shot out and I opened my mouth to scream, to warn Hades, but the Telechine was too fast. The blade entered Hades's ribs, just below his armor. A spray of ichor splattered the ground, as Hades roared louder than I'd ever heard before. His body curled and his face turned an unappetizing shade of puce as crackles of black raced from the edges of his wound.

Poison.

The Telechine rose to his feet. "You are lucky, deathless god, that this sword had not yet been finished, or you would already be dead. Instead, I will take pleasure in finishing you off."

Panic tore at my nerves. I needed Hades. Alive. A trembling began in my palms. It streaked up my arms and shot across my chest. I barely had time to react before a brilliant rose-tinted light burst forth from my body. I screamed in pain as the Telechine was blasted backwards onto his thorned back, three of his spines snapping off at the tip from the blow. The sword flew from his hands, splintering from the force of my light.

Without a second look, not even to gather his broken body parts, the monster turned and ran. "There's more where that came from," I shouted, hoping he'd think twice before attacking us any time soon.

Hades groaned.

Oh, shit. If my magic had scared a Telechine that badly, what had it done to Hades, my bitter enemy? I ran to his side and pulled him up, throwing his arm across my shoulder. He hissed, but I kept dragging us forward. "You can't die now, Hades. You got us into this mess, and you're going to get us out of it."

"Why are you so annoying?" he gritted out.

"That's what you're going to say with the little strength you have left? That *I'm* the annoying one? You are going down in history as having the worst last words ever. Seriously. The literal worst. I know, because I've heard all of them."

Hades let out a strangled noise that I took to be a laugh. That was a good sign. That had to be a good sign. Stupid, stupid god!

"Do you feel like you're dying?" I asked, my own strength waning with every step. My chiton caught on a jagged rock and tore, but I yanked it off and kept going. Safe... I had to find somewhere safe. I knew Tartarus better than Hades. There were safe places. I just had to find them. And get out of Kronos' castle compound.

I noticed something glittering behind us and sucked in a groan. Hades was still bleeding, trailing his golden ichor and showing any demon—or worse—exactly where to find us. Ahead was a darkened patch. As we drew closer, tall trees came into focus and then individual leaves. It was a crystallized forest, frozen in amber. It'd have to do for now.

I helped Hades limp to the nearest tree. He had lost so much blood, it looked like someone had tried to gild him with golden paint. It was thick and oozed over my fingers as I pressed against his wounds.

"Hades, I don't know what to do," I said, trying to sound steady, although my heart was beating much too fast.

"There was something on that sword," he grunted. "An ancient poison."

I put my nose next to his wound and smelled it, recoiling at the foul residue. "Okay," I said, jumping into action before it was too late. "I can handle this."

First, I peeled back his eyelids and peered inside. The black was veining its way through the whites. That couldn't be good.

"How's it look, goddess?" he slurred, his head flopping a bit.

"Well, we've always had different definitions of the same words, so my 'good' and your 'good' are probably miles apart."

"You're babbling."

I cracked a twig off of the crystallized branch and jabbed it into Hades' wound, ignoring his muffled moans of indignation. Quickly, before the poison had time to burn through the twig, I dropped it on the ground and covered it in the earth of Tartarus, rubbing the dirt into the residue to create a sticky mess of mud. With one of my few remaining lentil seeds, I cracked it open and let the tiny, furled bud flutter into the pit I'd made. I closed my eyes and hovered my hands over the whole thing, concentrating.

The lentil quivered under my magic, which bound the dirt of the deepest part of the Underworld with the cracked seed. Together they sprouted, and I forced a tear out of my eye and let it drip into the mud of my creation. In seconds, I was rewarded with a bloom of flowers and something a bit more scoop-able. I laced it together with the vines and whirled on Hades with what was surely a wild look in my eyes.

He blinked. "What the fuck was that?"

"I..." I trailed off. "Honestly, I don't know. Life and death are two sides to the same coin. Maybe just being here longer is working on my powers."

His eyes narrowed. "You're working some serious magic even though you claim not to have your precious pomegranate seeds. First, you pull some blinding power out of your ass, enough to blast back a Telechine, and then you create a random 'poultice' with your seeds."

He said that last part with air quotes and a rather rude voice.

I crossed my arms.

"You've seen my ichor. You know how weak I truly am. I can't help it if I've still got some reserves I can pull on in a moment of adrenaline."

He frowned at my explanation, but it was true. He had seen the sickly pale color of my insides. That couldn't be faked.

"Look, do you want the life-healing 'poultice' or not? It won't cure your dour attitude and sadly, nothing will help your suspicious little mind, but it will temper whatever poison the Telechine used. You know what? You're not capable of making these types of decisions right now. Just lay back and get comfortable."

"Those sound like famous last words I shouldn't listen to if I want to survive."

Thankfully, I had mostly tuned him out at that point. I bent to my work, layering the vines and my medicine around his wounds. The blood tapered off, slowly at first, before sealing itself behind a thin, watery line. Hades didn't even grunt, but it looked painful and it still had an angry, black tinge to it. Yet, the black webbing had begun to fade.

Hades said nothing as he held still, appraising me in his own time. It was unnerving, and I eventually had to look away, rubbing more dirt from Tartarus over the pit I'd created to scramble the evidence.

"We need to get out of here. That little spell will have

acted like a beacon, and your blood trail is pretty much a map to our location. This place is going to be crawling soon."

Hades got to his feet, his pain still evident in his body movements, although he masked it well to any outside observer. I, however, knew Hades better than anyone. He had a little crease near his eyes that shouldn't be there. If I stretched out to sense it, his life-force was just the tiniest bit ragged around the edges. He should be fine. For now.

Carefully, I put my head to the ground. A faint aura radiated from the surface. "I don't think any demons or souls you've tortured are this way," I said, nodding in the direction I wanted to go.

He lifted an eyebrow. "What about the souls you've tortured?"

"We'll just have to take that chance, won't we?"

Hades laughed softly, but he still followed like a loyal dog.

We passed through the barren gates of Kronos' old kingdom, each stone in the wall taller than a giant, which made sense since they were built by the giants themselves. There wasn't even small slits for arrows to be notched. Just towering rocks, stacked upon each other with impregnable dark magic woven into the porous stone. Impregnable, until now.

While the Underworld was much more beautiful and ecologically diverse than most mortals pictured, Tartarus was exactly what they feared. For the most part, anyway. The same rivers of pain and suffering defined this space, but it was also less tame. Dangerous mists drifted through the lowlands, and the hills swooped until they were ravines and gorges full of the darkest night where pits waited to swallow gods whole. Despite it all, we dropped deeper and deeper.

If Hades thought I had somewhere specific in mind, he didn't say anything, choosing instead to wait and to watch. He was always so good at that.

As we stumbled along, I noticed the familiar prickles of unease. Tartarus was vast. It didn't care who you were. Mortal souls or deathless gods, it would consume you. I actually felt a pang of gladness that Hades was here and I wasn't alone. Was I growing sentimental? Doubtful. As mortals like to say, in the case of a bear attack, I didn't have to be fast; I just had to be faster than the other god.

"What is this?" Hades asked.

We'd entered another forest. The black trees seemed to stretch to the infinite. None had leaves. The ground had turned a pale blue color, like cornflowers. It still shocked me that Hades had never truly ventured past Kronos' palace. It would give me an edge.

To him, I merely shrugged and pointed. "There's water over there. I can smell it."

Hades knelt down by the protected glade and dipped his hands in the crystal clear waters. His face had become more pinched, and it made me wonder. Kneeling, I pretended to slip and caught myself on his arm. Instantly, I flinched.

"Hades, you're burning."

He continued scooping water down the back of his armor. It glistened on his paling skin. "In hell, yeah, I get the joke."

"No, your skin. It's warm," I said, placing the back of my other wrist to his head.

He grunted, his eyes flickering once. "Don't be concerned over me, goddess. I will heal. Just let me sleep. Then, we must find the Telechines before they forge new weapons for our enemies."

With that, he stalked to a tree, rolled over, and let his wings enclose his body.

"Fine. I guess I'll take the first watch. So you don't die and everything."

"If you want. But I put up protections around a perimeter. If anything trips them, I'll know."

"Well you just think of everything, don't you?"

Still muttering salty thoughts under my breath, I laid down in the dirt. Close, but not too close. I let my senses roam, feeling the life and death of the place flowing around me. I could feel creatures in the water, sprites in the air, and... Hades standing over me? I yelped and stood. He could sneak up on me? "What are you doing, you creeper?"

"Take my armor, goddess."

I looked up suspiciously. "Why?"

"Because I want you to wear it while you sleep. You're vulnerable. I only use the term goddess to be respectful of the status you once held, but for all practical purposes you're a mortal woman exposed to the many dangers of Tartarus. I may be the wounded one, but clearly, you need this."

"So this is to erase the debt you owe me for saving your life with that poultice."

"Think whatever you need to in order to sleep at night. As long as you take the armor."

I let out a thick breath. "Fine," I said, slipping the diamond plated breastplate over my shoulders and fiddling with the straps. It was entirely too heavy for my weak frame, and the armor began to slip.

As quickly as the season's first frost, I felt the ice of Hades near my neck. My skin pebbled in response. My nipples hardened as his fingers caressed the bone of my shoulder as he tied the armor into place. He was still icy. He was still Hades, after all.

As quickly as he came, as if my springtime sun burned away his early morning frost, he was gone, making a bed with his cloak on the ground. "Good night, Persephone."

I thought for a moment. "If you really want to erase that debt, you'd share."

Hades spread his wings, and I didn't think. I curled inside of it, cozying in the sudden familiar scent that reminded me of our previous life together. Then I berated myself and made my mind go blank. "Don't we make quite the pair? I have too little magic and you need to conserve yours to heal."

Hades' deep voice vibrated me when it got its rumbling start. I shivered as its waves rolled over me and did my best to ignore how it made my fingertips tingle. "What would you do?" he asked, and I sensed a mocking tone. "Make us a bed of roses?"

"I have soft edges, you know."

Hades was so silent, I thought he wasn't going to answer. His voice was quiet when he said, "I know, Persephone."

I huddled under the deathless god, his good arm draped over me and tried not to think about the fact I'd saved him or that he'd wanted to save me with this armor. Instead, I told myself it was for the greater plan. Both his and mine. Of course it was.

But for now, I merely enjoyed the burn of his ice.

52

HADES

I lived and breathed Persephone. During council meetings with Thanatos and Hecate, my mind wandered. Scally liked to tease me, but the others were less than thrilled. They never said anything, of course. Hecate merely snipped, "Don't mistake sweetness for weakness."

I never asked what occurred between them, although I felt the frost. That was fine. I burned it away with the fire of our burgeoning love.

Persephone had relocated to my bedroom in the castle. Every morning, she replaced the vase of narcissus blossoms with new flowers, and I would twirl one in her hair. Shade servants brought us breakfast and then Melinoë for us to cuddle. I was beginning to understand why mortals would risk eternal damnation to bring their true love back from death. I almost pitied Orpheus when he failed. That never would have happened before.

This morning, I took my wife by the waist and up against the bed. She was still mercurial; sometimes she wanted it hard. It was more like two feral animals coupling. I must, at dear cost to my appendages, look her directly in the eyes when we coupled like this. I had a feeling I knew why. Other times, she moved against me slowly and languorously, and I could stroke the space between her breasts and trace the golden lines of sweat wherever they took me. I could drink all of her in and savor the taste. Today, she smiled coyly and beckoned with the crook of her finger. She had something on her mind.

"Wife?"

Persephone merely shook her head and crooked her finger again. When she smiled like that, it was a task to keep my heart beating and my lungs inflating. She could spin the earth off its axis and all flowers bowed down to her. Me most of all. She slowly unpinned her chiton, exposing one shoulder, then the other. She looked up and let the silk puddle on the floor. Hot pangs of longing rocked through my body as I watched her sit on the bed and spread her bared thighs.

With a growl, I covered her body completely, cupping her back beneath my arm while her legs went around my back, encouraging me, urging me closer.

We heard nothing as we took our fill of each other. For hours, we ignored the world. Ours only existed here and now.

Finally sated, we laid entangled in the black silk sheets, curled around each other. "Will you tell me what is on your mind now, wife?" I asked, kissing the place on her forehead where her hair parted down the middle. She didn't usually wear a crown, but instead a gold chain with a single rose diamond draping from it at the part. I'd pulled it from the ground after the birth of our daughter.

Persephone propped herself up on an elbow. Goosebumps peppered my skin where she drew invisible lines down my stomach, her bottom lip caught between her teeth. "Do you still love me, Hades?"

There it was again. Questions and confusion. I never could figure her out. "What are you asking?"

She stopped her route. "After all that I put you through. Do you still love me?"

I took her hands. "Even when you didn't want me to, I loved you. Will you tell me what's wrong, wife?"

She glanced up, a softness in her eyes I'd only seen on a handful of occasions. My blood thickened at the sight, desire rolling through me again. She smiled and I could have sworn there was a shy quality to it.

"I am with child. It will be a son and he will be yours completely, my king."

53

HADES

My body ached as it hadn't since the last days of the Demon War. I was tired and slept fitfully, a burning blackness raging through my system. All night, I ran through the charred Underworld as demons died and Persephone was lost. There was an empty space where before there had been Persephone.

I woke fully and put my arm out to feel for her. It wasn't just my dreams. Persephone was missing.

I leapt to my feet, wings spreading with a dull ache. Had she realized my secret and found her seeds? Was she gone? I resisted the urge to open my hiding spot and reveal them in case she was watching. That would be exactly the kind of move she'd make. Instead, I tensely surveyed the landscape and called softly, "Persephone?"

A displacement of air vibrated to my left. I whipped my head around and saw my wife leap from a tree branch with a grin. "Did I startle you?"

"I thought you were gone," I said blandly. As if I needed the reminder, it was a good lesson to learn. Never let your guard down around Persephone.

"Nope," she said, entirely too cheerful for the way I was feeling. "Just scouting. I set a few more mud traps around us so we could sleep peacefully. Want to see the shade who had the misfortune to be curious?"

My stomach turned over at her tone. "Persephone, release the shade from whatever horror you have it in."

She smiled, a feral thing in the dim light of Tartarus. The memory of her one-time shy smile was gone.

"You're hardly any fun," she sighed as if truly put out, "but that's not new."

I ignored her as I tested my wings and the pain level. The poultice had slowly begun its healing work. I was sore, but I could manage. I would heal soon enough. Whatever that poison was, it wasn't the draught of immortal death. Add it to the list of questions. Who reanimated the Telechines and why? The how hardly mattered, did it?

"Let's get going," I suggested. "The Telechine is here somewhere. If we find him, we'll be better prepared to catch him off-guard and question him. "

"Because he was so willing to spill his soul yesterday," Persephone said stoutly.

"He will be."

"Unless you have something I don't know about, I doubt it. Do you not remember the last time? Did the poison addle your brain, too?"

I took Persephone's jaw with one hand before she could continue her tirade and brought her closer. Her mouth worked furiously, but I held fast. More than life in this miserable hell, I wanted to kiss her plump lips into oblivion as we used to, the fire and anger in her eyes sparking me further.

"Will you be quiet, please?" I asked.

"How dare you," she squawked. "After all I did, saving you—" she cut herself off and I let her chin drop so she could stalk away in dignity. I tilted my head, trying not to watch the bit of skin I saw through the rip in her chiton. Choosing not to argue? How very vintage Persephone. I didn't like it one bit. A silent Persephone was a plotting Persephone.

"As you said yourself," I needled as I followed, unsettled by her silence. "You healed me because then I couldn't, and I quote, 'get us killed with a blood trail.'"

Persephone's silence deepened into something colder, something I started to question. Instead of pushing her on it, I swallowed my comments and followed her adorable fragrance. For hours, we walked. I thought about nothing, or at least I tried to. Instead, I found myself drifting more to the swaying hips and hair of Persephone. Eventually, I gave up and enjoyed the view. To go from thinking I'd never see her again for the rest of eternity to standing in her intoxicating presence was heady. I was nearly drunk on her perfume alone. So drunk, I almost missed the scent of danger on the wind.

Demons. Demons I had no name for. They should be gutted, every one of them. Unnatural and a threat to my empire. I wondered how many of my predecessors thought that as well.

"Get ready," I ordered Persephone, slipping into my old stance, my bident ready to decimate. With only a little hesitation, she followed suit as the air pressure plummeted. The black trees bent, doubling over and breaking with long, sharp cracks. Boiling black clouds rolled across the gunmetal gray sky, cloaking us in darkness.

Demons were coming.

"Shouldn't we hide?" Persephone muttered.

"It's much too late for that. I want answers and they will answer them. Keep only one alive. Kill the rest."

She saluted with that infernal pink dagger and limbered on the balls of her feet. Her mouth quirked up, the gesture turning my stomach.

Before I could give the order to charge, Persephone body-slammed an advancing phalanx of ten demons, moving against them with a savage glee that reminded me of a marauding mortal. She took entirely too much pleasure in pain, I thought sourly.

Keeping my senses open to how she was faring, I stabbed and cracked ribs, yanked armor and stared into the depths of their fabricated eyes. Three ganged up to jump on me, and met a quick fate of being skewered. I used my foot to push them off my bident and swung around for the next, getting only momentarily distracted by Persephone's thigh.

Something wrapped its teeth around my arm, and I roared, seeing too late a smaller demon that had slipped through the chaos unnoticed and was now attempting to eat me. I shook it off and stabbed through its stomach so I could examine my arm. It didn't do serious damage. Not for lack of trying, though. It continued snarling at me in its death throes, even as I stepped over its convulsing body.

There were only a handful of the hated monstrosities left when I heard a scream. A demon had tangled Persephone's hair in its claw and was yanking her closer. His forked, red tongue scented the air around her, flicking closer and closer as Persephone's eyes rolled in terror. Her dagger was gone and she grappled at the demon's slick arms to no avail. Without her little tricks, she really could become quite powerless at the worst times.

I growled and took flight. No one treated Persephone like that except for me.

54

PERSEPHONE

There were two more demons loping behind the big ugly one that held me tight. I thought I heard a swoop overhead, but Hades was far too wounded to fly. So perhaps a third?

I kept twisting in and out, taunting the demon as best I could, but my strength was waning. He'd kicked my dagger away, snarling, but I just had to wait for the right moment to spring my trap.

He bent his head, presumably to bite my windpipe, and I re-summoned my dagger. It was the definition of infernal, its value bought at the price of my blood. But didn't all women buy things with blood? Our very womanhood was transacted every month in blood. I gladly gave it to have this dagger, impervious to earthly manipulations. Or to Hades. I was its only master.

The weapon appeared, heavy in my palm, and I stabbed my dagger in the space between his ribs and yanked it out fast, encouraging the blood to drain. If I was going to use it, I wanted it to hurt.

Hades descended, ripping the head off of another demon. He looked entirely too pleased with himself. I flung the dagger end over end just a thread above his head. Hades' look of shock would have been frozen for eternity if I had been aiming for him. Instead, it impaled the last demon in his eyeball. And then I nearly collapsed, my feeble legs betraying me. I managed a few staggering paces to lean against a tree while I inhaled painfully into my bruised chest.

Hades stood over me. Although demon parts lay scattered around us, his black eyes burned with a look of unleashed vengeance. His blade was soaked with black blood, and he looked well and truly snapped. The deathless god gleamed with divine light, and his cheekbones were pinched, capable of cutting the diamonds that always seemed to spring up where he walked.

"Hades," I said softly, "I'm okay."

He stared at me uncomprehending, as if still in the middle of battle lust. I moved a step closer, smoothing my fingers over his heaving chest.

With a growl, he pinned me to his body, and we soared into the air. I wasn't supposed to be turned on by my enemy, but the heat spiraling out of control between my legs didn't listen to reason. I shuddered and Hades felt it. He gripped me tighter and the world burned where we touched.

I couldn't help it. Curling into his back, a small moan escaped from my lips, urgent and low. Even hating Hades drove me mad with want. My moan was only half-faked, but it was all that Hades needed.

55

HADES

I was lost in Persephone.

Thousands of years of want and desire pummeled me all at once. Everything I had suppressed rose, fighting for air at the surface of my consciousness. Or was I drowning in it?

I wanted to punish her for her misdeeds, but the thought of spanking her drove me mad. I slid my hand up her neck and threaded my fingers through her long hair. With a tug sharp, enough to make her whimper, I pulled back her head and kissed her throat. She was a drug, and I never recovered from the yearning. I wanted to torture her as she tortured me. I wanted her bare beneath me in every sense, my own exquisite prisoner. She had always been the only thing I couldn't master in my domain.

A thousand images paraded through my mind of the thousand ways I'd had Persephone, and still it wasn't enough. I wanted her again and again forever.

All control leaked away, and I pressed myself harder against her, gritting my teeth at the way she clutched my hips and rocked against them. Memories of her body, how her lips matched her nipples, primrose pink, attacked me as surely as my Kako demons had.

My breath was hoarse and my voice even worse. "Tell me the truth, wife."

"You already heard the truth. You saw my reaction in your dungeon. I have missed you. It is I who doesn't know where you stand."

Even if she betrayed me every chance she got, even if she was evil, it didn't change how much I wanted her. How much I always wanted her. Heat, warmth, and life discharged from her body. Her hair ran like water over my fist as I pulled her closer.

"You have always known how I felt about you. It has been my greatest weakness." Her chiton hitched over her thigh, and I pressed the dimple of fat she'd left behind. It was something of wonder, something imperfect. It made her more real. After fifteen hundred years, Persephone would be mine again.

I could never trust this goddess; she had betrayed me at every turn. She had a hold on me that none could match. Hecate was right to worry, but I was finding it harder to remember the risks when Persephone was slick with want beneath me.

Her fingers joined me under her robes, sharing her wetness between us. Slowly, with great effort, she let out a low groan, animalistic and impossible to ignore. A shimmering piece of my Helm, the last missing piece, emerged from inside of her. My body went still as she draped the silky, watery material over us, providing us with camouflage from predators, defeated gods, and demon monsters.

All of her was laid bare without my deathless magic concealing her secrets. I saw the remaining seeds she had and her infernal pink dagger. I saw how she had kept my Helm as her secret. And how she offered it now. I was a mess of emotions, mostly ones I did not think I could trust.

"You say I am your weakness," she said, her voice rough. "Let's make it a strength."

56

PERSEPHONE

Even if he denied me over and over, I still enjoyed his touch. He was the antithesis of me—but did that not make him my perfect mate? There is no life without death. There is no death without, first, life. His hands worked their way over my body, and I let him kiss and suck on my skin. Desire, sorrow for all we had lost together, and above all, a fierce need pounded across my skin. I trembled wherever he touched me, but it wasn't enough.

I groaned again, pulling the soft fabric up a little higher. Hades froze, his hands pressing deep enough to bruise my thighs. And then—he snapped. The deathless god was in control and hellfire blazed in his eyes. He pulled off my chiton and lifted my legs around his waist. His biceps flexed and moved with every step.

My head swam at the headiness of something I hadn't done in fifteen hundred years—let myself get lost in Hades' touch. He had been touching me for thousands of years and knew exactly what I craved and what I liked. I had to give him that. The way he looked at me with that ferociousness, in that way that made mortals tremble and my own knees weak, was intoxicating. His black, pitiless eyes drank me in, and even the ground trembled and the earth swayed beneath our feet.

So what if I needed Hades to let his guard down and begin to trust me? I could enjoy the way my throat let loose these animalistic noises and the heat that flamed through me, only to be frozen away by his continued touch. I missed that more than anything else, and I'm not too big to admit I might have tried recreating such experiences in the ice lands of the Arctic, although even now, I would never admit it out loud, let alone to him.

The Titans had their stone-like stature and deep, wide shoulders. Olympians, like Zeus and Apollo, had their beauty, this otherworldliness they used to set themselves above their predecessors. They manipulated their images. Hades did none of that. I enjoyed how he never tried to fit into their aesthetics. He strode his own line, displaying the heft of a Titan with their longer, dark hair against the clean-shaven, effortless beauty of an Olympian. Mostly, I loved how he didn't give a shit what either the Titans or Olympians thought.

I'd always admired that, although I never said it, of course. Looking at him now, I thought how he could have made a fine sea captain; it wasn't hard to imagine him rowing those mighty triremes. Or becoming a builder of great palaces, hoisting blocks of stone halfway to the heavens. If only he hadn't been born the eldest son of Kronos and yet, the youngest at the same time. That was the great problem with Zeus and Hades and why they would never trust each other. Hades was first, but Kronos gobbled up all of his children except for Zeus. Zeus, with much help, was able to disgorge his brothers and sister in the opposite order they were eaten. It was a rebirth of sorts, making Zeus the eldest and Hades the youngest.

But the only one who ever cared about that? Zeus.

Hades' voice was husky when he broke me out of my reverie. "What are you thinking about, goddess?"

"You," I answered truthfully.

My breath was slow and halting. I was overheating and I couldn't get enough. Where I touched him, steam burned. His cold lips were a shock on the heat of my skin, and I gasped when they locked around my nipple, an icy shiver sending me into spasms.

His magic rippled over me like dark waters, and I fought for oxygen. His powerful body moved against mine and I rose to meet it. I hadn't felt this close to him in centuries, and now all I wanted was to devour this feeling and pin it away forever. I called his name, urging him on, refusing to close my eyes for even a moment and miss the way he looked as he filled me.

We had been one, once upon a time. There had been brief moments, centuries that felt like seconds, where we were united. Not only in the darkness of our bedchamber, wreathed with the glory of the waxing and waning moons of precious gold, but in the halls, in the gardens, in the orchard, in the throne room. We refused Olympus, so complete in our happiness. We had our babes and our kingdom. We wanted for nothing.

That was when I felt it.

My seeds. He had my seeds hidden on his body. His shields must have slipped the barest of inches at his climax, and I saw them. Joy and rage tore through me in equal measure, mingling with the height of pleasure, and my body shuddered at the swirl of emotions. I arched against him, screaming his name, and I couldn't tell myself which was more dominant, the pleasure or the pain. Or why I enjoyed them both so much my eyes were black as the cosmos. Every male deity I had ever been near had ill-used me. Only in the vaguest of terms could I say the same about Hades. By far, he had treated me the best.

Even now, he had done exactly what I wanted, found my seeds and kept them on his person, yet I couldn't get over the feeling of betrayal. He knew I had been stuck on Earth, that I was vulnerable, and yet he refused to give them to me. I could've died. He could've died back there. That, above all, enraged me. He would have rather died and taken my seeds to his grave for eternity than let me have them.

I didn't betray a single thought as the whirl of pleasure wound down and reality punched a hole through the haze.

Hades had done exactly what I expected him to do, and I still hated him for it.

57

PERSEPHONE

This was what mortal women must feel, *I thought dreamily. My son cuddled under my arm, suckling like a sleepy kitten in the hay. His little mews and snuffles were sweeter than any siren song. I couldn't get enough of his musky, baby smell. I inhaled it, needing neither ambrosia nor nectar with him in my arms.*

Hades fussed when I forgot to eat, though, so I went through the motions of sipping from my goblet and moving squares of sweet ambrosia coated in crushed pistachios. He always made sure all of my favorite foods surrounded me, although the only thing I wanted to drink was the sight of my son.

Zagreus, I named him. Hunter.

I kissed the tip of his nose and breathed deeply. Hades himself could hardly bear to pull away from our bed to oversee the dead, and I didn't blame him. It was mutual between the two of them. Just like Melinoë, our son Zagreus adored Hades' attention. He scooped it up wherever he could get it, and they were both greedy little things.

I wasn't too big to admit I adored it, too. This was bliss.

After a few weeks, the time arrived to ascend back to Demeter. Due to his birth, Zagreus would have to stay in the Under-

world. Neither of my children could follow, and so I was without them for half of the year. It was a dagger to my breast, and I cried bitter tears for the first two months every time. The lands were awash with rains from my misery. The mortals rejoiced in their spring rains. I tried not to hate them for it.

Now, I sat in a field, idly weaving flowers. Sometimes, I found it satisfying to embrace the stereotype. The sun was cold that day, and I wondered why. Surely Helios wasn't mad at his daughters again, but it was Helios. His fury powered the sun. Bees droned and white poplars swayed in the breeze. It was spring distilled that day, until the gods came to destroy it.

Hermes, that great messenger between the realms, fluttered down beside me on his winged shoes. His broad-brimmed hat was balled in his hands and he wouldn't look me in the eye. I stood, wiping the dirt from my clothing, although soil was crusted under my nail beds, and I hadn't combed my hair in days. What was the point? Only Demeter and her nymphs saw me during these months.

"Hermes," I nodded. "Does my husband send tidings of our children?" Which was when I noticed him shift his weight, as if uncomfortable. "Hermes," I said sharper. The wit and sparkle was gone from his eyes. My fingers were cold before he even opened his mouth.

"Zagreus is dead, Queen Persephone."

A loud ringing drowned out everything. Hermes was still talking. Something about a rogue Titan escaping from Tartarus and stealing my son from his nursery. A rogue Titan who managed to chop up my baby boy and boil him for dinner, consuming all of him.

"Stop," I snapped. Hermes balked, as if I'd cut off his tongue. I wished I could. My body was a live wire and I felt everything and nothing. It was all too much.

"Hades has punished all of the Titans. Their noses are bound

to a whetstone until someone talks," Hermes babbled, but I barely heard, my mind racing.

"If Zagreus is dead, then bring me his soul, Psychopomp. That is your job, is it not?"

Hermes' fluttering shoes betrayed his thoughts. He wanted to flee my wrath. "It was also devoured. The Titans have such powers. I am truly sorry, Persephone."

On cold currents, he was aloft and gone, relieved beyond measure to leave the women to their sorrow. I wanted to scream and beat my chest and rip out my hair. Or rip that traitor from the sky. I barely noticed what I did. There was only one goal. I was going home immediately.

As I fled, Demeter grabbed my arm. Of course Hermes had gone to her first. Now, she thought to stop me. "You can't leave. It is the agreement," *Demeter said. Like that was the end of it.*

I ripped out of her pathetic grip. "Damn your agreement."

"He is dead. What good will it do for you to go? What will it change?" *she demanded.*

I stopped my frantic pace to the meadow where Hades always met me. Surely he would be there waiting. Instead, I turned to face this goddess, this monster. Her eyebrow was raised as if it were the most reasonable question.

"You truly have no idea what it means to be a mother, do you?" *I said softly.* "You don't understand the sacrifice or the love. Well, let me tell you this, goddess. It will take more than a handshake between gods to keep me from my son's body."

"There is no body," *she said.*

"Then what is left of my family," *I snarled, forcing Demeter to take a step back at my wrath. I moved closer; I made myself tower over her. The great goddess Demeter cowered beneath my rage.* "And you? Did you have anything to do with it?"

Demeter shouldered my wrath. "I did not."

"No little whispers or suggestions to Zeus? Nothing about a rival to his power?"

"You think so little of me, daughter?" Demeter whispered, as if pity would move my stone heart.

"Yes." I turned, done with her. "And I am not your daughter."

But Hades was not waiting for me, and I had to descend alone. That was the year the mortals shook and cowered, convinced their gods were betraying them. Perhaps I was, because I couldn't care less what they thought. I would rage and burn the realms to ash. If Earth suffered, what was it to my grief?

58

HADES

Of all the gods, Persephone was the most complex. She embodied too many things, that thin line between life and death, a constant tightrope for her to tread.

Still.

I adored the way she looked at me through half-lidded eyes and the little gasps I could make break forth. She tasted like salt and honey, and I wanted to bury my nose inside of her and twist my fingers in her warmth. I wanted to grip the little roll of her belly that she'd kept from childbearing and graze it with my teeth. Sometimes, that was the only visible evidence that convinced me she still cared. She could have snapped back to divine perfection as all the other goddesses did. Yet, she did not.

But when I moved to embrace her, to kiss her, my body already responding to hers again, she pushed herself up and began straightening her chiton. I couldn't tell, however, if it was because of what we'd done or something deeper.

If she had sensed her pomegranate seeds, I would not be able to let my guard down. In no world should Persephone have that power again. She was a scourge on the land, a beautiful monster. There were rare moments when our souls aligned and the blackness was complete between us. Such torment, such agony was she to me.

I had lost her when Zagreus died, although I hadn't known it until it was much too late to save her. She became a hard shell, and supplicants at their moment of death found no sympathy from their Dread Queen. They stood in line before our thrones of obsidian and begged for life in the Elysian Fields or to be allowed to retain their memories. Anything to dull the existence of an afterlife in the Asphodel Meadows. They wanted to suck on their memories, as if memories were a pacifier to soothe themselves for eternity.

Persephone would allow them to come close, to bow, to beg, to grovel. Without their knowledge, she would keep the poor souls in her thrall for her entertainment. She could make them split their spine to grovel before her if she wished. She could make them speak their foulest desires, impulses, and memories from life. But the worst? She could make them think they had a modicum of control.

She would let her attention wander during their supplications, tapping her toes or picking between pistachio and rosewater treats on a silver platter. Sometimes, she would nod or lean forward with her elbows on her knees, an entranced look on her face. Shades, unnerved, would try to drift away and pretend to get sucked into the currents of the crowd, hoping she had lost interest like some great predator who'd tired of the game, and she'd let them take jerking steps as if they were winning the fight against her will, like a dog with a bit of leash, or that she had perhaps forgotten about them, until—*slam*. She cruelly yanked them back to her and made them move to her macabre dance.

I used to think she'd grow out of toying with them. That

she enjoyed having power for the first time in her existence. I thought it was grief and that she needed an outlet, some sort of faucet to let loose the emotions that drowned us both. It wasn't as if the shades in the Asphodel Meadows were pure, I told myself. The stories that poured from their lips at her sly urgings were dreadful to hear. *Persephone will process this and come back to me.*

I no longer thought that.

Melinoë's shocking death during the Demon War merely amplified her hardness, like a statue placed outside in the winter. Persephone, as I once knew her, had been long gone.

Keeping her power from her? Was I really guilty of anything?

When I looked at her again, attempting once more to divine her secrets from the lines of her shoulders, she returned my gaze. Something seemed to have shifted.

"I have an idea how to find the Telechines," she said.

* * *

A HUT ROSE in the distance made from bone and shards, daubed with mud from Tartarus. It was something I had never known existed. Tartarus was nothing more than a pit for my enemies. I had always operated under the impression that the ancient gods or monsters who came before would consume me, given the chance. I had no need to come. But the way Persephone tilted her head and studied it, she had none of the same fears. She knew this place.

"You have wondered what came before the Titans," she said.

"Yes, every day."

She smiled and went inside. Mistrust rising in my throat,

I followed. The briar rose and bident tattoo would not let me do otherwise.

Inside, I found a simple hut, clear of decorations or dangers, but the woman sitting in her chair among her broken and ruined things made me want to smite the place and tear it bone by bone to the ground. She was an unnatural thing, sitting there placidly or perhaps too naturally in this dark habitat. A creature of the black ocean where no light can reach.

This was some being that I did not know about. This was some horror, unnamed and unknown. This was the darkness.

59

PERSEPHONE

The Fate Weaver. More ancient than the Moirai who drew the fates of mortals, the Fate Weaver knotted the fates of gods. None of the young Olympians knew of her, however, and only very few Titans.

She sat, her blind eyes indifferent to the darkness, gently rolling a shuttle back and forth across a loom and beating the threads with her spatha. A basket of spindles, most broken, sat at her feet. Unbleached yarn unraveled around the room, weaving its way through a cracked distaff and shattered loom weights, but as her shuttle sped magically left and right, warp over weft, colors sparkled to life. As for the rest of the room, it was spartan. An uneven dirt floor. Broken slats in her rocking chair. A small window from which no light entered.

Her hair was as brittle as the last time I'd seen her. Her face was still a patchwork quilt of wrinkles. The whites of her eyes stared directly into my soul as she lifted an eyebrow. Even blind, she'd caught me staring.

She cackled. "You can remove your divine hauteur. It doesn't impress me."

I barely bit back a smile in time. "Nothing much does."

That caused Hades' head to snap up as he probed at me. "So, you have been here before?"

The Fate Weaver cackled. "Oh, my Queen. Still playing games?"

"Only when asked," I said haughtily. "Otherwise I'm not invited."

"I wonder why." She sighed and pushed herself to her feet to sniff me. "Are you still attempting to have both, Dread Queen?" I could feel her examining me in minute detail. She sensed immediately what I had done all of those centuries ago, but she didn't reveal my secret.

I gave Hades a look to be quiet and cleared my throat. "Hades has lost his castle. New demons are being created, and the Telechines have reformed. I need to know what to do next to win this war."

She pulled three threads that had tangled and examined them under her lap with only her fingers. "The future is not possible to read so precisely. Everyone knows that. Even mortals."

"What do you see then, Fate Weaver?" Hades asked. He had proper respect for such an ancient being. I was working on it.

"Things I could make happen."

Hades and I exchanged another look. She was powerful indeed if she merely told gods possibilities and, perhaps, just perhaps, only the possibilities she wanted them to see. Is that what she'd done with me? I still remembered how she gave me two choices, two possibilities, and what I had chosen. So many must have taken her counsel. Those brave and foolish enough in equal measure. In my youth, I was both.

"Can you tell us who created the new demons? Who is

directing the Telechines?" Hades asked.

"That is not where my interest lies."

"It should be," Hades said, more forcefully. "They are destroying the Underworld. Everything, including your home, will be thrust into chaos greater than the Titan War. Greater than the Demon War. Without the gods to corral them, the Accords will be overthrown and every realm out to defend itself from that chaos."

"No. The realms will be fine. They will always survive. It is the gods who do not. Were you aware that you were a fated love that was never meant to be?"

I tried to read her mood. Having only been in her presence one other time, it wasn't easy. But I thought I saw eagerness in the curve of her shoulders, in the way her fingers moved more quickly through these threads than they ever had for me, alone. This was an event worthy of her possibilities.

I gambled.

"Even the ancient gods survive," I said. "And they will as long as that mortal..." I trailed off into silence that hurt.

The Fate Weaver smiled placidly as if she didn't feel the pain of my dangling sentence, already back to shuttling threads and beating them tighter. Even queens and citizens performed this daily task in ancient Greece. Although women, citizens or not, were little more than slaves to men in the ancient world, bound by their husbands at puberty and unable to even claim their children. Instead, they had to wait for their husbands to run around the hearth or to throw the babe in the woods for the wolves to devour. Even so goddesses, it turned out. Even so the Fate Weaver. We were all bound by men in some way.

"Take the headwaters of Lethe and the Pool of Memory where they mingle at the only point in this world. You'll need to bind that water with the ichor of an old god and a new to reveal the possibilities you desire."

"This is your prophecy?" Hades demanded. He was too abrupt, too *male*. "Bind headwaters."

The Fate Weaver kept her counsel, and her thoughts, to herself.

Of course, Hades had never been here before, and this interaction confirmed it. That was gratifying in some small way.

"We need one of our blood, and one of the Titan's to mix with headwaters for the potion?" he persisted, a minotaur, bulldozing his way forward.

"No," she cackled, weaving those iridescent threads seamlessly. "Older than a Titan."

Hades was careful. He picked his words with the care of picking his mate. But he had chosen wrongly in me, then, too. "What exactly is older than a Titan?"

The Fate Weaver only ran her fingers through her loom weights, admiring the jangle of their music. I nodded to Hades that we could leave. We'd get nothing more out of her. "Come on," I urged. "We've gotten all she can give."

"Or will give," Hades countered. "We don't know where to go, or how we're going to find anything. We need to question her more firmly. She can give more answers."

"She could. But she won't. I know where to go. Leave the Fate Weaver to her loom."

His voice was incredulous. "You?"

"Yes. And lucky for us, it's also where the beings more ancient than the Olympians and more ancient than the Titans reside."

"Convenient."

"Something like that." Yes. I knew where to go. I had also been there before.

60

PERSEPHONE

Despite the pleas of Demeter, I stayed in the Underworld that next summer, too. Zeus didn't interfere. He dared not. The land was barren and cold. Famine plagued the mortals, but I took some grim joy in the shades that populated our kingdom more frequently. Look how my power grew. Look how the dead began to outnumber the living.

Our son was gone and he wasn't coming back. He was not even a shade. He was nothing but a memory.

Hades went to my room every night. Every night, I let him in, but I could only stare blankly at the crackling hearth fire. I couldn't look at him. I saw Zagreus if I did.

One night, he finally spoke. "Persephone, where do you wander? Won't you let me beside you?"

A tear slipped down my cheek, but I thumbed it away before he could. His voice was pain incarnate. "We are supposed to be in our grief together. We were supposed to shoulder it together to ease the burden. We were lost, but we were supposed to be lost together, choking on the same thin air that lets grief blossom."

"Pretty words," I said dully. "But they are just that. Words."

"What actions do you want, Persephone?"

"I want you to kill him."

I felt Hades move sharply, but I still didn't look at him.

"Who?"

"Who else has the power to set a Titan free?"

"I can't kill Zeus."

"Why?" I asked bitterly. "He killed your son."

"We don't know that. I can't start a war between the gods based on assumptions."

Finally, I rose, and my legs shook from the effort. "Someone must."

"Persephone, be reasonable—"

I snapped, coiling and striking like a snake. "There is nothing reasonable in this! I want him dead. I will tear down everything to kill him."

Hades' face was horror, and he didn't try to hide it. I'm sure he felt as if he'd lost me, but I refused to stop. I had let my hatred for Zeus dampen as I enjoyed my children and look what happened. Zeus hadn't let it falter, and he had struck when I was least expecting it. He murdered my sweet baby.

I would never let my guard down again.

I turned my face away from my husband. I would venture where he was too afraid to go.

61

HADES

Persephone was miserable. If she thought she was hiding it, she forgot how well I knew her. I yearned to take her in my arms, to comfort her, but her stiff shoulders told me no. If that was the case, I might as well get some answers from her.

"When did you visit the Fate Weaver?" I asked. "During our marriage or after the Accords?"

"It doesn't matter."

"It does. Either you've been sneaking in here without my knowledge or this was before you left and you kept something else from me. I would be more shocked by the former, however."

"Neither of those sound like great options."

"No, Persephone. They do not."

"Fine. You're right. It was during our marriage. The day you got those scars on your back. Does that satisfy you?"

"Not even close," I said truthfully as I remembered the pain of Zeus' thunderbolt piercing my back that day. The day I thought Persephone and I might come out on the other side of our grief together.

"I allow you your secrets. Give me mine. Or shall I

attempt to shame you with all the power you hold and the little available to me? I came here asking for help. Not once have you cared."

"You were stuck on Earth. How and why is not my concern. Keeping you away from the Underworld was. Now, I am concerned with keeping an eye on you and discovering how you are so capable of killing these new demons when you claim to not have your seeds." Here, of course, I was embellishing.

"So I'm a suspect?" she demanded.

"Always."

"This is a great partnership."

"We stopped being partners long ago."

Persephone laughed, a perverse little laugh that sounded more like a tiny bird, hurt and flailing. "And here I thought I was the only one good at holding a grudge."

I turned away from her, beginning the long journey to the lands beneath the end of the world. Of course, Persephone would ultimately have to lead us. She picked her way to the front, quiet again as we trekked to the headwaters. Mercurial as ever.

The landscape swiftly melted from dreary to something light and bright. Improbably, the air smelled of brine and fish. There were temples painted with white lead and red ochre in the near distance. Broken abalone and cockle shells cemented together to form well-worn, meandering pathways through the ancient city. Leaping bulls and bottlenose dolphins were frescoed in vivid palettes of blue and green on even the lowliest houses. All of them were constructed of stone walls and thatched roofs.

Cypress trees lined the streets, and there were even raised edges for walkways. Magenta rock purslane flowers and viper's bugloss sprouted between the stones while vines of plump grapes and flowering climbers poured from window sills and draped between houses as if they were their own wild masters. The wet air smelled like plumeria and salt.

I knew what this mirrored. This looked like Crete in the days of the Minoans. Quietly, I asked, "Was this here when you came?"

Persephone nodded once. "It was busier then."

"Busy... with what?" In the depths of myself, I already knew the answer before she spoke.

"Ancient beings," she whispered as all my darkest nightmares came to light. "Creatures I couldn't name. Creatures of soot and fog. You know how mortals don't know what is in the depths of their oceans and everything they find fascinates them? This place beneath the Underworld, in the deepest parts of Tartarus... that's our black ocean bottom."

"These are homes," I pointed, aghast at their luxury and beauty. "Seaside villas. In Tartarus."

"I'm honestly not sure this would still be considered Tartarus," Persephone replied, bending to smell a bush of yellow broom flowers. Cypress trees lined the seashell sidewalk, and there was a green mountain looming in the distance. Volcanic, most likely.

I didn't have to ask what it was. I already knew. This was where the rulers who came before the Titans rested. Only, I didn't see anyone home. Persephone's face mirrored my concern.

"Where do you think they are?" she asked. "Last time, I basically disguised myself and didn't run into much trouble. I have no idea if they're violent or peaceful or even awake after all these centuries."

"Keep quiet then, and let's find the headwaters. You're the resident expert. Where should we go?"

She nodded her assent. "Mountains. Rivers always start on mountains."

Jetting my hand, I grabbed her arm and pulled her close, relishing the quick intake of her breath. "Where did you go on your first visit?"

She only wiggled a little, knowing it was futile to try to break my grip. "Not the headwaters, I swear."

"Then where?" I pulled her closer, her chest touching mine as she took a deep inhale.

"I went to both the pool and the river," she said. "But it doesn't matter. In the end, I still remember that day in the meadow."

I uncurled my fingers one by one from her bicep, choosing to let her think that I believed she went to forget about Zeus, or that she was unable to actually do it. As we walked, my Helm only slightly distorting us in order to keep the seeds a secret, I took in the eerie silence of what was once a sumptuous city. I could feel it in the way the briny breeze rustled cypress trees and in the echoes of our footsteps. Sparks of unease ran down my spine as I felt something watching us.

If possible, Persephone was even more distant since our night together. I had to consider the possibility that she knew about her seeds, but I wouldn't act on it. It was better to let Persephone play herself out. She always did, eventually.

We quickly crossed the road, small traces of life visible in the dirty footsteps left by the roadside and the smoldering smell of half-burnt offerings. I wondered how the inhabitants received them. There were small signs of life, including an odd creature that scampered into the underbrush when we approached.

As soon as we left the city proper, with its colorful

temples and precise streets, the dirt road became more of a suggestion. Trees crowded thicker, and we had to jump over fallen and decaying logs, their loamy scent thick on the windless air. The mystifying smell of the sea abruptly disappeared as well.

There was a small trickling noise that we followed as the hill inclined. The lack of living things—or dead—was more unsettling than I wanted to admit.

The light grew weaker as the trees became more dense. It bathed the edge of the mountain in silvery shadows that played with my mind and leached away my confidence that we'd find anything useful. I'd idly wondered about a place like this, never giving into the desire to investigate. I had duties. A kingdom. Responsibility. That kingdom relied on me to save them from threats, like the demon goblins that were trampling my castle as we wandered these hills.

This better not be for naught.

"There," Persephone whispered. An opal column rose in the distance, its first three iridescent steps submerged by dark waters. When I looked at it, I felt feelings of familiarity and fear.

Fear, I could handle. Oddly enough, it was the innate familiarity that terrified me. Why was this place so familiar? It must have been Lethe. Familiar, yet just out of reach.

"Keep down," I told her. "And stay behind me."

The temple was an open-air peak sanctuary. From the pool at the steps, the water began its descent down the side of the mountain. It seemed as if it bubbled up from the ground, a hidden spring of headwaters. The temple was small and unimposing. Zeus would have scoffed at its size and refused to listen to the pleas coming from within. I could just see beyond the opal columns into the middle of the sanctuary where an altar stood. There was something white on it, but blurred. As if... I didn't know, exactly. We crouched and inched closer.

Crunch.

Something fragile shattered underneath our feet. Persephone paused, her foot mid-air at the noise. Her eyes were wide, and I could feel the fear pulsing in waves off of her. This was something too new and too frightening to be nonchalant, so we took safety in each other. At least we knew who the other was.

Bright blue eyes stared up at us. White lead pottery and votive statues of humans and animals littered the ground, creating a trail that lead to the submerged temple steps. Their faces were uncannily alive looking, the artist clearly a master of their craft. Silently, I picked Persephone up and sailed the last few feet to the temple steps to avoid more unnecessary destruction. As I held her, I could feel her heartbeats get stronger and faster. Fear, surely.

Small, delicately shaped flowers littered the temple's floor. I couldn't tell what they were; every one of them had no color, but it was the corpse sprawled in the center that commanded my attention.

It was clearly an ancient goddess, her ruined body draped backward over the altar. Her diaphanous robes and even her very skin had been leached, leaving her as ethereal and pearly as the opal altar that served as her gravestone. Her hair flowed down the side as if floating in water. In the entire sanctuary, there was not one speck of color.

Persephone clapped a hand over her mouth, and that slight sound reverberated through the temple. "That's the Poppy Goddess," she said in wonder, circling the corpse. "She's dead. How..."

I bent my head to the drained body and inhaled deeply. There was no decay. Instead, she almost smelled sweet. Like flowers. I knew what it seemed like now. She was as matte and lifeless as a moth that was sucked dry by a spider in its web. I tried swallowing my distaste. This was how my daughter had looked. How Hermes had looked. How every god killed during the Demon War had looked.

"Who was the Poppy Goddess?"

Persephone, looking more shaken than I'd ever seen, licked her lips. "She distilled poppy flowers into opium for her mysteries. That's all I know. No one was allowed access to her mysteries except for mortal women, and all those who knew them died out hundreds of thousands of years ago. Let's hurry and get out of here. It's giving me the creeps."

"You're talking too fast," I said, suspicion blanketing me like a wool robe. "Shouldn't we try to see if there's anything left of her?" I jerked my head at the Poppy Goddess. "She's clearly one of the most ancient gods, from a time before the Titans.

"There's nothing left of her," Persephone brandished her arm. "She's completely gone, sucked dry, kaput. Okay?"

Persephone's breast was heaving. This place scared the Dread Queen, but I couldn't decide if it was because she was weakened in her mortal state without her seeds—or if it was something more. Despite the tranquil setting and open atmosphere, it had the claustrophobic feeling of a mausoleum. Death had settled into this place.

"We'll be fast," I said, soothingly. "And we'll end this thing. We're close now."

Seeing Persephone fearful stirred that old part of my protective spirit. The part that was my predictable, fatal flaw. As I began to collect the cold, crystal waters, I said, "You're not technically an original Olympian, so we'll have to use my ichor for that part of the ritual. Then we'll get back down the mountain, maybe find one of those ancient beings."

Persephone pulled her rosy bottom lip under her teeth and nibbled. Hard. She was coming to a decision of some kind. Suddenly she stuck out her arm and rolled back her chiton to reveal creamy white skin and a pounding purple-blue vein.

"I am more ancient than the Olympians and I am more ancient than the Titans. You may use mine."

62

PERSEPHONE

Hades' eyes iced over, and his stance went from casual to warrior. The air crackled between us.

"What exactly are you saying, Persephone?"

I swallowed, hard. "I am not Zeus' daughter, and I am not Demeter's, either."

"I don't understand."

"The day we met. That was why I was there on Olympus. After Zeus raped me, Demeter told me the truth, thinking it would make me feel better to at least know neither one of them were my true parents. It didn't, of course, but because she'd kept that secret from me, I wrangled a promise to visit Olympus and she'd agreed. I was so curious, and I wanted to see if Zeus had the guts to look me in the eye."

Hades looked so taken aback, I thought he might stop me, so I jumped ahead, spilling a few more of my closely guarded secrets. Not all of course. I kept a few to myself, like how I planned on meeting Hades that day on Olympus and beguiling him into marriage.

"That was what the Fate Weaver wanted me to see when I came to Tartarus the first time. I went to the Pool of

Memory and drank from its depths, so I never came up here to the headwaters. Instead, I saw my past before I came to live with Demeter."

"Which was what?" he asked flatly.

"Mine," I replied. "You don't need the details to know that I was betrayed by everyone who was supposed to love me. By everyone who was supposed to protect me."

"I never betrayed you, and I loved and protected you."

My heart furrowed at the past tense. "You slept with Minthe after Zagreus," I said softly. "Argument number 1002."

"Argument 1002b," he said back, his voice equally soft. "I never betrayed you."

I turned away. I knew that he had betrayed me; he had my seeds. But he must not know that I suspected. It was vital to everything I had put in place to be here at this exact moment. All of the years of planning would soon coalesce, and everything I strove for would soon be within my grasp. If only I kept my facade. Yet, this moment was also when things got interesting, when the unknown, those things I didn't control, made their way onto the scene.

"Stalemate," I replied, facing him again. "Feel free to derive pleasure from spilling my blood. Just remember, I get to cut your wrists next." I handed him my dagger, pink handle first.

His knuckles whitened around it, and I had to stifle a gasp when the cool metal slid past my palm. I could practically feel my blood pressure rising as we were caught in each other's orbits one last time.

"Are you ready, Persephone?"

I nodded once, leaving my hand extended. His eyes never left mine as the blade kissed the center of my palm. Together we mixed the blood and the headwaters, the power of the tripartite glowing gold and blue in Hades' hands.

That's when we heard the noise.

I jerked away as Hades called his bident from the ether. "What was that?" I whispered.

"Stay down," he commanded, alert and ready. It sounded large and clumsy, whatever it was. Rabbits and chipmunks suddenly bounded through the sanctuary in great, terrified leaps. Squawking birds winged overhead, and all of the pine trees creaked and groaned as the earth trembled beneath our feet.

Something was coming.

Hades twirled his bident, knees bent at the ready. "I'm serious, Persephone. I can't worry about saving you. Stay back."

He didn't have to tell me twice.

A creature, no, a hideous monster, emerged from the depths of the forest. Even though I expected it, my hand flew to my mouth at the sight as it lifted its head and roared. It had small, beady eyes set close together because it didn't rely on its eyes to hunt. There was no discernible nose, either. Instead, a huge, gaping hole took up most of its mud-gray face. Fear coursed through my body. It was instinctual, like a mouse staring up at a lion.

But here's the thing about mice when confronted by a lion: they're not worth his time.

I shrank back, crouching beneath the Poppy Goddess sprawled across her altar. Her strands of gray hair brushed the tops of my shoulders, and I could feel it straight through my thin chiton. I shivered and huddled my knees together. If Hades wanted to play hero, he was welcome to it.

The creature paid me no attention. He only had eyes for Hades, and I couldn't blame him. Hades rose in the air in full death armor, his bident glowing red. Smoke and shadows poured off of him. I could feel his power radiating from here.

The monster could feel it too. He pawed at the ground, thick strands of saliva dripping from the hole where his face should've been. Then, he reared back and roared, before attacking. He moved on a body that looked like it was made of muddy rocks stacked haphazardly upon each other by a drunken god, one who only vaguely understood humanoid shapes.

Hades dove to meet him. Their clash shook the temple, loosening pebbles and cracking the marble floor. Both were thrown backwards, and both leapt to their feet ready. The creature moved faster than I would have guessed from his massive girth. Then again, the Hulk had no problems.

Hades rose again into the air, his enormous wings lifting him out of reach. He stabbed down, a direct hit, and the creature wailed, but he didn't pause in his advance.

In his weakened state, I wasn't sure how long Hades would be able to hold out. Already, I saw long streaks of black resurfacing on his cheek from the Telechine poison. So I did something that was incredibly stupid.

I improvised.

Well, technically, I threw myself at the monster in what I hoped looked like an extreme act of heroism, but it wasn't in my script.

63

PERSEPHONE

The Underworld, 100 BCE.

His name was a drumbeat from which I couldn't escape. Zeus. Zeus. Zeus.

I would kill him.

Long ago, Demeter told me the truth. I was not his daughter. When the goddess found me shivering and broken in her fields after his attack, she finally revealed her truth, thinking at least that would bring me some comfort. That at least my own father had not raped me. At least it was just the king of the gods.

I was about to learn it was not the whole truth. Not even then did she tell me everything. It took much more wrangling and begging and crying before I got the truth from her. I was nobody's daughter.

I craved to know what created me.

I had heard rumors. Noises about ancient beings. I spent so many centuries researching these beings. Tartarus was beneath the Underworld, but what was beneath it? I craved to know more than I craved ambrosia or nectar.

After Melinoë was born, I had abandoned my research for wedded bliss; I was an idiot, and it cost me everything.

Frantically, I ripped through the notes of lost knowledge I had accumulated and stored like a chipmunk bracing for winter. I had been scared of losing it all over again—had almost let myself. Now, armed with tantalizing hints, I followed the River Lethe, the river of forgetting, as it wended and wound past Kronos' kingdom—more folly!—and even deeper. I followed it until I found a small hut and I entered it.

The woman inside had a way of seeing through you. She was blind. That much was obvious. It clearly heightened her other senses, for she took my measure immediately. Before I uttered a word, she cackled.

"*You are not Persephone.*"

I clutched the edge of her scarred loom, the only thing of meaning or with any sort of presence in her hut. Everything about her made me uneasy. It was as if invisible things were skittering over the nape of my neck whenever I looked at her. "*And who are you? You are not a Titan. How is it that I don't recognize you?*"

She raised an eyebrow. It was pure white, as wooly as a lamb in spring. "*Who do you think you are?*"

"*Even if I am not Persephone, I am not Kore,*" *I said defiantly.*

"*No,*" *she agreed.* "*You are not that, either.*"

She began to work the peddle of her loom. Zoom, thwack. Zoom, thwack. "*Would you like to hear a prophecy?*"

I snapped, "*And who are you to give prophecies to the gods? You are not much if you are here,*" *I spread my arms.* "*This is a place to grovel and to beg. This is not a place for ancient powers. I think you are trying to trick me.*"

Zoom, thwack. Zoom, thwack.

The silence outside of the loom began to hurt. The old woman spared no silly words. Everything she did was economical. I swallowed to relieve some of the dryness of my mouth.

"*Is that what you believe?*" *she asked.*

I deflated, all ire melting away. "*No. I would not be here otherwise.*"

Zoom, thwack. Zoom, thwack.

She said nothing, and I found myself clearing my throat and speaking again. "*I heard you are the Fate Weaver. Is it true? Do you weave the fates of gods?*"

A pale yarn of unbleached cream became a shimmering gold. She held it up to the light of her single candle, a bronze horn with a nutty smelling oil and a thick wick formed of twisted hairs. Sesame seeds. Goat hair.

"*I tell you this. A choice. You will bring down a king of gods or you will drink from the Pool of Memory. You will not do both.*"

Her words staggered me. I had to catch hold of the loom, upsetting the yarn as I did so. I have always wondered if that affected my prophecy. But in that moment of silence, I considered her words, for they were too tailored. Yet, there were two kings. Zeus may have been king of all of the gods, but Hades was a king, too. A king of the dead, a king of deposed gods. This prophecy could be trying to trick me into destroying my husband instead of Zeus. I was constantly on alert for trickery in those days.

Additionally, I was afraid to let go of something so familiar and comforting: my hatred. Zeus would not get off so easily. "*If I drink, what will become of my memories?*" *I asked.*

"*You will keep them and decide which are most valuable.*" *Zoom, thwack. Zoom, thwack. The sound of her loom at work was too mesmerizing. I could lose myself in just those sounds, let alone the Pool of Memory.*

The king I would bring down could be Hades, but I was betting it was Zeus.

I looked at the overturned box of golden yarn, with shots of silver now thread through. What was at the Pool of Memory that I could not have both? It must be immense, whatever secrets my old memories held. Did it know who my parents were? No, it must be more than that. What was hiding in my subconscious for millennia? I thought about going instead to the River Lethe and forgetting all of it; my revenge, my hatred, even that dark day with Zeus.

But I couldn't. As I said, I desired knowledge too much, I would consume the sun if the Fate Weaver ordered it.

So, I trekked to the Pool of Memory.

I drank from its waters.

I understood everything and nothing.

I would never bring down a king of the gods. Not by my hands, anyway.

When I finally found myself again after hours running through memories, I hurried back to Hades' castle in a daze. My entire existence was a lie. I needed time alone to process, but Hecate stood in my way, baring her teeth at me.

"What did you say to Hades?" the witch goddess snarled.

My stomach curled like maggots, wiggling in the sudden light of discovery. I felt ill.

"Nothing," I promised. Pushing past Hecate, my feet pounded down the corridor and to the stable. Alastor was gone.

His demonspawn horses did not like me, but Aethon was the easiest to sway. He was a burning, tawny-red color with flames that licked up his hooves. Cooing softly, letting my magic mask some of my fear, I approached him, wishing for a carrot or a mortal arm. Whatever it was they snacked upon.

Still, he shied away. Yet, I was too worried to be cautious. I jumped on the horse's back and fled to Olympus as he jerked and tried to buck me off. The chilled air burned hotter as we ascended, my arms tiring from bracing myself against the reins. Then, Aethon's eyes rolled to their whites.

The earth shook as bolt after hurled bolt hit the ground. They weren't even in Olympus. No, my husband had told Zeus to meet him in the same field where Zeus had taken me—the same field where Hades had taken me home. It was supposed to be poetic justice, I believe.

I wheeled Aethon around as the horse shied from the next lightning strike. "Go forward, beast, or I will feed you to Tartarus," I commanded, digging my heels into his gut.

Both gods saw me at the same moment. Their great clash, centuries in the making, paused as black clouds swirled around us and the air sparked with maddening currents. I dismounted and went to stand next to Hades. Aethon knew better than to run away with his fear. He stood trembling, his eyes continuing to roll to their whites.

Zeus was lambent, but I could smell his sweat, and it smelled of fear. "Two against one? So this is mutiny? This is a coup?"

I thought about the prophecy. My eyes squeezed shut, knowing whatever we did would not work. I had taken the other path. I could not have both. At least, for now. Yet, in time, I knew I would always find a way to thwart those in power.

"No, Zeus. This is not mutiny. My husband and I are going home."

Hades found my hand. We looked at each other, Zeus hardly mattering in that moment. Hades would have done the impossible for me. He would still try if I told him to. Hades truly loved me. For this moment, it was enough.

We turned our backs on the king of the gods. For this moment, I considered letting my grudges go. I considered what it might mean to love my husband unconditionally and forget Zeus existed. To indulge in love.

When reality hit, it hit hard.

The jolt of electricity passed from fingertip to fingertip where Hades held my hand. His back smoked as he convulsed from a direct hit, and I was thrown clear. My husband's robes disintegrated, and I already saw crackles of lightning spider-webbing his skin where the bolt exited his body. Hades groaned and caught himself on the burning grass. I barely pulled myself to my elbows, my skin smoking where I'd felt the lightning pass through our fingers.

Zeus' eyes flickered with hatred and desire when we met, but I called up darkness, the darkness I knew was inside of me thanks to the Fate Weaver, and I let it bubble across the ground, leaving a trail of decaying rot in its wake. I called up the ancient spirits I knew would answer me, and I threw them at the king of the gods with only death in my heart. I could never turn my back on him. Never.

Of course, he wiggled away. I wasn't quick enough, too new in my regained memories to be effective. Zeus ascended to Olympus, unharmed. Even his look of fear at what I could do to him was not enough to diminish my own anger. Zeus and I could not rest until one killed the other.

64

HADES

The monstrous creature, its skin brown and cracked like dried mud, had a gaping mouth with no teeth. For some reason, this unsettled me more than fangs would have. Fangs, I understood. They were meant to pierce, to draw blood. A maw? That meant to suck. What it wanted to suck... that was the question.

Saliva dripped down its chin at my sight, as if it were staring at an exquisite meal. Clearly, I contained what it desired.

"The thirsty ones," Persephone shouted. "Remember... the way they looked."

"What does it do? What are its powers and weaknesses?" I twirled my bident over my head and brought it down to keep some space between us.

"They... suck ichor. They steal immortality."

It all came together. The Poppy Goddess had been sucked dry. Just like Melinoë. This monster was what the mortals used to defeat us, to finally kill the gods. For perhaps the first time in our long lives, we were truly in mortal danger.

For some stupid reason, that's when Persephone decided to attack the monster. She leapt from the temple, her pink dagger in her hand, and lunged for its neck.

"What are you doing?" I angrily lunged for her flying legs, intending to yank her from the sky. "Trying to get yourself killed?"

The creature screeched and reared on its back paws like a bear as the dagger dug into its rocky skin. Persephone executed a perfect backflip onto the ground and stabbed its toe. The monster roared.

"Are you trying to make us both mad?" I asked. "Because that's all you're doing."

In response, Persephone screamed as the monster, moving faster than should've been possible, gripped her leg, lifting her in the air, feet first, its maw around her thigh. I could hear the sucking from thirty feet away as it tasted her lifeless ichor, bleached white from her years on Earth.

I had seconds, maybe less to act. Looking past the poison still pulsing in my body, I found that kernel at the heart of every god. Then, I pushed all of my immortality to the surface. Smoke and fog swirled around me in a kaleidoscope of black and blue. My bident glowed in my hands. "I am Hades," I declared, my voice booming off of the marble of the temple. "The oldest and youngest born of Kronos. I am the deathless god. I am the god all mortals fear."

At the sight of me, the monster's head swiveled back, and Persephone dropped to the ground like a forgotten crumb falling from the plate of a feast. She groaned through the pain, but at least, she was still alive. For now.

"Still hungry, are we?" I taunted.

The monster screamed in my face. Somehow, the hole in its face seemed bigger than before.

I lashed out with my bident, checking its reflexes and

drawing it away from Persephone. It pawed at my head, and I spun clear of its reach. Despite its size, it had preternatural speed and wicked strength. No wonder Hermes never stood a chance. He always relied on his winged shoes.

Before I could thrust a second time, it caught the spiked ends and attempted to yank it away, roaring spittle flecked with Persephone's blood in my face. It took nearly all of my strength in my still-weakened state to pry my infernal weapon from its grasp before it did real damage.

Feinting one way, I whirled and dropped my shoulder, body slamming the creature. It sailed through the air and smashed into a column of ancient ruins. The drums of the column cracked at their mortar points and began to groan.

At least it had no strategy or flair; it just attacked, and brute force could be manipulated. Slowly, I began working it toward the staircase of the headwaters. I only had the ghost of a plan forming. Something about throwing it over the edge of the steps and waiting for the oblivion of Lethe to take hold. I had no idea if it would work, but perhaps I could settle on drowning it, instead.

"Hades!" Persephone shrieked.

I glanced over, my focus slipping for a second, and the Dipsioi immediately attached itself to my neck and began to feed. It felt as if all of my life force was being drained, sucked out of a hole like a straw. I clawed at it, stabbing over and over with my bident and kicking at its mass. My wings beat uselessly, succeeding in only lifting both of us off of the ground for a moment, but I couldn't unseat the monster. It barely noticed or cared, so intent on my ichor.

Never had I felt such physical pain, such anguish. It seemed as if I were a dried husk being battered and kicked along the ground. Was this how my sweet, dear Melinoë felt as her life was sucked away from her? For so long, I at least comforted myself that it was quick, but like most things in my life, that was clearly an illusion.

Out of the corner of my pain, I saw Persephone crawling to my aid, her body destroyed, her skin pale. She looked like death. Anxiety pulled on her face. "No, I can't lose you again," she sobbed. "Hades, you must fight him, or we are both lost!"

In her hands, she held a piece of soldered iron. It formed a circle with spikes arrayed along the inside. I don't know where she found it, but it almost made me laugh. Did she really mean to control a beast capable of killing a god with a piece of barbed wire?

If this was to be the end for both of us, at least we would go down fighting. I felt for my Helm, already slick with drool and golden ichor, and pulled its invisibility to me like an old, worn blanket. Instantly, Persephone's seeds shimmered into view, pulsing with the power she craved so badly. "Here," I croaked, holding them out to my Dread Queen. "Take them and heal yourself."

She snatched them in one go, her nails raking my skin.

Then, my eyes went dark.

When I came to, the world swirled around me in thick smudges of color, the fog of my pain practically drowning me. The only thing guiding me back was the brilliant light beckoning me forward. It radiated before my eyes. I had never seen anything so beautiful.

I blinked, and the light came into focus. Persephone, fully restored. The power of her seeds suffusing every part of her essence. Next to her, the beast snarled but not at her, at me. She tugged on a leash and spoke a single word in an ancient tongue. It laid down on its haunches, its head resting on its paws like a giant Rottweiler.

I tried to focus, to search for the right questions. Like,

how the fuck did you do that? But my tongue felt thick and heavy, like gauze. Never before had I realized how much power it took to speak.

Persephone bent down and I felt something snap around my wrists. I met her eyes for just a moment. Something terrible lived inside them. Together, we both glanced down. A pair of nightless cuffs encircled my wrists, binding me at her mercy.

Unfortunately, even through my haze, I realized Persephone had none.

65

HADES

Even if I didn't realize it then, I had already lost her. My touch was unwanted, my attention ignored. Nothing mattered except her revenge. It consumed her like a fire. From the way she had taken my hand and the way she had cared for my wounds, the scars now crisscrossing my back, I thought we would survive this pain. Together.

Yet nothing could tempt her back into her old self. Eventually, I had to leave her alone. It seemed the closest to what she desired. At least, it was easier.

I spent my mornings on my throne, my afternoons with Cerberus, and my nights with Minthe. At first, it was just to see if there was any life left in my queen. The hated nymph was the one sure thing to get a rise out of her, and an emotion, even negative, would give me hope. Any attention was better than none.

Instead, my attempts were ignored. I knew every word of every language ever spoken and yet, I could find none to comfort my wife. They turned to ashes in my mouth, bitter and dry.

I never slept with Minthe, however, much to her chagrin. She flung her own insults before slipping into wheedling promises of making me feel better, of making me feel good. If only I would let her. Recently, I had begun to meet her in the throne room, just to see what would happen.

Minthe draped herself across my lap, entangling her fingers in my hair and jerking me closer to whisper in my ear. She moved against me, grinding as she whispered, dragging her tongue along my jaw. And I let her. It was only a matter of time before I let the nymph have everything that she wanted. Perhaps now was as good a time as any. Maybe I would actually feel something for once since the death of my son.

Something heavy crashed to my right. We both stopped to stare. Guilt coursed hotly through my veins as I saw my wife. Persephone only watched me for a moment before turning her back and walking away.

Dropping Minthe to the dais, I went to the pomegranate-soaked air where my wife had just stood. Minthe joined me, her eyebrow cocked up as if she'd won something. And then, a shriek, long and loud. Minthe turned and ran, fleeing the throne room in panic.

There on the marble floor was a mint plant, the pottery smashed into a dozen pieces.

66

PERSEPHONE

The nightless cuffs clicked around his wrists. *Finally.*

Our eyes met as I rose, his hands bound as mine had been. I attempted not to feel much guilt. Rogue emotions were the only thing I hadn't accounted for.

A thousand years of planning had led to this. Hiding my seeds in the Underworld for Hades to find. Biding my time on Earth to become weak and vulnerable so that the Dipsioi wouldn't view me as a threat, so that I wouldn't smell divine. If I had, it never would've let me get close enough to spring my trap without sucking me dry as it did to Hades. *But here's the thing about mice and lions: they're not worth his time.*

My clumsy arrival in the Underworld and my even clumsier attempts to find my seeds, all to ensure Hades kept them on his person. I would need them for what came next. I even planted the idea that he should explore Tartarus in search of the source of the new demons, and I anticipated Hecate binding us together so he'd have no choice but to bring me. Her hatred was so predictable.

Once here, I had led him to the Dipsioi's land and made an irresistible mix of power. My seeds, the blood of two gods, the power of the headwaters. For a beast that feasts on power, there was no resisting that. I'd hidden the cuffs here long ago, and I'd been lugging this collar with me since Earth, hidden with more potions and spells than Hades could ever dream of concocting. It had taken so very long to find it and wring the answer from that mortal woman's lips.

I even allowed myself to improvise a little by attacking the Dipsioi. I knew it would mortally wound me in my weakened state and that Hades would be forced to grant me a seed to heal myself. It was a gamble, which I hated to take, but it was worth it. Luckily, I knew my husband better than he knew me. He wouldn't save himself, but he couldn't bear to see me in true pain.

There was so much more to the story, so much planning and effort, ichor, sweat, and tears. I had to become practically *mortal* for this to work, and I'd had to wait centuries for that to happen. It meant leaving magical items across three realms, all while deciding which way my old family would zig or zag.

And now? I had the last piece of the puzzle. The thing I was missing all these years: the creature that could kill an immortal god, and it was under my thrall thanks to the Collar of Josephine.

As the humans say, it was my "trick shot," but it was only halfway to the net. Now, I had to take this creature, this monster, to Olympus in order to kill the greatest monster of all. Zeus.

I had placed everything perfectly for this moment when I would be reunited with my seeds and my full power given back in all its glory after so long apart.

If I'd had one true moment of weakness during this plan, it was under the tree of False Dreams after seeing so many memories of our children. When Hades rescued me, I thought perhaps I had punished myself long enough, but I knew I hadn't. Not with all this destruction I had wrought to be here at this moment. Hades was better off without me, anyway. I was only half a wife, half a woman, as long as Zeus was alive.

"Persephone..."

"Shh, it will be okay," I promised. The sweet lies were still on my lips as I swallowed my remaining seeds. Nothing, not even lies, were sweeter or more tart than my seeds, however.

HADES

End of the Demon War, 500 CE.
 Olympus.

A LARGE MAN *in a bear skin pelt lounged across Zeus' winged throne of white marble streaked with gold. His legs dangled over the side, and he picked his teeth with a deadened thunderbolt. The Olympians were in chains. What was left of us, at least.*

Zeus still held onto a hint of his old arrogance, although his knees were in the dirt and his robes crusted with stains. He had taken the brunt of the mortals' rage, but one could hardly blame them.

The great god coughed ichor as he tried laughing. A drip of gold slid down his chin. "What now? What happens now that the gods are defeated? You have some grand plan I assume."

The large man was silent.

"What?" Zeus taunted. "No one dares take credit for such a feat? You brought down the gods themselves! Surely someone wants the glory."

Of Thorns and Bones 291

The silence turned uncomfortable. No human came forward until a small voice broke in.

"You will answer to me."

A slight woman, her hair cut short around her ears and an antler crown on her brow, stood forth. She had been seated next to the man in the bearskin pelt, easily overlooked.

Even in his defeated state, Zeus couldn't help his sardonic laugh. "This is your great leader?"

The woman didn't even blink. It was as if she predicted Zeus would behave this way. "Surely you didn't expect someone so obvious, like an Alexander or a Pericles?" she asked simply.

The gods in chains moved uneasily. Only I gave a low laugh. She turned her head and watched me with that unsettling gaze.

"Tell us your terms, so Zeus may get on with his eternity," I said, wearily. This small mortal woman held the key to everything. How she came to find it and hold onto it was something else altogether. How had she killed so many immortal gods?

Still, the woman stared at me. My wrists ached where we were bound together. Persephone hadn't lifted her head once, but I could feel her body swaying as the fatigue and aches of a war settled on our shoulders.

"What is your name?" I asked suddenly.

The woman came closer. For someone no taller than a stalk of wheat, she took up a lot of space. She crouched to look in my eyes. "You are the deathless god," she said.

"What gave it away?"

She tilted her head, examining the mists that swirled around my body. "They called me Josephine. My parents, that is. Do you know them in your realm, deathless god?"

"I know what you're asking, and I'm afraid that would be impossible."

She sighed and pressed her palms to the ground to lift herself. "As I thought." She straightened and boomed out, "The

Olympians have no choice. You will live out your immortality here on Olympus."

Zeus began to laugh, but her general in the bearskin smacked the great god across the mouth with a thunderbolt. Red marks zigzagged across his face, and Zeus fell silent.

Josephine's eyes had never left mine, however. "Except for you, deathless god. You will remain in the Underworld. Demons under your domain may choose to stay on Olympus, the Underworld, or Earth. There will be no movement between the realms. What is chosen here today is for eternity."

"And me?" Persephone's clear voice rang out among the columns and temples of Olympus.

"You may also choose, Dread Queen."

"I may pick between Olympus or the Underworld?"

"Make your decision," Josephine said.

"Wife?" I asked softly. I couldn't help the little flare of hope after seeing her form. She had chosen a soft, feminine belly, curved just so from her labors. As a goddess, she could will it away, but she didn't. She kept just a touch of softness as the antithesis to Olympian hardness. She kept it for Zagreus and for Melinoë. And maybe, she kept it for me.

I should have known her choice the moment she refused to meet my eyes. Instead, I let her come close and felt her soft lips brush a kiss against my cheek. I imagined I felt a warm tear between us and could almost taste its salt, except I don't think I did. I think it was my own as she turned and didn't look back. She went to Olympus, her revenge more important than my love, or perhaps I was wrong and we had never been in love. Now, I'd never know. Persephone had chosen Olympus over me. Forever.

In that moment, I didn't wonder why she alone of the gods was given a choice. That came later.

HADES

"It will be fine, I promise," Persephone was saying. It was hard to care when my wrists were tied by own my cuffs, and I felt true weakness from the Dipsioi attack for the first time in my long life. Each time I tried to move or lift my arms, it felt like moving bags of concrete. I had been nearly drained by the beast, and I was unsure if I'd ever fully recover.

The pain wasn't localized, and my body couldn't figure out where to heal itself first. That was probably the point. This monster attacked all of your systems at once and left you in a blinding pain that immortals rarely felt before. It was a perfect assault.

Persephone knelt down, her eyes shining. "I promise I will make this better. Your war is over. Mine, however, is just beginning."

I was still trying to shake off the fog of pain, my eyes dilating every time I blinked, attempting to bring her back into focus. "You'll just snap your fingers, and I'll appear back at my castle? No harm done."

"Something like that." She looked away.

"Please tell me you didn't start this war."

"I did not. At least, I am innocent there. It was a true uprising. But I won't lie. I did take advantage of it."

I laughed mirthlessly. "The Telechines. The new demons."

"I had no choice. I needed to keep Hecate busy, and I needed the castle to fall."

"Why save it the first time?"

She paused, her mouth half-open. She seem flustered but wouldn't answer.

I gave an unpleasant laugh. "What? One of your precious stray cats got your tongue?"

"No. I just doubt you'd believe me after everything that's happened and I have to get going. So do you, if you want to make it back to the Underworld before more of these creatures come."

"And you're just going to call off the Telechines and fabricated demons?" I snapped my fingers. "Just like that."

"I will."

I tried to process what I was hearing. "Was the wound I received battling the Telechine planned from the beginning?"

"No. I needed you strong."

"To attract the Dipsioi," I said, finally understanding.

"You should've killed him before he stabbed you. You have too much honor."

I remained silent, trying to understand the complexity of it all. For weeks, I had been trying to put the pieces together, trying to understand Persephone's game in returning to the Underworld. No wonder I had failed. The puzzle covered a thousand years and three realms. I ground my teeth. "Persephone, you will regret this. I promise."

She still didn't meet my eyes. That was something.

I tried appealing to that. "Persephone, you don't have to do this."

She snapped. "Don't. Just—don't. You never could do what needed to be done. Not really."

"Your revenge will consume you. Is it truly the most important thing in your life?"

"Yes. It has to be. There is nothing else."

"But there could be so much else. With me." There. All of my cards, all of my hopes and dreams were hers. It was so very dangerous, but I had been living in a dream before this.

She hesitated.

I was sure of it so I pressed forward, unused to the pleading sound my voice made, but unable to stop it. I always came undone around Persephone. "We could rule the realms. You don't need this revenge. Kill this monster and come home."

I smelled it. The same chthonic stench that emanated from the demons. My eyes burned as I watched her check the bindings of the nightless cuff around my wrist. She raised her fist, her dark magic already pooling in mists around her arms, and I almost thought I saw regret.

"Persephone. Wife."

"This is difficult enough, Hades. But you lied to me. You kept my seeds."

"It's what you wanted me to do!" I shouted. "To hold them for you as you played at being weak."

"True. Still now I know you are capable of deceit and so I cannot trust you."

"What a perfect image of our marriage."

"No marriage is perfect, Hades."

"Your revenge will destroy you," I exploded. Anger and embarrassment at my honesty mixed together in a deadly combination.

"No. I will be complete once I kill Zeus."

I laughed derisively. "That's your epically grand plan? Take a Dipsioi to kill Zeus? You know this is so much bigger than him, right? Zeus hasn't mattered to anyone but you for centuries, because you will not let it go."

Her face twisted in pain. "You don't get to tell me when to get over something, Hades. You, most of all."

I kept my voice low. "Fine, Persephone. You're right. You heal on your own time, even if it takes a million years. In the meantime, I will worry about the Underworld alone."

"'If I cannot bend Heaven, then I shall move Hell.'" She spared me one last look, the ice in her eyes sending chills through my remaining ichor. "You're nothing but dead weight. As we both know, only I can go through the realms. You will only bring me down."

"Why don't you just kill me, too, then?" I asked, wishing not for the first time I could strangle my pretty little wife. And not for the first time, she turned her back on me.

"I said I would heal you, and I will keep my word." She put a finger to my mouth to shush me, although I could hardly fight back, bound like this. Her words glided over my body as she pressed her hand to my wound. Their meaning was drowned by my scream in the wake of the pain. And then—gone. The wound scabbed over to leave an angry scar.

"Goodbye, Hades." Bending down, she whispered in my ear, speaking words and stringing them together in ways they should not adhere. She was trying to sever our connection from Hecate; I could feel our link fraying like a rope as she continued sawing on it, hacking away. She would cut me off and never look back.

Persephone would be consumed by her hatred. I wished I could see her demise, but she took care of that, too. I truly would never see her again once she passed back to Olympus and took her revenge on Zeus. She had no reason to ever return, and I could not go where she went.

The link between us frayed faster into threads. I threw the last of my energy into halting it, into keeping the connection between us alive. I groaned with the effort, but much like our doomed marriage, our ill-fated love, I was the only one trying. In quintessential Persephone style, she had healed me, only to drain my energy so I could not follow.

When she walked away with her pet monster into the void, I could only lift my head to watch her leave.

To be continued...

AFTERWORD

If you have experienced trauma like Persephone, You're Not Alone. Talk to someone. To share the burden is to lift at least a small part of the burden.

A note about the word "rape" in reference to what first occurred between Hades and Persephone. The first Greek telling is by Hesiod. The word "*ἥρπασε*" is ambiguous, but essentially means "to abduct." In the subsequent Latin, "raptus" actually means to be carried off or seized, not sexual violence. *It should be noted that all stories and artistic archaeology from the ancient world do indeed depict Persephone as unwilling, and the Romans were a little... loosey goosey, morally-speaking, with abducting women. (See: Sabines)* While probably more ambiguous than a modern reader would like, here is the crux of where my story began to take shape.

Diving deeper than the Greeks into the Minoans before them (yes, if the Minoans are directly related linguistically to the Greeks is debatable, but no, I don't want to debate it. I would have stayed in archaeology if that were the case!) there's even evidence that Persephone was indeed more ancient than the Titans, along with the Poppy Goddess. How do you like them pomegranates? And so, we have our plot: Our motivation, our background, and a heavy dose of modern day feminism where Persephone gets to take back her story. #notsorry

On to the others: Kako demons are my own creation from the noun *kakos*; evil. While my Kako demons are neither good nor evil, their lack of intelligence allows beings to manipulate them. Dipsioi are also an ancient Mycenaean being, the word meaning, "the thirsty ones." I used it frequently as a singular noun, so please forgive me. Also, see my foreword on classical grammar if all the apostrophe s's got you down.

Totenpasses were real, used by supplicants to Persephone and can be roughly translated as "passports for the dead." Start your research here: https://en.wikipedia.org/wiki/Totenpass

It got a little meta there talking about Dante, but I love the idea of an immortal Hades running out of ideas for torture, so he uses medieval writers (weren't they creepy?) to administer new techniques.

Mint was, indeed, used as an herb to help with nausea, so I thought it proper for Persephone to be in the throes of childbirth when she created it. That's totally my own addition, the original myth implying she turned Minthe into mint from pure jealousy.

Zagreus, again, is debated as to whether he is the son of Zeus or Hades, but there is precedent for Hades from a fragment of *Sisyphus* by Aeschylus. I took the bit and ran. #stillnotsorry

I also apologize for all of the Hamilton and Survivor references. I've been binging.

The Deathless King will reign again, January 2022. Pre-order the conclusion to Hades & Persephone, *Of Flames and Thrones* for the discount price of $3.99. In the meantime, try out my completed Paranormal Women's Fiction series with another midlife twist, *Forty is Fabulous*. It's *Under the Tuscan Sun* meets *Practical Magic*—with more Greek mythology and even Egyptian mythology thrown into the mix! Join my newsletter here for updates, a cover reveal, and future discounts.

And I understand if this paranormal romance wasn't your cup of tea. I have other cups with other drinks. Like Champagne! Look for my next PWF midlife adventure in Spring of 2022. It's demonology in the South of France. There will be spell slinging, croissants, and plenty of bubbly!

ABOUT THE AUTHOR

Unlike her namesake of medieval infamy, Heloise doesn't intend to have her midlife crisis in a nunnery. She'd much rather drink espresso martinis and chant in fairy rings while wearing socially questionable clothing.

In her other pen names, Heloise writes romance, nonfiction, and epic fantasy with tinges of the ancient world all thanks to dual degrees in archaeology and Classics. She splits her time between St. Louis and Chicago with her husband, two kids, and ~~two~~ one cat, and is too heartbroken to plot how to bring in a puppy for the moment. Hug your real babies and your fur babies.

Printed in Great Britain
by Amazon